Actors Anonymous

also by James Franco

PALO ALTO

Actors Anonymous

A NOVEL

James Franco

ff

FABER & FABER

First published in the United Kingdom in 2013
by Faber and Faber Ltd
Bloomsbury House
74–77 Great Russell Street
London WC1B 3DA

Printed and bound by L.E.G.O. S.p.A. - Italy

The right of James Franco to be identified as author of this work
has been asserted in accordance with Section 77 of the Copyright,
Designs and Patents Act 1988

A CIP record for this book
is available from the British Library

ISBN 978-0-571-31169-9

2 4 6 8 10 9 7 5 3 1

Players and painted stage took all my love,
And not those things that they were emblems of.

—Yeats

Contents

Preface

We of Actors Anonymous are more than fifty men and women who have recovered from a seemingly hopeless state of mind and body.

In this volume, we relate our experiences in dealing with existence, modern society, and identity, in order to find suitable ways of acting and being in the world.

Sometimes it is painful to be oneself; at other times it seems impossible to escape oneself. The actor's life has provided escape for many that find their lives too dull, painful, and insular. But the actor–escape artist can go too far as well.

If one puts on too many different personas or goes too far into character, one is liable to lose oneself. Some have believed that this loss is a positive, and perhaps it is for those that enjoy a rootless swirl of personality in the void, but others, like those who have come to comprise Actors Anonymous, believe that there is a balance to be struck between life and art, between self-creation and the veridic self.

We have put down our experiences in these pages in order to guide others—professional actors, amateurs, and nonactors alike—to a way of life that both defies psychological determinism on the one hand, and freewheeling insanity on the other.

We are people who work in the world as professionals, whether we make our money from acting or not, and it is important for us to maintain our anonymity. There are centuries of prejudice piled on the actor and thus it is important that no one of us is thrust into the spotlight. (God knows that some of us get enough of the spotlight as it is.) So much money is made off the aggrandizement and defamation of actors already that we ask the press, especially the tabloid press, to hold their pens, video cameras, paparazzi flash blasts, and blogs, and respect our organization's anonymity.

This is a serious text that is intended for actors: "actors" in the most essential sense, not necessarily actors of stage and screen, but actors in the sound and fury of life. Anyone who wants this message is encouraged to glean what she will.

We are not an exclusive club; the only requirement for membership is a desire to change oneself, to be able to act decently in a controlled manner. Everyone can act, but not everyone can act well, and not everyone knows how he actually presents himself to others.

We have no spokesperson, and there is no hierarchy. We have no dues or fees, and we are open to all regardless of race, religion, nationality, or acting style.

We do not oppose anyone—even those actors trained by I_____ C_____ or L_____ M____ or any of the other charlatan acting teachers sucking actor blood in dark classrooms across the Los Angeles sprawl.

Our simple desire is to help. Not to train, but to save individuals from training, whether that training was given in a classroom, by a parent, or by what can only be called contemporary life.

We of Actors Anonymous subscribe to the following twelve steps and twelve traditions, not because they were handed down from on high by a bully studio, nor from a dictatorial director; we have no concern for deskbound screenwriters proclaiming Napoleonic ambitions of control, and we are certainly not adherents of the steps and traditions because we are beholden to the hordes of critics, both high and low, who proclaim to know something of which they write and speak but hardly do, these sideline vipers who sting and snare and then duck into their holes when the real animals of acting turn on them in anger.

We salute and live by these principles because they were generated by the blood experience of those who have lived through the profession, its trials both on and offscreen, on and offstage, for surely the pitfalls of everyday life are increased in proportion to the heights one reaches in the realms of performance. One cannot live solely in the airy realms of the imagination.

Let these steps and traditions guide you to a balanced life of creativity and truth in a world of surfaces and untruths, through realms of materialism and jealousy, past the vortices of public humiliation, and the private, tooth-ringed maws of self-doubt. We are here for you. Let us love you and guide you.

We speak of what we do.

The Actor's Opinion

We of Actors Anonymous believe that the reader will be interested in a professional opinion regarding our situation. There are so many hucksters in the world of performance training that it is important to receive some corroboration from a professional with experience on all levels of the acting strata.

To Whom It May Concern:

I have been a professional actor since I was eighteen. I trained for eight years, and I have been working as a professional actor for fourteen years. I have met many actors from all over the world. It is hard to find a common denominator, but there are many similarities in most of the actors I meet. There is usually an ingredient of self-hatred that underlies actors. This hatred manifests in different ways; sometimes it is so buried that it is virtually unnoticeable, but don't be fooled, it's there. Anyone that is driven to play dress-up for a living is trying to hide something either from himself or from others. Or the self-hatred may be manifested in the drive for success and fame, the algorithm being: "If many people love me, then I must be important." This can be written a different way: "I hate myself, but I am going to transform myself into something charismatic so that everyone loves me, and if people love me, then I won't hate myself anymore."

Most actors are doomed, because the self-hatred never goes away—even for the few that achieve the kind of success that is recognizable by the greater population. I speak about *fame*. Roughly one tenth of SAG is made up of actors able to support themselves by their acting alone, and only 2 percent approach what might be called famous. So even for those fortunate few, the demons of self-doubt inevitably whisper songs of unworthiness, or else the subject is so insulated in fantasies of grandeur that he lives a life of hermetic madness: He might function in the world, but his eyes see hardly beyond his own pumpkin head. Nothing lasts, not even the films themselves: Look at Edwin S. Porter's *Jack and the Beanstalk, Life of an*

American Fireman, and *The Great Train Robbery* and George
Cukor's *A Star Is Born*—works of art, ripped and deformed.
This speaks of the destruction of film classics, the ostensibly most durable vehicle and storage facility for actors' souls,
nonchalantly defaced—and these are the respected films of
their day, goodness forbid the contemplation of the fates of
the lesser known films, ships of fool actor souls adrift and
lost in the tides of eternity. So, the actor is someone with the
need for immortality who will never find it, often a locus of
intensely driven ambition that can only flare out or burn up in
a quick bright moment. This situation has left generations of
actors broken on either side of the divide of success, and until
now there has been little consolation outside of SAG funded
actors' homes for the elderly.

I can honestly say that until this volume I thought actors
were fucked, but here hope has miraculously touched down on
earth, one hundred years after the advent of the moving picture,
six hundred years since *Everyman* and the religious morality
plays, four hundred years since Shakespeare played Hamlet's
father's ghost, and thousands upon thousands of years since the
Lascaux population did ritualized dances for campfire roasted
venison. Here is a collection of experiences that can give the
actor not a way to act better, but a way to live better. For so long
actors have carried the conscience of the world across screen
and stage and in their personal lives, but they have received little consideration for their pain. They are considered arrogant
and self-centered by their fellows, at the same time that they
are being applauded for their brave explorations of the dark-
est places of human experience. Now, with the advent of com-
puter-generated images, actors glance timidly at the future in

which their luminosity will be dimmed to the dullness of the poet, novelist, and painter. But all is not lost; there are others who understand, and that understanding in conjunction with a spiritual connection is already guiding dozens if not hundreds out of the wasteland of Hollywood into Elysian Fields.

Peace,
James Franco

The Twelve Steps of Actors Anonymous

STEP 1

We admitted that life is a performance—that we are all performers, at all times—and that our "performance" had left our control.

STEP 2

Came to believe that there is a power greater than ourselves, some sort of directing force, that could restore our "performance" to sanity.

STEP 3

Turned our will and our "performances" over to the Great Director.

STEP 4

*Made a fearless and searching moral
inventory of our "character."*

STEP 5

*Admitted to the Great Director, to ourselves, and to
another actor the exact nature of our "character's" wrongs.*

STEP 6

*Were entirely ready to have the Great Director
remove all of these defects from our "character."*

STEP 7

*Humbly asked the Great Director to remove
our "character's" shortcomings.*

STEP 8

*Made a list of actors our "character" had harmed
and became willing to make amends to them all.*

STEP 9

*Made direct amends to such "actors"
whenever possible, except when to do so
would injure them or other "actors."*

STEP 10

*Continued to take our "character's" inventory, and
when he was wrong, promptly admitted it.*

STEP 11

*Sought through prayer and meditation to improve our
conscious contact with the Great Director, praying
only for knowledge of his will for us and the
power to carry out his direction.*

STEP 12

*After our "character" has had a spiritual awakening as the
result of these steps, we tried to carry this message to other
actors and to practice these principles in all our scenes.*

*We admitted that life is a performance—that we
are all performers, at all times—and that our
"performance" had left our control.*

———≈≋≈———

I Am the Actor

I AM THE ACTOR.

I am alive in 2013 and I was alive in 1913.

I am an actor, so I can play everything. Everyone is in me, and I am a part of everyone.

I am a part of your consciousness. You don't think so? You want to deny that I have made my way inside? Just because you think you don't know me doesn't mean you don't know me. I am all actors.

I am Jack Nicholson and Marlon Brando and Jimmy Stewart and Jean-Paul Belmondo and Steve McQueen.

I am Meryl Streep and Natalie Wood and Cate Blanchett and Marilyn Monroe.

I am Nicolas Cage and Robert Pattinson and James Dean and Rock Hudson. I am Sean Penn and Robert De Niro and Cary Grant.

I am Bette Davis and Barbara Stanwyck and Kathryn Hepburn and Audrey Hepburn and Grace Kelly, Jean Harlow and Lauren Bacall and Judy Garland and Greer Garson. I am Norma Shearer and Lillian Gish. I am Garbo. I am Joan Crawford and Joan Blondell, Jean Moreau and Anna Karina and Marlene Dietrich and Monica Vitti. I am Ann Dvorak and Lucille Ball and Louise Brooks. I am Vivien Leigh and fucking Shelley Winters.

I am Clark Gable.

I am Montgomery Clift.

I am W. C. Fields.

I'm here to entertain you, but I don't really care about entertaining you, know what I mean?

Audiences have a taste for shit, so I am not trying to entertain them anymore. Even the smartest critics have a taste for shit, at least when it comes to acting.

Yes, every once in a while people will get it right and appreciate good performances. We have plenty of awards shows. We have the Oscars.

But where were the Oscars for Nicholson in *Five Easy Pieces, The Last Detail,* and *Chinatown*? The Oscars for De Niro in *Mean Streets* and *Taxi Driver*? What about Brando in *A Streetcar Named Desire* and *Last Tango in Paris*? What about Clift in *A Place in the Sun,* Dean in *East of Eden* and *Giant*?

I used to care a lot about acting, but now I see that you're only as good as the material you're given, and if you have good material, you're only as good as your director. There is so much dependence on others that I can't care about acting anymore.

I'm like a sophisticated prop. I'll give you all the feeling you want, all the accents you want, all the hairstyles and wardrobe changes you want, and I'll say whatever you put in front of me. But don't ask me to take pride in the work.

Did Brando deal with fame by getting fat and bitter?

Did McQueen fuck himself to death?

I was alive when Shakespeare wrote all that crap. It was good then, but it wasn't Shakespeare.

I performed for money, and I performed for free. It's better to perform for money if you hate the director; it's better to perform for free if you love him.

I used to care about how I looked. Now I don't care as much. Maybe it's because I'm so handsome.

Jack Nicholson used to worry about losing his hair. You can see it going as early as 1963 in the Roger Corman film *The Terror,* and it's definitely going by *Five Easy Pieces.* But he's ten times sexier in all his films of the '70s (post–*Easy Rider*) than he is in the shitty films he did before that. When he had more hair.

Many actors want to direct. Nowadays, many actors end up directing. It's weird how their films feel small and cliché when they do. I don't even like thinking about most of them.

If you work in Hollywood, you usually have to play the game. It's damn hard to only do movies that are good. Even Daniel Day-Lewis did *The Boxer, The Crucible,* and *Nine.* Not that he was bad in any of them, but if you think about how he only does one film every two or three or five years, he must have felt pretty shitty after those films came out.

I hate actors that make their performances more important than the project. Get the fuck over yourself. What's the point? Don't you know you're in a collaborative business? Your career isn't that important.

I hate books that try to give advice about how movies work. This is how it works: do what you love and believe in. Sometimes you can do a project that will not be the best movie, but it has aspects about it that make it worthwhile, like you get to work with a cool actor for a week, or you get to work with new technology, or you get to play a crazy role for a little bit. But who cares about movies that work? The only people that care about those are the people that care about money and praise: the executives, the agents, and the nonartists.

Yes, film is a populist art form, but it's been losing its populist standing since the '60s. Of course you can still produce movies that make tons of money, but so what? Even though books are dying, you can still publish books that make tons of money. That doesn't mean that the movie industry is going to stay dominant forever.

Theater used to be the place where the stars were.

What about all the vaudeville kings and queens?

It's great when you travel for a film. You get to stay in a hotel, get fed, see new places, and lots of people from the cast and crew screw each other.

There are some people that are very serious about their acting. But the ones that are too serious are boring and usually end up strangling their own performances.

Daniel Day-Lewis never breaks character, even when he's in the makeup chair or at home. Can you imagine being Bill the Butcher for half a year? Wouldn't you feel silly walking around town dressed like Abraham Lincoln? If you were eighteen? If you were twenty-five? If you were forty, fifty years old?

What if you walked around as an insecure loser character for thirty-three years? Wait…

Would you hurt another person to help them give a better performance? If it meant a better performance for yourself, would you slap someone? Cut someone? Punch someone? Spit on someone? Call someone a kike or a nigger offscreen, meaning it wouldn't be heard in the film, but you would do it to catch the person off guard in hopes of producing a genuine reaction?

Some actors hate doing photo shoots (mostly guys) because they feel phony. But isn't posing for a still camera the same thing as acting for a motion picture camera? Is it because the photo shoots are ostensibly capturing the real person and the roles in films are characters? I guess.

Acting teachers are fucked up. They are unlike any other teachers, because they deal with their students' emotions and bodies. They get inside their students' heads. Even if they have the best intentions, they can't help from becoming gurus and therapists for their students, because they deal on such intimate terms. When you have a bunch of students looking up to you because you liberated their emotions, it's hard not to play the role of mentor/lover/father/mother.

As in any profession, it's the people who break the rules that become special. The problem is that for every innovative rule breaker, there is a whole army of rule breakers without talent that you never hear about.

Harmony Korine dropped out of NYU. So did P. T. Anderson and Woody Allen and Steve McQueen (the artist/director). You'd think dropping out was the way to become a great writer/director.

What do you think is good acting? The most revealing performance? The biggest transformation? Being the most charismatic? The biggest hero? The sexiest? The funniest?

Are film actors the most respected of all actors? And by whom? The general public? By other actors? Is it the renown that makes them seem bigger and better than the rest?

Do we like to kick film actors when they step outside of their comfort zone? Or do we like to praise them? Julia Roberts got criticized when she went on Broadway. Scarlett Johansson won a Tony.

What do you think the best performance on film is?

What is the best theatrical performance? Marlon Brando as Stanley Kowalski? Laurette Taylor in *The Glass Menagerie*?

How many people are alive that saw those performances?

Shakespeare was an actor.

So was Sophocles.

It's funny when people say actors can't write. Most of 'em can't, but look at Woody Allen. Look at W. C. Fields.

And what is good writing? Even the best writers resemble the best actors. They have a few good projects in them, and the others don't seem to add up.

Screenwriters and directors. Weird people. They're of a different breed. I don't know if I like them. I mean, I do; I really like some of them, but I'm also prone to hate them.

At acting school I was taught to hate directors, because they knew nothing about acting. My teacher said Elia Kazan was the last great director of actors because he came out of the Group Theater. But this was stupid thinking. Directors might not know much about acting, but there isn't much to know. Be simple, be in the right place, and go with your instincts.

Basically, if you're relaxed in front of the camera, you'll be good.

Acting wasn't and isn't always this way, the less-is-more idea. In some cases it's good to be tense, to be over the top, not to know your lines, to be too loud, or to be too quiet, to jump up and down, or to scream out everything you say.

If you try to look cool, you can sometimes pull it off. Steve McQueen was cool (in *Bullitt, The Getaway, Papillon, The Great Escape*), but how many books did he read in his life? His characters outsmart everyone, but it's the smarts of the streets, where the rubber hits the cement. Isn't it lonely in that place? Where thoughts are feelings not articulated ideas?

McQueen's intelligence was all body and machines: the way he moved and the way he handled machinery, the way he came out on top.

At the height of his popularity Steve McQueen would make people pay him before he would even consider a script. He made tons of money. At one point he was the highest paid actor in the world. I guess that's something to aspire to.

Arnold Schwarzenegger got paid a record breaking $30 million for Mr. Freeze in the *Batman* film that had ice skating and nipples on the Batsuit.

Steve McQueen stole Ali McGraw away from Robert Evans while they were shooting *The Getaway*. He married her, then made her quit acting.

McQueen was a sex addict and would have threesomes all the time. He wanted to do Ibsen's *An Enemy of the People* for the longest time, and then when he finally did it, no one saw it.

He would just sit in his hot tub all day and drink beer. He would only watch his own movies. He got cancer at a very young age. He tried to cure it with a bunch of quack doctors in Mexico. He thought he was cured. He died at fifty.

Jack Nicholson struggled for twelve years before *Easy Rider*. He started as a gopher in the animation department of MGM at eighteen. He loved basketball even then. Eventually he took an acting class with Jeff Corey, James Dean's old teacher. Later Jack studied with Martin Landau, James Dean's old friend.

Jack might not have even wanted the role in *Easy Rider*. It was intended for Rip Torn. Dennis Hopper was a nut that Jack knew from the coffeehouses on Sunset, and then was in a movie that Jack wrote for Roger Corman called *The Trip*, about LSD. The story goes that Jack did the role in *Easy Rider* as a favor to his friends Bob Rafelson and Bert Schneider, the producers, in order to look after Dennis.

Dennis's director's cut of *Easy Rider* came out at four hours. Everyone from Bob Rafelson to Jack to Henry Jaglom helped cut down the film. Sometimes it's bad to have an actor in the editing room; sometimes it's okay.

Then the movie was released and hit a nerve with the young. Jack was nominated for an Oscar.

Jack grew up in Asbury Park, New Jersey, thinking his grandmother was his mom, and his mom was his sister. By the time he found out who was what, both were already dead.

James Dean's mother died when he was eight. She had loved Jimmy; his father didn't. After the death, he sent young Jimmy back to Indiana to live with his aunt and uncle on the farm. Jimmy traveled back on the train with his mom's coffin.

It's no surprise that Dean's characters so desperately needed the love of the father figures in *East of Eden* (Raymond Massey), *Rebel Without a Cause* (Jim Backus), and *Giant* (Rock Hudson). Or maybe he just hated them.

Dean had tons of natural talent and a strong drive to succeed. He seemed like he was all instinct, or maybe that's just a way of saying that he put all of his energy into acting.

If Dean had lived, he probably would have made some flops. He was supposed to play Billy the Kid and then Rocky Graziano in *Somebody Up There Likes Me*. After Dean died, Paul Newman did it. It wasn't very good.

Newman was older than Dean. He tested alongside Dean for the brother in *East of Eden,* the role eventually played by Dick Davalos, the guy on the cover of the Smiths' *Strangeways, Here We Come* album. The Newman test still exists. I think Jimmy is playing with a switchblade in it.

Newman must have been frustrated that Dean got all the roles.

River Phoenix was supposed to play Brad Pitt's part in *Interview with the Vampire* opposite Johnny Depp (in the Tom Cruise role). Then he was demoted to the interviewer part for commercial reasons. Then he died before it was shot.

River was supposed to have been interested in the book *The Basketball Diaries* and in the play about Rimbaud, *Total Eclipse.* Leonardo DiCaprio was in both movies based on these books.

Lots of famous actors hate acting, or say they do. Partly because they hate the lack of control.

Lots of actors turn around and love acting when they get praise for a performance. It's easy to blame a director for a bad movie, and it's easy not to give him credit for a good movie.

Everyone thinks Scorsese is the best director. His best movies are *Mean Streets, Taxi Driver, Raging Bull,* and *Goodfellas.* Now his movies are huge. It's hard to go back to the good old days when you were making audacious things for no money.

And no one went to see them.

Quentin Tarantino's best films are *Reservoir Dogs* and *Pulp Fiction*. They had heart and soul. His new movies are fantasies. He is an authority on the LA underworld and B-movies.

He has recreated history. He killed Hitler.

Somewhere along the way his characters became their dialogue and lost some of their heart.

I am a good actor, but sometimes I look like a bad actor. And I don't care.

I used to want to do a bunch of accents and physical impediments with every role. Now I don't care. Now I want to be as simple as possible, just slip into the world I'm in and be as natural as possible.

When they get older, some actors that were once respected become clowns.

It's like young women: When they have great bodies they don't want to show them, but when they're older, and they're no longer pretty, they do.

Al Pacino was in such high demand he turned down roles for three years before doing *Scarface*.

In *Sunset Boulevard*, Erich von Stroheim plays Gloria Swanson's butler and ex-husband. When she screens a film for her new lover, played by William Holden, what they show are shots from *Queen Kelly*, an actual silent film starring Swanson that von Stroheim directed. It was financed by Joe Kennedy because he was Swanson's lover at the time, but Swanson had such a bad time with Stroheim she had Kennedy pull the plug before it was finished, and it was never released.

Would you rather be Buster Keaton or Peter Fonda? Charlie Chaplin or Leonardo DiCaprio? John Wayne or Phillip Seymour Hoffman? River Phoenix or Mickey Rourke?

Mickey used to be so beautiful. Look at *Diner*. Yes, he looked like he was falling apart a little even then, but there was no indication of the creature he would become. But he did some things that were pretty amazing, even if they were crazy. He opened a boxing gym, and he became the highest paid four-round fighter in history ($500,000 for a fight in Japan). I heard he had a little soda shop/cigarette stand in Beverly Hills. Bikers would hang out there, also, and under the counter young people could buy beer.

How can you do good work? How can you *always* do good work?

There are so many people in Hollywood that make your good stuff into bad stuff. They even turn you against yourself so you don't know what is good. So, you're just standing there waiting for something safe to come along. A real fucking snorefest.

It's weird. Many actors have great runs of success and then they seem to lose their taste, or lose whatever it was that made them great. Or do they not get the same kinds of offers anymore because they're older?

Marlon Brando cut a great figure in *The Wild One*, but the movie falls apart halfway through.

Marlon Brando was great in *Zapata,* but in hindsight he looks a bit silly with all that strange makeup on, trying to play Mexican.

When I see an actor with bad makeup I think about how he has been let down. Not by the makeup artist, but by the times. Look at how *Breakfast at Tiffany's* is ruined by Mickey Rooney playing Japanese. I guess back then that was comic relief. Why didn't Rooney protest such a racist caricature? Why didn't Audrey Hepburn?

Actors get worn out by doing small movies and never having them seen, so they just do things for the money.

John Cassavetes did it right. He used acting to finance the films he cared about, and then he didn't need those movies to make money, because he made his money off his day job, acting.

Even though he didn't seem to care about acting as much as directing, he was still a great actor. If your day job is acting in *Rosemary's Baby,* that's not too shabby.

Actors are treated like royalty on-set. The extras are treated like peasants.

There is a hierarchy on a movie set and a hierarchy in Hollywood. Everyone has his place. There are all kinds of skilled positions, but the actors are the ones that are most visible, so the people in different departments, even if they don't like the actors, treat them with deference.

It seems that the old wisdom of keeping a private life is not appealing anymore. Back in the day, the stars would present a public façade that was probably quite distant from who they really were. The young people today share tons, but I suppose it's just a bunch of the same kind of old bullshit.

There are tons of actors who are well loved by the public who are not what they seem. Tons.

I wouldn't want to be in movies with half of them.

The problem is that when actors are successful, they build up asshole capital. That means they can be assholes for a while and get away with it. If they keep having successes, they can keep being assholes. I guess this goes for anyone: directors, writers, producers, etc.

If you have a bunch of flops, it's harder to be an asshole and get work. No one wants to work with you.

If you have a bunch of flops and you're a nice person, it doesn't really matter: No one wants to work with you.

Some actresses fuck just as many crewmembers as their male counterparts.

Lots of actors like to screw the extras. It's pretty easy.

When you're portraying a romantic relationship onscreen, you can usually score with your acting partner after the first makeout scene. This applies even if the other person is in a relationship.

On-set relationships rarely work out. Don't make any life plans while you're in the middle of a film, especially if you're shooting on location. It's like going to camp: Everything changes after you leave.

When you're shooting on location (away from your home, which usually means away from LA), you have a bunch of people around you that are your world for a number of months. They create an environment that is part of everything you do, even your private relationships on-set. Think about it: If you're fucking your castmate, you're either keeping it secret from the crew, or you're open with the crew, but either way, they're helping to define the relationship. When the movie ends, that feedback network from the crew and the regular schedule of the shoot disappear.

When you play a role, sometimes you take on characteristics of that role. In subtle ways. Like if you play a lothario/magician, maybe you don't start doing magic, but you might start sleeping with a lot of women.

If you play a dictator, people might start treating you like you're an evil, powerful man. Or if you play a monkey, people might treat you like an animal.

Sometimes actors behave badly. They show up hours late to the set every day, or they don't come out of their trailers. I'm not saying this is acceptable behavior, but they do it because they have spent years waiting for the crew, namely the director of photography, to set up lights and shots.

Of course cinematographers have their own gripes, and of course the position is invaluable; a cinematographer is one of the director's closest companions on-set. But from an actor's POV, the DP takes up all the time on a movie set.

I'd say the ratio of lighting time to acting time is on average 3:1, if not 4:1 or 10:1.

An actor needs to learn how to fill his time on-set when the lighting crew and the camera crew are setting up for shots.

Some actors like to chat and gossip. They will chat with anyone. Usually the other actors, but definitely with any cute women or men on-set.

Some actors read on-set. Some actors go to their trailers and play video games or watch TV. Some actors do yoga and work out. I'm not sure how they keep from getting sweaty before they have to act again.

I heard Nicolas Cage used to have a workout regimen that he would do between setups. It was about forty-five minutes long, and once he started, he couldn't be interrupted.

DPs can be the ruin of a movie. But they are also the ones that producers feel they can replace most easily if a movie is going slowly. It's harder to replace actors because they are onscreen.

I hate when directors say, "I couldn't do what you do in front of the camera; it's too scary." It makes me think they're saying *What you do is embarrassing.*

It also makes me think they're saying, *You can't do what I do behind the camera; you're an intellectual baby.*

But I also hate actors that try to take over and direct a movie.

I used to be one of those actors. But only as far as my performance went.

It's not like I tried to suggest shots or anything.

Setting up shots is one the most fun things on the set. People who try to tell you that directing is just working with the actors are stuck in the old days of theater. Films involve cameras and editing in addition to acting; if you're a director, why wouldn't you want to get mixed up in those things as well?

The problem is that some directors get too wrapped up in all the camera crap. Their movies are cheap and hollow because they're all flash and no human substance.

I don't know if that's the problem either. I think all flash and no human can be cool as well. But when it's immature flash, it's like they're making movies for twelve-year-olds.

I know most movies are for twelve-year-olds, but still, come on, grow up.

Some of the best actors are really uneducated, but somehow they understand people well enough to fake it. They have behavioral intelligence and emotional intelligence. Like an athlete has physical intelligence.

I hate being limited. If all you have is emotional intelligence, then the directors can just use you like clay.

Nowadays, I like being used like clay (if I like the director) but that's only because I get to direct my own movies between the acting parts.

Jack Nicholson wrote quite a few screenplays for Roger Corman in the early days. He had almost given up on acting and thought he would become a writer/director/producer, but *Easy Rider* pulled him out of that.

Warren Beatty thinks that everyone wants to be an actor because they all want to be in front of the camera. I'd say yes and no.

After *Easy Rider* and *Five Easy Pieces,* Jack Nicholson cowrote and directed a film called *Drive, He Said.* It was about college students, basketball, and the Vietnam draft. It was not well received, and it didn't make much money.

After Nicholson became a star off *Easy Rider* and *Five Easy Pieces,* two films that he had filmed years earlier that had been shelved were released. One was a western; the other was a biker film. They didn't do very well.

I wonder what happened on *Drive, He Said.* He must have worked hard on it; he had good people around him. But it's a bit of a mess.

Nicholson didn't direct again until *Goin' South*; it's nice, but pretty goofy. Later he did *The Two Jakes,* the sequel to *Chinatown. The Two Jakes* is not as good as *Chinatown.*

Ben Affleck acted in a bunch of horrible movies. But now that he directs movies, he's not too bad. Isn't that crazy.

Sometimes it's good to act badly. It's good to mix things up. When everything is so precious, it becomes difficult to grow. It's hard to be around someone that takes himself too seriously.

Jack Nicholson never does television interviews. It makes him mysterious.

I make millions of dollars on some movies.

I've spent millions on movies that didn't make it back.

Everyone likes to talk about movies because they think that they can. Everyone's a specialist.

Robert Bresson liked using nonactors. He called them models. His actors are almost blank, but they suggest something more, something transcendent.

Yasujirō Ozu let the characters just breathe.

John Cassavetes let the characters go crazy.

Stanley Kubrick was a painter.

The Dardenne brothers find great drama in the simple.

W. C. Fields was great because he was so dark.

Charlie Chaplin was great because he was an icon. The tramp could go anywhere and do anything.

Laurel and Hardy, like creations out of Magritte or Beckett.

Andy Kaufman was the greatest.

If you read everything written about me, you won't have a sense of me, but of how stupid our journalists are.

If you are a film actor, get ready: You will be treated like a fool.

If you are famous, you will be both a hero and a subject of envy. This is why the idea of building someone up and then tearing her down is so easily understood.

Of course, the other problem is that some famous people are liked for doing one thing, and then they think that they will be liked if they do anything.

Sometimes actors hate acting because it comes so easily to them. They want to break out of it because it makes them feel silly, especially when they are adults (dressing up, putting on makeup, playacting), but they are scared to leave it because it's all they have. It's hard to put work into something else and start over.

I had a friend that had a great personality. He was a funny guy and came from money. But he did drugs from age sixteen to thirty-four. When he finally got clean, he wanted to break into the movies. Instead, he stepped in front of a train. It was probably pretty daunting to start life at thirty-five.

Ken Kesey worked at the VA Hospital in Menlo Park while he wrote

One Flew Over the Cuckoo's Nest, not far from where I grew up. Jack Nicholson changed his role from what it was in the book. He made the character much more intelligent, more fully dimensional. The guy in the book was just a cowboy.

The character in *Five Easy Pieces* is perfect Nicholson: a working-man who has great talent and intelligence. Nicholson didn't want to break down at the end of the film in the scene with the father, but Bob Rafelson forced him to cry. I think it was okay because they were friends. Nicholson was nominated for an Oscar, so in hindsight he was probably fine with the crying.

We think that movies are separate from our lives, but they aren't; they are how we see ourselves. Actually, it's television that is the mirror. Movies are now mostly fantasies.

Superheroes.

Money.

Fame.

Sex.

If you're an actor, you can get a lot of pussy. If you're an actress, you can get a lot of dick. Or dick and pussy, or pussy and dick.

If you're an actor in film, people will think that you are like your roles. If you smoke pot onscreen, you are a stoner; if you kiss a dude, you are gay; and if you murder John Wayne, your career will be over.

Most people don't know the level of criticism that most actors have to deal with. You can understand why actors are insecure. If everyone in the world faced the kind of criticism that actors deal with, they would probably quit their jobs.

Of course, actors—the famous ones—get enough good things to balance out the criticism: hot spouses, nice tables at restaurants. They can tell stupid jokes and people will laugh, they can always find friends.

There was a time when I wanted to teach. I thought about working with kids, as a charity thing. But I looked at my skills and all I had was acting, I didn't even know how to teach it. I felt like all I could do was put on different masks, and they weren't even very good ones.

Just relax.

I guess this is a monologue about film acting, not other kinds of acting. But no one really cares about other kinds of acting because it's theater and there is either no complete record of it, or because it's television and it ages really fast.

No one really cares about movie history either.

So don't worry about actors if you're not an actor; they're all going to become animated things after a while.

And if you're an actor, make some money if you can, and live it up while it lasts.

*Came to believe that there is a power greater than
ourselves, some sort of directing force, that could
restore our "performance" to sanity.*

~~~~~~~~

Peace

AFTER I ARRIVED in LA, I started going to this acting class in
the Valley. It was on Lankershim Boulevard down from Universal
Studios. It wasn't a glamorous area. There were car dealerships and
apartment complexes and bars with names like Residuals and the
Casting Office. Everything was run down, like it had been put up
really fast, and then they tried to make the best of it by adding creative signage.

The thing about the acting school was that it was serious. There
are a ton of acting schools in LA, but most of them are scams. They
claim to teach you how to book auditions or work well on camera. At
my school, they did everything differently. It was like they didn't care
if you booked anything. They used plays to teach, not movie scripts,
and they were above all the Hollywood stuff.

I lived in an apartment close to the school with two other actors that also went to the school. They were called Peter and Pete. The rent was $650 a month, and I paid $150 and slept on the couch. There was a Taco Bell and a Jiffy Lube and a Ralph's on the corner where our street hit Ventura Boulevard. An earthquake had hit the area in the mid-90s and everyone had scattered.

All I did was go to class or prepare for class. I was nineteen, and I was one of the youngest. I worked as hard as I could at my acting, and it paid off because people in my class said I was pretty good. All the girls in their midtwenties said I was cute.

There was one girl in the class who had had some parts in big movies. Maybe it helped that her father was a producer. Her name was Bree. She had blond hair and huge eyes, almost too big. They were just peculiar enough to make her even more pretty. She was a good actress but weird. When she was acting, it was like she was secretly laughing at everyone.

Bree didn't talk to me; I just did my work in class and hoped that she would be impressed. I did scenes from *Hurlyburly, Glengarry Glen Ross,* and *Tea and Sympathy.* I was pretty good in all of them, even if I was too young for all but *Tea and Sympathy,* which was a play about a little gay guy and an older woman. Then one day something changed. I came out of the bathroom backstage, and Bree was there in the dark.

"Hey, Jerry," she whispered.

I stopped and then stepped toward her in the dark. There was a scene happening onstage, and we were the only ones in the back.

"You're pretty cute, you know that?"

Even though it was dark, I could see her big eyes from the light that spilled through the crack in the stage door. The roundness of them.

"Thank you," I said. "I think you're great."

She smiled, and it made me realize how young I was. It was a sweet smile, but it was also like her smile when she was acting, as if she was secretly laughing at me.

Then she whispered, "I think you're really talented."

"Thank you." Her eyes were there and her smile, and I was there with them, in the dark.

"I'd like to do a scene with you sometime, okay?" she said.

"Yeah, sure. I mean, yes, that would be great."

"Okay, cool. Let's do one next week."

"Great."

She gave me her number and we planned to do a scene in a week or so. But then it was her birthday. She invited the whole class to her party. It was a big party at a huge house in Hancock Park. It was her father's house, the producer. Everyone was in the backyard drinking beer and talking. I hardly had a chance to talk to Bree because she was so busy with her friends and her two sisters. One of Bree's sisters was an opera singer and sang her a song in Italian, and then sang her a grand version of the birthday song. I stood in the grass in the backyard and talked to my two roommates, Peter and Pete. Peter was a nerd and Pete was a bodybuilder. We had nothing much to say, but we kept each other company. It seemed like Bree didn't know I was there, but I also had this feeling about her and things.

Before we left, we heard that Tobey Maguire and Leonardo were going to show up because they had been in a movie with her.

The next day we rehearsed for the first time at her apartment in West Hollywood. It was a nice little place on the top floor with a great view. We picked a scene from a book of plays by John Patrick Shanley. It was a little one-act about two young people in love. The girl in the scene wears a red coat, and the boy talks about it. He talks about how much he loves the coat, but really, he is talking about how much he loves the girl. And she says she feels invincible in the coat. At the end of the scene, she asks him to kiss her.

The characters were too young for us, but it was okay, because it was just for class. We read it over a few times, and when I got to the part about the red coat, I did it very passionately, because I wanted Bree to know that I had feelings for her. The third time we read it, at the part when the girl character starts talking about kissing, I leaned in and kissed Bree. She kissed back and I opened my mouth and kissed her that way too. She pressed her lips back at mine with an open mouth and her tongue was there, small and sharp. Then she broke the kiss and held my face with both hands so she could look right into my eyes.

"That was pretty bold," she said, with her face very close to mine.

"Yeah," I said.

I felt good, but I knew that I needed to kiss her again—that if I didn't kiss her I would lose her.

"I'd like to introduce you to my agent," she said.

I didn't kiss her.

"I think you're an amazing actor and you're going to be huge."

"Thank you," I said.

"I'll set it up," she said, and stood up. I left soon after, and then we didn't talk until the next class. But I thought about the kiss a lot, and I could feel her soul on my lips.

In the next class, I saw her sitting in front. Then, at the break, she saw me. She handed me a piece of paper.

"Here's my agent's number. She's expecting your call."

I was in love with Bree. Not only was she beautiful and famous and unusual, but she was also helping me. I felt so indebted that I didn't speak to her for the rest of class.

That evening, I called the agent, a woman named Sabrina. On the phone, Sabrina was brisk and without emotion. We set up a meeting for the next day, and she told me to bring a headshot.

The next morning, I took a good shower and put on one of Peter's light-blue polo shirts and a pair of jeans. I didn't have a headshot, so I brought a photo of me sitting in my Honda Accord just before I drove from Chicago to LA. I was smiling big with my head hanging out the window, and I was wearing black Ray-Bans. I looked happy.

At the agency, the girl at the front desk directed me to Sabrina's office. I knocked on the door and she opened it. She was about thirty-five, tight skirt, attractive. She said hello without smiling and walked back and sat behind the desk.

"Did you bring your headshot?"

I handed her my little photograph. She took it and looked. She said nothing. Then the phone rang, and she answered.

"Oh, hey, Charles, yeah, hold on a second..." She tucked the phone into the crotch of her neck and said to me, "You look like Corey Feldman here." Before I could respond she dropped the photo on the desk and continued talking to Charles. She said some things and absentmindedly pushed the little picture around on the desk with her forefinger. Then the call was over and she hung up.

"Bree thinks you're a good actor," she said to me.

"Thanks," I said.

Silence. She picked up the picture again, and then she put it down.

"She said you are like a young Sean Penn."

"Wow, I love Sean Penn," I said.

"Yeah, he's good."

"Yeah," I said.

"*Dead Man Walking*, amazing," she said without any enthusiasm.

"Amazing."

She handed the picture back to me.

"Here, I assume you only have one of these," she said.

"Oh yeah, thanks." I put the picture in my front shirt pocket.

"You have a great look," she said.

I smiled at her. She didn't smile back; she just stared at me for twenty seconds.

"What kind of movies would you like to do?"

"Um, I'd like to do dramas. Like Marlon Brando."

"Great," she said. There was silence. Finally, she said, "Well, I'll need to talk to the rest of the partners if we are going to take you on."

"Great," I said.

Then she began to mess with some papers on her desk. I stood up.

One day, soon after the agent meeting, Bree and I rehearsed our red-coat scene before class in the park near our acting school. From where we were sitting on the grass, you could see the top of Universal Studios. We rehearsed a little, and then we talked.

"Is it hard being a famous actor?" I said.

"I'm not really *famous*..." she said, a little embarrassed.

"Well, you're in really big movies, and I know that people recognize you."

"That stuff doesn't matter," she said and looked toward some trees. Beyond them was the 101 freeway.

"Oh," I said, and looked at her white cheek. It made me aware of how we have skin over bones and there are different shapes underneath that are arbitrary. There was something under my skin that wanted to come to the surface and grab her.

She looked back at me, and her eyes were large and wet.

"You're amazing," I said, hoping that she would get the full meaning. I wasn't just saying that. I meant a world of things, but I was using simple language.

"*You're* amazing," she said. "You could be such a great actor, like Sean Penn."

"I love Sean Penn," I said.

"He's the best," she said, and I leaned in and kissed her. We were sitting in the grass and kissing, and I felt like I was turning my life into something great. We kissed for five seconds, and I licked her lips a little and they were soft. Then she pulled away and smiled. She looked into my eyes and I looked back.

"Yeah," she said, like she was answering a question.

After that we went to class. In class we did our scene. When I did the part where I talked about the red coat, I tried to pour all my real feelings for Bree into the speech. As if everything my character was trying to say about the girl he loved through the red coat was what I was trying to say to Bree—as if the scene and the acting were my red coat. I felt like everyone could see how much I loved her, and it felt good.

After the scene, we sat onstage, and Mr. Smithson critiqued us. He said Bree was good in the scene, real.

"But you were forcing it," he said to me.

"I was?"

"You don't have to *show* us that you are in love with her, you just need to *feel* it."

"I *was* feeling it."

"No, you wanted the whole class to know what a great actor you are, so you hammed it up. That was actually the most in your head I've ever seen you."

I stopped talking and let him go on. It made no sense. I was usually a good judge of my acting, and I had never felt so emotionally engaged with someone before in my life. I looked over at Bree and she gave me a smile, but it seemed a little sad, like she was embarrassed

for me, and I knew something that had been alive in the park had
already died.

The next day at 11 in the morning, I called the agent, Sabrina. It had
been a week since our meeting. The assistant told me that Sabrina was
in a meeting, but she would call me back.

I had the whole day free. I got some movies on VHS from the
library around the corner and sat at the apartment and watched. First
I watched *Taxi Driver* and then *East of Eden*. I was alone in the apartment because my roommates worked. Peter was a tutor for kids at a
private high school and worked until late. He thought he was really
smart. And he almost was. He also thought he was really handsome,
which he wasn't. Pete was dumb. He was a trainer at a gym. He used
to compete in Mr. Universe contests when he lived in Michigan.

I had Campbell's soup for lunch with toast and butter and a glass
of water. There was still no call from the agent, so in the early evening
I walked over to the library again and got *Lust for Life,* a movie about
Van Gogh. As I walked back to the apartment, the sun was sinking
into the smog. Back in the apartment, the light was a tattered gold-
brown. I watched the film about crazy Van Gogh.

The real Van Gogh used to walk a whole day just to see the girl
he loved step out of a church. I had almost watched the whole movie
when the phone rang. I pressed pause and Van Gogh was stuck at the
asylum missing half his ear.

It was Sabrina.

"Hi, Jerry. I talked to the partners, and we think that you need a
little more experience, okay?" she said.

"Okay," I said. "But how do I get experience?"

"Well, you need to work more."

"Okay."

"You understand?" she said.

"But how do I get work if I don't have an agent?"

Pause.

"Yeah, well, we just all thought that you need a little more experience."

"Uh, right. That doesn't really make sense, but okay."

"Okay, thank you. Talk to you later."

She was waiting on the line. I heard paper.

"Good-bye," I said, and she hung up.

I paged Bree, and then I turned the movie back on. Van Gogh fussed about, and then he went to the field where the black crows were and shot himself. I put in *A Place in the Sun*, which I owned, and then Bree called.

"Are you mad at me?" I said.

"What? What do you mean?" She sounded good, almost as sweet as usual. Her voice transmitted something solid, light blue and reassuring.

"I don't know," I said. "I didn't do well in the scene in class, and I thought maybe you didn't like me anymore."

"Jerry, that is ridiculous. I don't care about a stupid scene in class."

"I know, but I really thought I was good. I mean I really believed what I was saying, and I can't believe he told me I was faking it."

"What do you mean? Believed what?"

"Just about my feelings. Nothing, never mind."

"Jerry..." she said, and then nothing.

"Do you like me?" I said.

"Of course I like you, don't be silly."

"Okay, sorry." I almost felt good, but I knew something was gone between us.

"Don't be sorry," she said. "You're great, you're such a cool guy and such a good actor."

"And so you're not disappointed that your agent didn't want me?"

She answered really quickly.

"Oh no, she liked you. She just thinks you need more experience."

"Right."

Then there was silence. The soft blue thing was there, hanging in the black space between us, but it was just out of reach, and I was suffocating. In the real world, the sun had long ago dropped behind the palm trees and apartment buildings, and the living room was black except for Monty Clift on the TV looking sensitive. He had Elizabeth Taylor in his arms and was telling her something very important, but the sound was down and I couldn't hear him.

"Well, do you think I could see you again?" I said.

"Of course," she said. "I'm working on a new movie, but we'll get coffee or something soon, okay?"

And that was it. I turned the sound back on, but I didn't watch. I just lay on the couch, which was actually my bed, and stared at the ceiling as the movie played. The light flickered in black and white on the ceiling and walls. I was in my own movie with light all around. There was a vague storyline running in my head, something dramatic. The most obvious part of the daydream/movie was that I was the star. I was an antihero lying on the couch thinking of stardom and wanting to be something so cool and sensitive that a whole generation would want to know me, and *be* me, and let me lead them. After a while of thinking like that, Shelley Winters started whining in the background. I looked up and they were in the boat. And then Monty killed her.

Bree didn't come to class for a while because she was working on her new movie. Class wasn't as exciting without her there. I would do my scenes and work really hard, but there wasn't the same kind of satis-faction, because she wasn't watching. I wanted that light-blue feeling. And I also felt shitty because of the agent. I knew that I could do well in class, but it wouldn't matter to the agent. I needed professional experience. My life was in a vacuum.

Finally Bree and I planned to have coffee. I was very excited because I hadn't seen her in three weeks. Not since the day we had kissed in the park. I hoped she hadn't forgotten the kiss and that she still liked me. We planned to meet at Buzz Coffee on Santa Monica Boulevard, which was near her apartment. She was still working on the movie, so we planned to meet at 10 p.m.

I waited at Buzz. The night was hot. The café was full of gay men in T-shirts and tank tops. While I waited, I read *A Streetcar Named Desire*. I almost read the whole thing, and then at 11:30, I got a page. I went out-side to the payphone. I checked my messages. One was from my scene partner, Ben, who wanted to rehearse; he had a David Mamet scene he wanted to do. He worked in a bar and got off at 2 a.m., and wanted to rehearse at 2:30. The second message was from Bree. It was her voice, but I hardly felt any of the light-blue stuff. It was there but hidden deep below her words. She said that she had an early call the next day and couldn't make it to Buzz and that she was sorry.

I went back into Buzz and read *Streetcar*. I was feeling very alone and was on the last page when a guy sat next to me. He was tall with wiry arms and hair all over them and his hairline was receding but combed to the side in a sleek way. His presence was like a gazelle's.

He was pretending not to look at me, but when he saw that I was looking at him, he turned to me and said, "I love that play."

"Yeah," I said.

"Tennessee," he said, shaking his head like there was something he just couldn't get over about Tennessee Williams. "He was a tortured soul."

"Yeah," I said, and tried to read the last page, but the guy started talking again. His voice was high and had a slight whiney upswing at the end of his sentences.

"I heard that Tennessee was Blanche in that," he said. "That he was refined and sensitive like her, but that he also was attracted to the brute side of things, and that is why he wrote Stanley—because all his boyfriends were brutes like Stanley."

"That's interesting," I said.

"I'm John," he said, and put his hand very close to me.

I shook it and said, "Pete," thinking of my roommate.

"What a funny name, Pete. Ha, how did you get *that* name, *Pete*?"

"I don't know. It's just a name. Normal." I knew that this hairy guy wasn't going to let me finish the last page, so I got up. "Nice to meet you, John. Sorry I have to go; it's past my bedtime."

But the guy followed me outside.

"It's so hot out," he said, but I didn't say anything. I just kept walking. I walked to the parking lot behind the café. The guy was pretty nice, so I wasn't scared, but he wasn't going away. When I was almost to my car, I turned to him and said, "Can I help you with something?"

"Oh," he said. "I'm just an artist, and I thought maybe I could paint you some time."

"Paint me? Like naked?"

"Oh, well, I was just thinking about your face, but sure we could do that too."

"No," I said.

"Oh, well, are you an actor?"

"Yes," I said.

"Yeah, I can tell. Oh, man, you are so hot, you are going to go so far," he said, standing close to me, making his breath heavy. "Brad Pitt has nothing on you, baby," he whispered. "You are going to be a motherfucking star." And then he leaned in and kissed me on the lips, and for a second I let him. His stubble pulled me out of it. I put my hand on his chest and pushed him away. His gazelle body was full of energy, but I got away from him and to my car.

He was still by me.

"Fuck *off*," I said over my shoulder. I got in my car and slammed the door, but he was standing right there at the window. He stood still as marble as I pulled away.

There was a 7-Eleven close by. I went in and got a rose with plastic around the stem. The gay kiss made me excited, like life was happening. I drove over to Bree's feeling romantic and wild.

It was an old art deco place, all white. I parked the car across the street and walked up. There were sculpted bushes all around and a black-and-white check pattern on the ground in front of the main door. Her unit was five stories up. The lights were off up there, so I climbed the fire escape ladder onto the roof. It was about midnight.

At the top, I leaned over the side and saw her window. I knew which one it was from when we had rehearsed there. I tried to hit it, but the angle was bad. I missed a bunch of times, and the coins fell onto a dumpster in the parking lot below. I tried all my coins, quarters too, but she didn't wake up. I sat on the roof, holding the rose, looking at the sky. The moon was bright, and I could see the dark part, not reflecting anything back.

I sat for twenty minutes feeling something like sadness and also feeling very romantic, like a poet. I was getting cold; I only had a T-shirt on. I got up and walked around on the roof quietly. It was steeply pitched, and I could have fallen off. There were apartment buildings across the street, and if someone looked they could see me being a prowler. I scooted on my butt to the edge of the roof on the side of her apartment opposite her bedroom.

I gripped the rain drain on the side of the roof and went for it—I swung through the void onto her balcony. Once I landed, I felt like I had accomplished something. My blood circulated fast; everything else was quiet. I wraith-floated across the balcony to the door, and, like a wish granted, it was unlocked.

Inside, the place was in shadow, and I made my way across the wood floor toward the back rooms. Bree had a roommate who slept across the hall from her. I was about to see Bree, my love, and I was going to make something happen. I pushed open her door, and there she was on the bed beneath a thick white comforter. Her eyes flickered, and then she jerked up into a sitting position. That's when I knew that something was off.

"Hey, it's me," I whispered.

"Jerry, what are you doing here?"

"Um, I brought you this." I handed her the rose.

She didn't say anything. She was hunched up against the headboard beneath her comforter.

"I miss you," I said.

She said nothing.

"You must be tired," I said.

"Jerry, how did you get in here?"

"I climbed onto your roof and then swung down onto your balcony." It was all different when I said it out loud.

"I'm sorry I didn't show up for coffee," she said. "I have to get up at five-thirty."

"Oh, that's okay," I said, talking as if I was very calm and nothing was wrong. "I just wanted to see you."

"Jerry, you can't just break into my apartment."

"I didn't break in. I love you."

She said "Jesus," but it was quiet.

"Have you ever loved anyone?" I said.

"Jerry, stop."

"No, I wonder if you have ever really loved someone so that you feel like you want to be a better person because of that person? You are so amazing, so amazing, that I just want to be the best person I can be when I am around you."

"Jerry, if you're in love you don't break into someone's house."

"I didn't *break* in. And Romeo did."

"*What?*"

"Broke into Juliet's place. Nothing, never mind, I just want to be with you. I want to be the best actor I can be, and you make me a better actor and a better person when I'm around you. I am sorry that your stupid agent didn't like me, but I know that I'm good; *you* know that I'm good. I'm like Sean Penn. I'm really good, right? Isn't that what you told me?"

"Jerry, you have to go."

"What, you don't think I'm good now? The fucking gay guy said that I am going to be bigger than Brad Pitt. I know it was because he wanted to kiss me, but still, everyone can see—can't you see? Everyone can see that I'm going to be great!" I was talking loudly and getting closer to Bree. Then her roommate came in.

"You better get the fuck out of here," the roommate said. "I just called the police." She looked like hell with her curly hair sticking out all over the place.

"The police? What the fuck, what? I'm just…"

"Get the fuck out of here, Jerry," said the ugly roommate. "I'm serious."

I turned back to Bree. "Bree, you're not scared, are you?"

"Jerry, go," said Bree. She couldn't even look at me.

The roommate said, "You broke the rules, motherfucker. Now get the fuck out of here. *Now.*"

I stared at the frizzy-haired roommate for a long time. She stared back, real hard.

"Don't you know who I'm going to be?" I said.

"I don't care if you're JFK," she said. "If you don't get out of here I'm going to tell the cops to shoot you."

I walked out of the room, then through the dark living room. I unlocked the front door, which was difficult in the dark. I took my time. I didn't care if the cops got me. Maybe they would shoot me and all would be better.

"Get out, moron!" said the roommate. And then the door was open and I was outside. It was cold again and when I closed the door behind me I knew my life was over.

In class that week we did an improvisation for our scene from *Sexual Perversity in Chicago* by David Mamet. I was too young for the role, but it was a cool scene. I did it with my scene partner, Ben, the bartender in real life:

"So, last night, how'd it go?" he said.

"Sheeeit."

"Wha?"

"I said, 'sheeeeeeit.'"

"I heard you. For real?"

"For double fucking real."

"Don't bullshit," he said.

"No bullshit."

"So tell me. And no bullshit."

"So tits like melons, no bullshit."

"No shit?"

"No shit, and an ass—momma."

"A momma ass?"

"No, an ass like butter. An ass like candy."

"An ass like *that?*"

"An ass like an onion, bring a tear to your eye."

"Holy . . ."

"Holy fucking shit is right. And young."

"Like . . ."

"Like eighteen, twenty."

"Motha-fucka."

"What?"

"MOTHA-fucka! You're a beast."

"Sheeeeit, you think she's a virgin?"

"Ain't no virgin, hungh?"

"Puleeeeease."

"Little slut, hungh?"

"Are you fucking kidding me?"

"Big slut?"

"Sheeeeit, her fucking *name* was Slut. Slut Mackenzie."

The scene went on. Bree wasn't there. I didn't think about her or anyone else. There was no use.

*Turned our will and our "performances" over
to the Great Director.*

~~~~~~~~~~

The Great Director

THAT'S THE BIG QUESTION: Who is the Great Director?

If you want, I will be your director.

But if you don't want me, then you need to realize that there is always a director. Even when you're a director, there is a director of the director.

Directors nowadays are trying to serve the public taste. The taste is changing. As it always does, and the directors and studios try to cater to that taste.

Movies are dying, right?

But they've always been dying. When were they not dying?

Movies still make tons of money.

Video games, Internet, YouTube, shit like that. It's taking over. But television was the same way when it came around.

Movies. I guess that's what we're talking about. Movies. But when we think of movies, we think in terms of feature-length films: ninety minutes to three hours. That's how we conceptualize movies.

What about the movie of your entire life? Boring or exciting? Good scenes?

In the movie of your entire life, do you want drama and conflict or a straight shot to the top, unencumbered?

In the movie of your entire life, is there a soundtrack? It must change over the years, yes?

How about the cast of players? That changes too? A great big cast, yes? I hope so. I hope there are some good actors in there.

Now, in the movie of your entire life, do you want to be happy? That's not that interesting for other people to watch. Just saying.

Who is the cinematographer? Is the cinematography dark and moody? Fast and bright? Video or film?

Is there a lot of action in your film? Comedy? Are we laughing at you or with you? Are you in control of the comedy or its victim? Who is your foil?

Who are the villains in your film? Do they get punished? Are you the one to punish them?

What role do you play in other people's films? Are you the comic relief? The villain? The mysterious lover? The femme fatale? The father of the bastard?

It's nice to think of your life as a film because then it just feels like play-acting. That the consequences are insubstantial, as they are when your camera eye pulls out far enough. If we're watching your life from space, your personal dramas don't mean much.

Who is directing your film? I mean, really?

Who are you acting for? Who is guiding your performance? It is very hard to act and direct at the same time. I've done it a bunch of times, but I always depended on others for help when I did so. Friends.

Does your film end tragically? You probably don't know. Can't control it. Maybe you could if the character committed suicide.

I knew a young woman whose grandmother committed legal suicide in Europe. She was sick of life.

My grandmother is full of life at age ninety because she is vitalized by my career. All of her friends are jealous that I'm her grandson.

Even the friend who is the mother of Judith Butler.

Actually, *especially* the mother of Judith Butler.

Movies and entertainment dominate. That's all there is. They rule the world.

I guess they are dependent on a stable country, but when we have that, there is nothing more influential than popular entertainment.

Maybe when things are unstable, entertainment is just as influential. A nice escape, they say. But if your life is in entertainment, is it an escape? And if everyone just watches videos now, aren't the videos life, and real life is the escape?

It's safe to say that entertainment *is* life.

Do you differentiate your life from your art? Sometimes it's best to.

It's great to read *Hamlet,* but you probably wouldn't want to *be* Hamlet, or even hang out with him.

Horatio. What a good guy. Like Razumikhin is to Raskolnikov, he is to Hamlet. In life, it's better to be Horatio and Razumikhin; in art it's better to be Hamlet and Raskolnikov.

When I was in fifth grade, I copied down the character lists from all the Shakespeare plays.

I wanted to own all those characters. It was an attempt to encompass all of Shakespeare.

I had the same impulse in seventh grade, when I wanted to draw a diagram of all the people at my junior high and how they were all socially connected, all the cliques and shit.

These were two early attempts to make sense of both my artistic world and my social world.

Both worlds are made up of people. Even abstract art has a human creator.

Art is given different definitions at different times, but those definitions will be destroyed.

My director? The poet Frank Bidart.

Read Frank's poem, "Advice to the Players." It talks about all of this, about the human need to create.

Fuck business. Fuck money. Fuck fame. Fuck coolness.

I am in a great position. I *can* say fuck all of those things because I am a famous actor and because I *have* money and I can do whatever I want (within a range) and I will look cool.

But I still say fuck it all.

My work is my life and my life is my work. And something like this—this book—is totally free of the pressures of being popular, because I don't make my living off of books, I make my living off of acting.

Always have one artistic thing that is pure, at least one thing, where you don't compromise. You can do other things to make money, but have one pure area.

Now, being pure doesn't mean that you don't listen to others' opinions or don't listen to your director (whether he be actual or in your mind), but it means that you listen for the right reasons: for artistic purity, not for reasons of money or popularity.

But there is also something to be said for being successful for the sake of being successful, or getting rich for the sake of getting rich, or being famous. Maybe in the end, this is all there is.

But I would prefer a nation of artists than a nation of businessmen.

This is how they get the kids to go to Wall Street: The banks recruit at the top Ivy League schools. They make it seem like Wall Street is the next step in the elitist rise up the ladder. The young Ivy Leaguers want to continue their dominance, so they join the ranks of rats.

Business. It's all business. Culture is business. Art is business. They call it the *movie* business for a reason.

Here's the new game, or the same old game (French New Wave): Get one over on them while still playing their games. Make movies that fit into their system but also subvert their system.

That's the best way to go. Just don't let yourself become Disneyfied or Hollywoodified or indiefied or dramafied or comedyified.

Sometimes you can get into a situation where you can be the actor in some pieces, the director in others, and the writer in others. Sometimes you can be all at once, but that is usually not the most fun. Unless you're Charlie Chaplin.

Or Woody Allen.

Must be nice to control your whole world the way Woody does. His whole world is his movies, his music, and everything he loves. He's brought everything he loves around him.

Create your world around your work. Create your work around your life. Let other people help you shape it.

The film lovers and the crazies: Sometimes they're the same people.

Some people love the characters, and some people love the actors behind the characters.

Sometimes the characters take on attributes of the actors; sometimes the actors take away attributes of their characters into their own lives.

John Wayne became a cowboy because he played so many. He grew up in Glendale.

The Marlboro Man probably thought of himself as a cowboy.

If a real cowboy posed for a Marlboro ad, he'd be a phony, no?

You need to be able to take on all roles and laugh at all roles. To be able to mock the role you're playing *while* you're playing it.

You also need love. Your characters need to love something, otherwise they will be unlovable.

That's one of the big secrets. Make your characters interested in *something*. Striving for something. In need of something. Good at something. This will make them likeable and interesting.

You want to be interesting? Be interested.

You want people to open up to you? Open up to them.

I was a brat when I was little. Closed off. At camp, with strangers, I didn't want to share my secrets.

But I had no secrets worth keeping. Be open, open, open.

Your experiences are your most powerful resource. Share them.

When I was twenty-seven, I had to teach myself how to talk to people, how to be social. How not to be shy.

Being famous also helps. People will just talk to me. I am never alone at a party. People will chat my ear off.

Or I'm like Santa Claus: Everyone needs a picture sitting on my knee.

The ones I don't mind are the young pretty ones.

Eat everything up.

Don't worry about rejection. Keep trying.

If you are a player, it's fine; you'll just have more experience when "the one" comes around.

The people who hold back and wait for "the one" are usually too obsessed once they find the one that they pressure the relationship to death.

Be free.

Your life is not in your control anyway. You are made up of everything around you. So choose your characters and play them out.

Don't worry about the consequences so much—they're just roles, right?

Life is but a stage. Life is but a film. Life is death if it is not recorded.

Create.

Made a fearless and searching moral
inventory of our "character."

River Poems

1. River in Idaho

River gets a blowjob from a fatman
In the first scene. He gets money.
He meets with Keanu, they are young hustlers.

Gus's idea to use pop stars of the day
To play *gay for pay* Portland prostitutes
Was the first time anything like that went down.

Back when playing gay was as cool
As getting raped. But River had balls.
He played his role like James Dean

Mixed with Charlie Chaplin,
Mixed with the most vulnerable,
More vulnerable than any

Prostitute ever played before.
And funny.
That's the trick, he was funny.

2. Beautiful River

River died when I was in high school
I read his biography in college.
I became a vegetarian because of him.

He was so damn cool.
What about him?
Probably just his good goddamn looks,

That's all. I used to want to look like him
And I do a little.
But he had this long blond hair

That would do anything he pleased
And he had a great nose
And beautiful eyes.

Sometimes an actor will like another actor
Because he looks like him,
And sometimes an actor will hate another actor

For the same reason.

3. River Died

He died in front of the Viper room
On Halloween, in his brother's arms.

How can you blame the Phoenixes
For shutting down, for saying nothing

To no one, their darling son died in public.
The scum broadcast the recording

Of his little brother's high pitched pleas on the 911 call.
If I were a Phoenix, I'd tell the world to go to hell.

But that means that the last word on River
Was the tabloid word, the twisted word

That used River to sell papers, to turn his name
Into something flat.

But River was the coolest person
That ever lived. He was a force,

An actor and a musician, he could create
Something natural and ethereal,

Even in something like a teen thing,
Or a caper film, or the third *Indiana Jones.*

In *Stand by Me,* the boys go looking for a body.
River, I'm looking for your body, stand by me.

4. James, it's River

Hello, James, it's River.
Where do you think I'm calling from?
Deep in hell, deep in the Florida wilderness?
Deep from the cement bowels of LA,
Beneath the neon, and the signs?

It's me, River, calling you
From the underworld. Did you think
I went to heaven? Do you think
You'll go to heaven? We all die, James,
I died at age 23, ten years before your age now.

James, you're the Jesus age.
Are you even close to Jesus?
Are you close to what I was?
You fucking egomaniac,
You're not even close.

James, you think you know me?
James, I tried to be something good,
Something that spoke to people,
I was pushed into acting, but I loved music,
You're in acting because you chose it.

Pick up the phone, James, it's River,
I'm calling to say it's over.
You know that choke feeling,
Like the air is gone, because there is no
More of a life? I've left just a little,

I know you want more, James,
But I left only a little.
And what time do we have for others
Anyway. I did a bunch of movies
You haven't even watched them all.

You say you love me, but not really.
I've been gone for decades,
I've been forgotten.
I spent my two decades focused
On work and family,

You spend your time all over, James.
You're all over the place, James.
I was a River that flowed straight
And pure, you're like a king
That orders one thing,
And then orders the opposite thing.

*Admitted to the Great Director, to ourselves, and to
another actor the exact nature of our "character's" wrongs.*

———≈≈≈———

Experiences

MY DAD DIED WHEN I was twelve. I took it like a man. I grew
up near Cleveland in Shaker Heights. That's where Paul Newman
grew up.

I went to college for a year at Ohio University. I studied English
literature, which was okay. I also took one acting class in the theater
department. It was an introductory class for first-year students. The
teacher's favorite exercise was to make us act like animals and trees. I
liked being a turtle. I moved very slowly on all fours and didn't smile.
My teacher thought it was shitty. He said I should be a more expressive animal, but it's cheesy to be a tiger or a gorilla. So I just did a turtle and then I did a frog.

I hated school. Mostly because I didn't like my classes, and I didn't
like my friends. No one was special, and we just got drunk every
weekend. One weekend I got drunk, and this girl on my dorm floor
got drunk too. We were in her room. She passed out on the bed, and

when she was unconscious, I pulled up her skirt and took her panties off and I had sex with her. She woke up in the middle of me doing it, but I don't think she knew what was going on, she looked at me for a bit and then closed her eyes and moaned a bit. I didn't use a condom, but I didn't finish inside her. I did it on the sheet. Then I put her panties back on. She was this little blond girl, pretty cute. I liked her, but she left school after that. I thought I might get in trouble, but no one ever said anything. At the end of the year I dropped out too.

After I left school, I went to Cleveland and worked in my uncle's bar. I was nineteen, and wasn't supposed to be working in a place that served alcohol, but my mom asked him to work it out. I slept in the storage room above the bar. There were old liquor bottle boxes that said Seagram's and Bacardi but were filled with papers and checkered tablecloths and Christmas tree lights. In the corner below a frosted window there was a small bed with a fuzzy orange blanket. My uncle said he used to take hot women from the bar up there and do 'em. For the first week I slept with my clothes on because I didn't want to touch the blanket.

After a while, I got used to the place, and I ended up spending a lot of time in the storage area above the bar. Whenever I wasn't working, I would go up there and read and think. I still had a few acting books from school and this big play anthology, and during the day I'd lie on the bed and read them. I hardly ever went out except to work in the bar downstairs. I'd lie on my back on top of the orange blanket, and I got to like how it scratched the skin on the back of my arms and the back of my neck. Above me the ceiling slanted up to a peak and made a crotch where there were layers of cobwebs, as thick and white as milk. When my brain was tired, I'd stare up at the spiders sitting like raisins in all the white. As I slept, they probably crawled all over

60

me and in my mouth, but I didn't kill 'em. More would just come. Sometimes during the day I would look out the window. I couldn't really see out of it because it was frosted, but if I looked down toward the street I could see blurry shapes and colors moving by.

I read all those acting books. They were mostly craft books, about getting into character and analyzing scenes as an actor, how to behave naturally, and how to make things interesting with props. But I had no one to practice with, so I did all the exercises in my head. I read a ton of plays too, all the ones in the anthology and some others. William Inge and Tennessee Williams, Arthur Miller and Eugene O'Neill. And Lillian Hellman. All the Americans. And Odets, all of his early stuff. Maxwell Anderson and Robert Anderson. I'd act everything out in my head, and I'd play all the parts. And I had this book called *The Fervent Years* about the Group Theatre, which was exciting. And I had a book on Ibsen, Strindberg, and Chekhov by Stella Adler. She insisted that Russian names be pronounced correctly. I read all the plays those guys wrote: *Ghosts, Miss Julie, The Seagull.* I read all that shit, and then I would work at night. No one talked to me in the bar, I just bussed the tables.

Except one time this lady started talking to me. She was probably thirty-five. I was wiping down the bar and she asked me to bring her a vodka cranberry. I said I couldn't but I asked the bartender to bring her one. After he brought it, she asked my name.

"Ben."

"That's a pretty plain name, Ben."

She took a sip of her drink but kept her eyes on me at the same time like she was being sexy.

"I didn't choose my name," I said.

"I wonder why your parents gave you *that* name."

"They didn't. They called me Benjamin."

"That's even worse. *Benjamin.* It sounds like corduroy. Or cardboard."

"What do you mean?"

"I just mean it's boring."

"I guess it's a biblical name."

"A boring one."

She took another little sip and then smiled at me as she swallowed. There was evil underneath her face; it seeped out of her smile lines.

"What's your name?" I asked. She kept looking at me but stopped smiling, so then it was like everything was very serious. Then she said "Jenny."

She lifted her glass to take a drink but then she didn't drink; she just held the glass in front of her mouth and stared at me. It was like she was trying to be very mysterious.

That night I took her up to the storage room. She had had five more of those vodka cranberries, and by the time she was on top of the orange blanket with me, she was slurring her words.

"Boring Benjamin," she said while we were kissing. We were kissing hard so that when she said things she said them right into my teeth and the back of my mouth. Her breath was hot. She said it again, "boring fucking Benjamin" and I could feel it in my throat. I was trying to kiss her and ignore what she was saying. The kissing was very messy, saliva all over our chins and across our cheeks.

She was not bad looking. The only problem was her face was flat: Her cheeks were pushed forward onto the same plane as the rest of her face, and the whole thing was oval and really pale. It was like a plate. But she had big eyes that I liked, and I held her around her back and pressed my chest against her breasts, and I could feel that everything was firm.

I grabbed a tit over her shirt and squeezed a bit. She said, "You like that shit, don't you, boring Benjamin?"

I said, "Yes, this cardboard wants to fuck you."

She pulled away from the kisses and looked at me like she was inspecting me. Her big eyes were half closed from the drinking, and the evil was really showing now. She inspected me and then she started laughing.

"Okay, you little cardboard fucker, fuck me. Do it, fuck me."

When we were doing it, she got really into it. I was on top, and she grabbed me around the ass with both hands and pulled me down into her with fast, hard jerking motions. Then she flipped me down on my back and got on top. She put her hands on the wall above me and made weird quick motions with her pelvis that whipped her vagina back and forth really fast. She started breathing huffily and heavy, and she wasn't looking at me; she was looking at the wall above me, then the ceiling, and then her eyes were closed and she was moaning like she was chanting. I looked up and knew that all those spiders were just above her head like a crown of thorns.

After she had her orgasm I flipped her onto her back and I got back on top. I reached under and grabbed her ass so I could control her and keep her from doing those quick movements. I held her ass and pulled myself into her again and again as hard as I could. I wanted her to know that it was *me* inside her. But I guess she liked the hard stuff, because she held my ass, and my back, and helped me thrust into her really hard. I tried to go harder, I wanted it to be so hard that it would hurt, but it wasn't working, she just got more excited the harder I did it.

She whispered in my ear, "Fuck me, little guy, fuck me."

It made me want to go harder, but I was already going so hard I was panting. My hip sockets felt like air from all the motion. I looked down at her flat white face. *Fuck you,* I said, but not out loud. Then I got into a rhythm: With each thrust I said *fuck you,* but only in my head. I was going really hard and fast and I was looking right in her half-closed evil eyes, like a snake's eyes, and I was screaming in my head *fuck you, fuck you, fuck you.* But I couldn't come. After a bit, I was really tired and lightheaded. I stopped moving.

I lay on top of her and didn't pull out. I put my face on the pillow next to hers and tried not to pant. I was so tired and pissed, but mainly I was pissed because I knew this woman was so hollow and lonely and she had pulled me into that hollow space with her. Whenever I imagine the dark back rooms of the world, the cold corners full of lonely people, I think of that storage room with that flat-faced, evil woman.

I lay there, and my breathing started to slow down. Down below, I moved my pelvis only, going in and out very slowly so that I would stay hard. She was gently stroking my back with her fingertips.

"You have such soft skin," she said. I guess she was being nice.

I turned my head and spoke into her ear, and I was so close my lips brushed the shell shapes inside. I whispered, "I want to eat a meal off your face."

After a second, she stopped stroking my back. Then she pushed me off, quickly pulled her dress over her head, and left. I lay in the bed naked, my wet dick sticking to the fibers of the orange blanket.

Nothing happened to me for months after that. One winter night it was raining outside, and the place was pretty empty. I had read all the acting books by then, and I was restless. I sat in the bar and drank a little in secret and stared at the few pointless people that were in there. This girl Pam came into the bar. Pam was a little older than me and she used to go to my high school. She was ugly, but she tried to look pretty. She sat and had a drink, and then after a bit she said she was supposed to meet some friends, but they had ditched her. So we started talking. She had been in Los Angeles for a couple years but now she was back. She told me about an acting school in LA.

"LA is fucked," she said out of her bulldog face. "But if you go, I recommend Valley Playhouse. It's great because it's very intense, not like a lot of the bullshit schools out there. The teacher, Mr. Smithson, is amazing. So smart."

"But you left?" I said.

"Listen, LA is a shit pit. There are five million people out there trying to be actors, and only a handful of them make it and the ones that don't just hang around and rot. It's depressing. That's why I left. I mean, I worked a little, some TV shows and stuff, but it was soul-crushing. Everyone is a vampire there."

I worked in the bar for six more months. Then, in the summer, I drove to Los Angeles.

It took me five days to get to LA. I had my dead grandpa's Nissan Stanza. My grandma had given it to me after I crashed my first car. I loved my grandfather. He was an oral surgeon, but he loved literature, and we talked about books together. The car still had his smell, which was like aftershave. And his hair was under the seats. If I dropped something in the car, like a pen or some money, when I reached down I would come up with clumps of his soft white hair.

I drove through deserts and on long boring freeways. I passed a ton of cows. It was so hot that summer. There were McDonalds and Burger Kings all the way across the country. I ate a lot of beef jerky too.

I arrived in LA on June 16, 1996. It was night. I exited the 405 and drove up Sunset Boulevard. First I drove through all the residential areas with the huge mansions all lit up: Brentwood, Westwood,

Bel Air. I passed UCLA and went through Beverly Hills. It was dark, but the mansions were blasting their lights, so the windows were like square fires. And then I got to the strip and then there were tons of lights. It felt like an important moment, like an entry into something. I drove slowly and took everything in. There were people standing in lines outside the clubs and punks walking in the street. I passed the the Roxy, Whisky a Go Go, the Viper Room, and Tower Records. Then there were a bunch of restaurants with outdoor seating and a red Ferrari and a yellow Lamborghini and some other fancy cars parked by the valet in front. Driving past, I saw a bunch of backs in backless dresses, and legs, and some asshole-looking guys. I said *fuck you* in my head to those people and drove on. There were billboards and big lights, but everything was a little dirty. I took Laurel Canyon through the Hollywood hills to get to the Valley because the acting school was over there.

The first night I stayed in a Best Western on Ventura Boulevard, near Universal Studios. It was a hot night and I laid on top of the green and white paisley duvet. The bed was stiff. I laid there and let the night soak into me as I sweated. It was all starting.

At 1 a.m., there was a fight in the room behind my head. The man told the woman she was an asshole.

"Don't be such an asshole!" he said.

"Richard, it's true. I don't care what you say. It's *true*."

"Of all the assholes in all the world, *you*, I gotta be here with *you*."

It was great. It was great to be in LA and to have people screaming.

The man kept saying she was an asshole. It was weird to hear a woman called an *asshole*.

"I swear to God," Richard said. "I just...I just want to beat the fuck out of you, you fucking *asshole*."

"Shit, didn't stop you at Disneyland did it? Fucking shit."

"Motherfucker! Motherfucking *asshole!*"

Then there was some stuff thrown and more shouts. There was something heavy that made a hollow sound on the floor and then something broke.

The screams continued. I turned my head toward the window. In the middle of the cement courtyard, there was a kidney-shaped pool. On the surface of the water, there was a bit of yellow and pink neon reflected from the hotel sign above. The yellow and pink danced with each other and went in and out of each other, and the people screamed next door, and I knew that everything was good in the universe.

The next day at noon, I drove down Lankershim Boulevard to the acting school that Pam had told me about called Valley Playhouse.

It had a plain brown front that you would miss except for the sign. I parked and walked in. I was a little late for the noon class; I have a problem being on time for anything, even things I care about. There was a lobby area with a bunch of movie posters and clippings. No one was there. Everyone was inside the theatre; I could hear voices. I opened the door as quietly as I could. The place was dark except for the little stage at the front. I saw a few faces in the audience turn back at me. I closed the door and discreetly walked to the back row and sat. I was next to a woman in her forties; she looked at me briefly and then back to the stage. She thought she was something.

It was a fifty-seat theater with a few raking levels that descended toward the plain gray rehearsal stage. There were students in most of the other cloth-backed chairs, about thirty of them. Everyone was looking at the stage. Onstage, there was a couch against the wall, a circular table in the center, and some folding chairs.

There was also a guy and a girl up there, both in their twenties. They were screaming at each other. The girl was seated at the circular table knitting something and the guy was standing over her. The guy looked like a model that had been doing drugs for a few years and the girl looked like a stripper. It didn't seem like there was a script, they were just yelling and cussing and saying whatever. They sounded just like the people back at the motel. There were tears on both their faces but neither of them stopped yelling.

"Oh, you're just going to keep knitting, hungh?" the guy said.

"Yeah, I'm going to keep fucking knitting," she said.

"Oh, so what? I'm going to stand here and you're going to fucking knit a…a little fucking *thing?*"

"Yeah, I'm just knitting a fucking *little thing!*"

"Oh, that's great! That's fucking great! You're going to knit, while I'm fucking standing here."

"Yes, I'm going to fucking knit! I'm fucking *knitting!*"

"You're knitting. You *fucking* bitch. You're fucking knitting, while I'm standing here and it is so upsetting! I want to cry!"

"You're standing there? You're standing there and you want to cry? Well *don't* stand there, asshole!"

"I'm *standing* here, *bitch,* and you're making me cry!"

"Don't call me a *bitch, fucker!* Fucking pussy, go cry, you fucking pussy motherfucker."

The guy got on his knees in front of her.

"Don't you understand? I'm going to *die!* I need the money! They're going to kill her! They're going to fucking shoot her if I don't give them the money!" The guy stood up and was now holding the girl's shoulders and shaking her.

"Don't fucking touch me!" she screamed, and stood up.

Then the guy grabbed the little square thing that she was knitting and pulled at it violently. It didn't quite come apart, so he kept pulling. The girl screamed and snatched for it, but he threw it on the ground and ran out of the door at the back of the stage and slammed it behind him. The girl collapsed on to her knees and picked up the little destroyed knitted thing. She blubbered out deep sobs and everyone watched for a full minute. Then someone started talking.

"All right, Sean, come on out."

At the foot of the little stage there was a tall man in a large chair. He had gray curly hair combed back in a bouffant. This was the teacher.

Sean came back in through the stage door.

"Don't slam our doors," the teacher said. He had a slow resonant voice. But when he accentuated anything, his voice went up into his nose and sounded high and nasally.

"Sorry, Mr. Smithson, I was just so into it, the situation." said Sean.

"Shut up." Mr. Smithson turned to the girl and said in a deep voice, "That was good, Tiffany."

"Thank you, sir."

"What did you *feel?*" said Mr. Smithson. He was playing with a rubber band in one hand. He wrapped it around his index finger and stretched it with his thumb.

"I felt angry..." said Tiffany.

"Yes, *and...*" The rubber band stretched.

"Well, I felt angry and upset and I felt like I really had to get this knitting done and Sean was really pissing me off and upsetting me because he was so needy and he didn't understand that I needed to get this done."

"That's *good,*" said Mr. Smithson. "Good, you were really feeling the situation. You were connected to the imaginary circumstances. Good. Now why did you have to get that knitting done?"

"Because my baby died. And I needed to knit him a shawl before the funeral started." As she said this she started crying again.

Mr. Smithson let her cry, and then when she was done, he said, "That's very good, Tiffany, very good. Obviously you had a connection to those circumstances."

"Well, if anything ever happened to my son I would just die, so yeah, it meant something to me."

"Very good. Now, Sean, why did you come to her door? What were you after?"

"Well, I needed money from her because I was tangled up with the mob and I had made a bad bet at the races and if I didn't pay them fifty thousand dollars they were going to murder my girlfriend."

"Sean. No, that is not real."

"But I know someone that that happened to."

"I highly doubt that."

"I did! He was this guy..."

"*Sean*. I don't care!" Mr. Smithson was using the nasal voice again. The woman in her forties sitting next to me was whispering to herself. "What an idiot," she said.

"Listen to me," Mr. Smithson said to Sean.

"*Listen* to him," the lady in her forties whispered to herself.

"I don't care if that happened to you or someone you know," said Mr. Smithson. "It has no resonance with you. And I highly doubt it ever happened. It's false. It's a made-up story. Didn't you see how upset Tiffany was?"

"Yes, but..."

"No, shut up! Did you see how upset she was while she was doing her activity?"

"Yes."

"Then why didn't you work off that? Why didn't you take that in? You were so wrapped up in telling your false gangster story that you didn't connect with her. You could have taken her in and experienced a connection with her, but instead you were wrapped up in gangster land."

The class laughed at this. Even Sean laughed a little.

"I wasn't in *gangster* land," he said.

"*Quiet,* Sean," said Mr. Smithson. "I don't want to hear it. That is your problem. You always play the *story,* instead of engaging with the other person. Acting is *not* an isolated exercise! It is about connecting with the other person. If you are playing your story, or off trying to smell a lemon in your imagination, or doing anything that is going to take you away from what is going on with the person in front of you, then it's *false.* What you're doing is *false.* Do you understand?"

The woman next to me whispered, "Yes, *yes.*"

"Yes," said Sean to Mr. Smithson.

"You do? What do you understand?"

"That I need to connect to the other person more," said Sean.

"That's right. Okay you two, rehearse, rehearse, rehearse."

"Yes Mr. Smithson," they said and got up and sat with the other students in the audience.

Mr. Smithson called two names from a list and two people went backstage and two more people that had been backstage came out onstage and started improvising and arguing like Sean and Tiffany. Mr. Smithson was stretching and stretching his rubber band.

The class went on for three hours. At the end, Smithson told the students to rehearse and dismissed them; then he turned to the auditors in the back row and said he would meet with them. Mr. Smithson moved to the circular table onstage and all the auditors lined up. I was last in line, behind the lady in her forties. Mr. Smithson sat with each auditor and quietly asked questions. When he got to the lady in her forties, I could hear what they were saying.

"Have you acted before?" said Mr. Smithson.

"Well, I was part of an improv group in college, we did comedy skits and things like that," said the lady. She was holding her purse in her lap and kept readjusting the position of her hands.

"And what do you do now?" Mr. Smithson was stretching the rubber band.

"I'm a paralegal, but I hate it."

"Mm-hm, and why do you want to be an actor?"

"Well, I just love it. I find it incredibly liberating and I want to express my feelings." Her hands moved and then moved back. She was gripping the purse hard. "I feel so constrained by the structures in my life and I want to be able to be free, to be uninhibited."

"Good, I see. How old are you?"

She paused, and then she said, "I'm forty-six, but I have tons of energy. I know that I am older than most of the students here, but I will work as hard as anyone. I *need* this. My husband says I am a fool for wanting to do this, but I don't care. I can't keep doing what I am doing; I am going to kill myself. I am cooped up in an office all day filling out paperwork for megacorporations. I would rather die than continue doing what I'm doing."

She was getting emotional like she was in one of the improvisations from the class.

"Okay," said Mr. Smithson. "You can start next month, okay?"

"Oh, thank you, thank you," she said and shook his hand. She walked out with a huge ugly smile on her face.

Then I was up. I was the last person in there. It was just me and Mr. Smithson sitting across the table on the stage.

"How can I help you?" he asked.

"I want to be in your school," I said.

"Why?"

"I want to act."

"Why?"

Suddenly I didn't know what to say. Then I said, "Because I hate myself and my life and I want to be someone else."

Mr. Smithson's face was blank. I looked down at the tabletop. From the corner of my eye, I could see him working the rubber band.

"You're a little young," he said. "We usually like people with some life experience. You need to have something to *act*. You understand? You need to be a little brokenhearted and a little beaten down. Does that make sense?"

"Yes," I said.

"Have you ever been in love?" he said.

I thought for a second, then said no.

"Right, well, what have you done?"

I didn't know what to say. I hadn't done anything in my life. I was proud of nothing. I really did hate myself. I was just boring Ben.

"I don't think I've done anything. That's why I want to act." Then I said, "My father died."

He made a noise but said nothing else. I kept going,

"I want to live in an imaginary world because my world is so stupid. I mean my dad died when I was twelve, and it was so dumb and worthless. Like I couldn't even feel it, or I didn't let myself feel it because it seemed like such a cliché, and so many people lose their dads, so who cares? Nobody really felt bad for me. I mean, not *really*. Not to the point that I ever felt like talking about it with anyone. Even my mom, she was so wrapped up in herself, I couldn't talk about it with her." Now I was crying as I spoke. It was the first time that I had cried in a long time.

"And my dad was okay, but he wasn't like a great guy or anything. He just owned a few fast-food places, and then he had a heart attack and died. It's so boring, I hate to even think about it. And my grandpa died, and my cat died, and that's about it for people dying. And I went to college for a year and studied literature and took a little acting, but it was so horrible, not like here."

"University acting courses are worthless," said Mr. Smithson.

"I *know*, they just made us pretend we were animals and it was so pointless that I would just pretend that I was a tree and stand there and no one cared; I would just stand there while everyone else was slithering on the floor, or growling, or jumping around. I stood in the corner with my arms down, a limbless tree, and no one said anything. After a while even that was too much, so I pretended I was a rock and sat on the floor."

Mr. Smithson didn't say anything; he just worked his rubber band.

I didn't know what else to say. Then I said,

"I raped a girl once. Well, it wasn't rape, but I guess it was." I didn't look at him, I looked down at the tabletop. The story came out while I looked at the pattern of the wood grain, little rivers of different shades of brown. "We were both drunk and I think that she liked me. I mean, we were getting along before it happened and we kissed and everything, but then we were watching a movie and she passed out. I knew that I should have probably waited, but I didn't." All this stuff poured out, and I felt small but also like it was stuff I should say, and Mr. Smithson was the guy I should say it to.

"I never saw that girl again. Her name was...well, I can't think of her name right now. I think she might have left school after that. Maybe I ruined her life, I don't know. I just did it, and it didn't seem real, but then she woke up for a minute and looked at me, and then it felt so real. So I guess that is *something*. I mean, I have feelings about

74

that. I mean, I shouldn't have done that. I know that now, but I can't take it back. And I've never told anyone about it until now. You're the first person I've ever told about that."

I was crying, I was crying so much and it wasn't stopping. I felt so great.

*Were entirely ready to have the Great Director
remove all these defects from our "character."*

〰〰〰

Windsor Girl

I'M JUST A STUPID little girl who wants to be an actor. James wouldn't want me writing this but I've taken over. I know I'm young, and everything I have to say is a cliché, but I also feel like I have a right, because he took my virginity. Maybe he took a lot of girls' virginities, I don't know. Well, maybe I do know, and yes he did. But I'm pretty damn sure he didn't like any of them, at least the young virginal ones, as much as me.

I was a student at NYU (still am). I was raised in Windsor, Canada, just across the river from Detroit. I was a virgin through high school, but I hung out with punks and idiots and actors and did some stupid stuff anyway. My parents are from Croatia. Actually, I was born in Croatia and my parents had to put me in a bag and keep me quiet as they crossed the border to escape from the war. My father held his hand over my little mouth. So I was in Croatia for only a year. But I'm still Croatian. I go back to visit family: my grandmother, who I love, but she is also a typical Croatian woman, meaning she is dumb and does whatever my grandfather says.

My mother is a nurse. She is also a typical Croatian woman and she lets my father say whatever he wants to me. He is the boss in the house, but I tell my mother *everything*. We have a close relationship. Now that I'm in New York, my mother texts me all day long. We talk every night. I told her, but not my father, when I had sex with James. Sometimes my mother is annoying and I get bratty in return, but I still love her so much. I just don't want to become her.

I want to be an actress like Meryl Streep. Or more like James Dean or Marlon Brando (I wish I was a boy sometimes). I don't want to be a girly girl (sometimes I do), and I don't want to be a Croatian bride. I want to be a punk rocker riot grrrl. I want to be able to show my pussy out loud. But I'm shy of my pussy. I'm afraid it smells. It doesn't, and it's not an ugly pussy, but I'm still shy of it. I'm prouder of my tits. I have perfect tits. I'm very comfortable with showing them. I've shown them in a bunch of James's projects. But that was all later.

My father drove a cab in Canada while getting his law degree. He worked very hard for me and my little brother. In Croatia he was a very successful lawyer, but he needed to pass the bar in Canada too. He yells a lot, but only because he's passionate.

My parents are supportive of me going to Tisch drama school, but only if I work hard and get good grades.

Kurt Cobain is my god. He is the most beautiful man that ever lived. Except maybe James. I used to hang out with punks in Windsor. We'd go to this old abandoned house and have little concerts in the basement. Death metal type stuff. At NYU I had a band with my dormmates. We were called DaDa. I wanted to tag all the stop signs around NYU so it would say "STOP DaDa" everywhere. Like *Stop Daddy*. But also like the art movement. Chaos.

My first month of being in New York, I lost my virginity. Just like Marlon Brando. He wrote about it in his autobiography, *Songs My Mother Taught Me*. Maybe I'll have a book someday, or people will write about me.

I kinda doubt it, I don't know if I'm good enough at anything.

Going to New York was the most exciting thing in my life. I signed up for all my classes. I was put in the Stella Adler program—NYU has different studios that students are assigned to for their four years: Stella, Strasberg, Musical Theater, the Atlantic Theater (David Mamet's place), and Experimental Theater. I thought Stella was a good fit. It's where Robert De Niro and Benicio Del Toro and Marlon Brando went (but when Stella was *alive,* oh well).

One month after I got there, I was hanging in my dorm room one night (it's in a big tower on 14th Street), and I got a text that James Franco was at the Starbucks near school. Me and this redheaded girl from acting class I was rehearsing with jumped in the elevators and ran the three blocks, giggling, to Starbucks. It was the wrong one. So we made our way over to the one near Washington Square Park, this time walking. As we walked, I told the redhead everything I loved about James and his work. After seeing *Freaks and Geeks,* I knew he was a kindred spirit (I was like the Freaks in high school), and after seeing him in *James Dean* I knew he was a genius. He was the actor I wanted to be like. I also watch a lot of cartoons and comedies. I've memorized everything he says in *Pineapple Express*. Saul is a character for my generation. Pure genius.

We walked down to the park and took a left to hit the corner of West 4th Street. It was October and chilly; I wore black leggings and my muscular legs looked pretty damn good.

Romance.

I want to be the voice of a generation. I want to be an artist. I want to be famous.

When we breached the frame of the window, I could already see the crowd of undergrads surrounding him, whispering and giggling to each other; I wanted to hate them, but they were just like me.

What is a person? Nothing. Destroy the person. But also I want to be a special person. This is a way to destroy the person that I am, that I hate. I don't like my nose, a Croatian nose, my father's nose. And I have big eyes, but they're blue and pretty. Or so I've been told. Mostly my mother is the one who says I have pretty eyes. I've had one boyfriend. He was an asshole. A wannabe punk who liked to beat me a little bit. I mean, not really, but he pushed me a couple times and was emotionally cold when I tried to be emotionally warm.

How many times must I give myself to others, be a good friend, open myself up, and then get squashed? I want to be loved. Like James Dean, I *need* to be loved. I will act and make music in order to be loved.

Inside, a group made up mostly of giggling Asian girls went over and asked him something. He didn't look up right away; he finished his page and then lifted one side of his large headphones and asked them to repeat. I couldn't hear, but there was more giggling, and then they were obviously asking for a picture. He turned them down.

I got my hot chocolate with the redhead. Then, with a glance, we silently decided to go over. Like with the Asians, he didn't look up right away, but then he did, and slipped off one side of his Bose headpiece. He was smiling. We told him we were actors and that we really admired him. We didn't ask for a picture, and he kept talking to us. I told him about Stella, our school, and about the different classes we had to take: History of the Theater, Ibsen, Shaw, Chekhov, etc. Then he got my number. He got the redhead's too, but I figured he was just doing that to look uninterested in me. Just a hunch I had. It was cold out, so we ran all the way back to my dorm. We screeched down Broadway, yelling because we wanted our voices to sew themselves into the night, because it felt like New York had opened up, like a big orifice, a ragged mouth or vagina, and in a deep, unheard voice said, *Here is your wish come true.*

We were liberated cunts and legs in the winter wind, whipping, flapping, and flying. We must fly. We were students and we were sirens. At least I was.

I was so obsessed with Kurt Cobain that I wrote a short story about him. Not exactly about him like a biography, but about a teenage boy who was like him (and like me too, if I was a boy) who was so depressed and artistic he committed suicide. Later I showed this story to James—this was much later, after he had come into my life, when he talked to me about marriage and children, after I had started working with him on his art projects, but before I had traveled the world with him—and he read it in my dorm room, but he didn't have much response. He said it was good and smiled like he knew something.

After Starbucks, James didn't call me. Later, when he was in my life, we would talk about that time, back when I was just getting to know him, and I would tell him how upset I had been then, but how I felt like I couldn't be because what could I have expected? He was James Franco and I was a stupid NYU freshman. I went to my classes and tried not to think too much about him. I focused on Arthur Miller, but James was the only thing alive in me. All I had to hold onto was a crinkly-eyed smile, because we hadn't really talked much. I tried to warm myself from the impression that was still inside me, to make his face visible in my mind, the version of it that looked right at me and was conscious of me, and maybe if I made it clear enough in my mind it would send out energy to him and he would know I was thinking about him.

One week after I met James, I got a text message from him at 10 o'clock at night asking me what I was doing. I was reading *The Glass Menagerie*. I wrote back that I was doing homework. He asked if I wanted to come over later, and I said yes.

At 11:30, I went to the address on 13th Street. He buzzed me in, and I walked up a twisting stair to the third floor. His apartment was a three-story place with its own circular stair inside. He offered me water, and we went over to a leather couch in front of a flatscreen television. It was dim in there, but I could see books all over the place. He showed me some pictures on the wall. One of them was an early Warhol, a sketch of a boy's face that looked like James Dean. We watched a little bit of a weird art film called *Scorpio Rising*, gay guys on motorcycles. Then he kissed me. His tongue was in my mouth. It felt good. I was pretty surprised. I had kissed four guys in my life and none really like this. Then he asked if I wanted to go upstairs. I said sure. We went up the winding stair past pictures of naked girls (later I learned they were photos by Francesca Woodman), and then we were in his room. It was small, with a mattress on the floor next to the window with a view of the street. There were a couple shelves with more books next to the mattress.

It was dark except for the streetlights through the window. I kept thinking of the word *haunted* for no reason. Nothing else was in my head except that I was from Windsor, Canada.

We got into the bed. And pretty soon after we were kissing. Then my shirt came off and then my bra and my good tits came out. And

81

then my pants were off. He tried to go down on me but I wouldn't let him. I was too shy about that, so I pulled his head up. Then I went down on him. I wasn't that confident, but I tried my best and he guided me a little. Then he put on a condom and we were trying to have sex. He was on top of me, pushing, but it really wouldn't go in. It felt like it wasn't supposed to fit. I was pulling my torso away in an awkward way while trying not to make a noise because I was so embarrassed. Then it was making its way inside and then it was all the way in. I managed to whisper, "Slow. Go slow," and he did at first, but then it started moving easier and he went faster.

I really didn't know that this was going to happen, or if I did, I kept it from myself so that when it did all start happening I just went with it like I was innocent but also because I really wanted it.

I had to stop him in the middle because it hurt, and I was embarrassed about the blood. But then we kept going.

Later that night, I woke and lay there beside him. His arm was over me, and I was naked under the covers except for my panties. I looked out at the lights. We were high up enough that the streetlights were level with us. There was one just outside his window; it was in an old-fashioned style, as if it were from a London fairy tale, even though I'd never been to London. I felt like I was in *Mary Poppins* and I was about to fly out to Never-Never Land.

For a second.

*Humbly asked the Great Director to remove
our "character's" shortcomings.*

~~~∧∧∧~~~

McDonald's I

I WAS BORN IN THE LA and I never left the LA. I lived in the
Valley. For about six years, I did heroin all the time. I had two boys,
but I never saw them. They lived over the hill with my ex in West
Hollywood. I was twenty-seven at the time. And then I stopped
using heroin. I moved back in with my parents in North Hollywood.
My mom didn't work and my dad was a priest at a little church on
Magnolia. He was happy to tell the church that his son was now clean
and was trying to get his life together. He said it right in front of the
whole church one morning so that everyone would be happy for me.

After the service I talked to all the people. "Sean, you keep praying
and the Lord will deliver." I shook their hands and smiled. I always
had a good smile. The heroin had worked on my face a little, but I was
still a good-looking guy. Maybe my hair was going a little in front.

I went to these alcohol and drug meetings, and before I knew it, I
had six months without using heroin or any drugs. I liked going to the

alcohol ones because they were more organized than the drug ones. I still had a car, and every morning I went to this men-only meeting on Vineland Boulevard, called the Valley Bucks Meeting. It met in this little burrito place called El Jardin Encantado at 7:15, before the restaurant opened. The guys were there every morning; what a group of characters. The men were all ages. Some were professionals in suits and others wore sweatpants and let their balls show in bulges. Some sat in the booths and others sat at the actual bar. I never talked, I just sat and listened, but they all told jokes and talked about their wives and about God.

I got to know all the guys there because I went there every morning. I got a sponsor named Sonny. Sonny was a washed-up actor. He was a million years old, but he acted like he was twenty. He loved to talk about acting, which was okay with me because a long time ago I had wanted to be an actor. Sonny had been onstage with Bert Lahr, the Cowardly Lion from *The Wizard of Oz*. They traveled all over the states doing a play about aliens back in the '60s. Sonny didn't work anymore. He had turned his daughter into an actress, and when she got on a hit TV show, he used her money to buy a house. She was my age now and was crazy and now that she wasn't a cute child star anymore she couldn't get work. But Sonny had his house. So he just went to the alcohol meetings every day and hung out at his big house in the valley. He always wanted me to come over.

I'd go about once a week. He would keep me there for hours. We'd lie on his bed in front of a huge TV and watch old movies. I'd lie on his wife's side of the bed. She was never there during the day because she worked as an extra. It was great at first. We'd watch Chaplin, and Laurel and Hardy, and the Marx Brothers. We'd watch *Dracula* and *Frankenstein,* the *old* versions, with the slicked hairstyles and the funny monster makeup. They were all old-fashioned and stupid, but also good because of that. And he'd tell me stories as we watched.

"I did *Picnic* in Miami. It was the premiere run in Miami, and William Inge had me over to his house. Funny man with a high voice. So I didn't know what was up. I mean, I knew some gay guys in the theater, but *this* guy ... he went into the bathroom and while he was in there I saw this container of Vaseline on the dresser. The cap was off and when I looked in I saw there was a little bit of brown *shit* in it."

"Oh, man," I said. "A fucking faggot! Using Vaseline on assholes!"

"Exactly. But back in the day we called 'em queers. Well, when he came out, I didn't say anything about the shit, but he wanted to take my picture and I said 'Oh, yeah?' And he said 'Yeah, with your shirt off,' and that was it for me. I didn't care if he had written some great plays, I was out of there, *fast*."

"No shit. I don't know why you were there in the first place."

"Well, you're right. But you know, when he was a young actor, Brando rode his bike out to the beach and fucked Tennessee Williams to get the part of Stanley in *Streetcar Named Desire*."

"Shut the fuck up."

"I did Brando's voice once. For another Tennessee thing, *The Fugitive Kind*. Sidney Lumet needed some voiceover lines for Brando and Brando wouldn't do 'em, so I got a call to do Brando's voice."

"That's cool."

We'd watch the old movies and lie on his bed and then he would talk about getting spiritual. One time, just after I went six months with no heroin, he said, "You need to get a job."

"But I want to be an actor, like you."

"I don't give a shit. You can be an actor all you want, but if you don't take care of yourself, then you're shit."

"But no place will hire me. I've never worked anywhere before."

"I don't give a shit, Sean, that's what being *spiritual* is: taking care of yourself. Being responsible. *That's* spiritual. You're just a selfish little prick, and you want everyone to serve you."

I wanted to mention that we were lying on a bed on the second floor of the house his daughter bought him, but I didn't. Instead, I listened to him, because I wanted to change. I didn't want to be selfish anymore, and I didn't want to be a drug addict.

"I want to be good," I said. "I just know that no place will hire me. I have no experience, and I look like shit."

"You've *never* worked *anywhere?*"

"I worked at a golf course in high school, but I got fired because I fell asleep while driving the ball-fetching cart on the driving range; I was on some drugs, and when I fell asleep, it drove toward the people hitting the balls and then into a person. An old man."

"That was stupid. I'm an old man, you gonna hit me with your golf cart?"

"No."

"Damn right, because I'd fuck you up, young buck." He laughed. That was his joke: that I was young, but he could still fuck me up. And that he called me "young buck."

Then he said, "Well, what you're going to do is clean up. You can shave, can't you? And comb your hair?" I nodded. "Well, do that, and put on a good shirt and go get a job."

I tried. That night at home, I cleaned myself up. My hair was pretty long, not long like a girl, but long: curly and 'fro-y, so I cut it with some scissors in the bathroom. It was uneven at first and I kept trying to correct my work until it ended up really short. My mom tried to come in but I told her to go away.

"What are you doing in there so long?"

"Nothing, just shitting." I guess she was worried about me going back to heroin, so she still watched my every move. I lathered my face with hand soap and shaved off my blonde scruff. I looked okay. When I came out my mom started crying. I'm not sure why, but I didn't ask. She came in to hug me, and I let her.

The next day I wore a white button-down shirt and jeans because they were all I had, and I drove around looking for a job. I had a Ford Fairmont from when I was using. It was very square and brown, like a long box. It had no heat, no AC, and the parking brake didn't work, and there were spiders and living things all over the inside because I couldn't close the driver's side window all the way.

I mostly went to restaurants. The ones I went to in the morning had me take applications because the managers weren't in yet. An Italian place, a place with a French name, a steak place. After an hour I had a stack of the forms on the passenger seat. The forms asked for prior work experience, and I knew that was going to be a problem, and some of them asked if I had been arrested in the past ten years, and that was going to be a problem too.

Around 12:30, the sun got hot through the windshield, and there were wet circles under my arms. I needed something to drink. I went into this Italian place not far from my parents' house, which is off Riverside on Tujunga. It was called Isabel's. It wasn't a bad place, but it also wasn't gourmet. The manager was there. He was a medium-size Italian guy with dark hair and a square head. All the lights were on, and the place was empty except for a couple Mexican-looking guys that were setting the tables with candles in red honeycomb glass and another Chinese one was putting out silverware. I asked the manager for a glass of water. He brought one with ice, and when I told him I was there for a job we sat at one of the tables. The other guys worked in the background.

"Why do you want to work here?"

"What do you mean? Because I want a job. I mean, right?" The water tasted really good, almost blue.

"I know, but why do you want to work at Isabel's?"

"Because I want to work really hard."

"Yeah, yeah, but I mean, why *here?*"

"Because I love Italian food?"

"You do? What's your favorite dish?"

"…Spaghetti?"

He considered my answer like it was a good one.

"You know?" he said, like it was a follow-up to something that hadn't been said. "Do you know what this place is? Isabel's?"

"A restaurant?"

"This place is a *shrine*. To my mother." Then he stared at me.

"Okay," I said. "A shrine. Cool. I thought it was an Italian restaurant."

"It *is* an Italian restaurant, but it's dedicated to my mother. That's what Isabel's means; it's *her* place, a place dedicated to her. You know what I mean?"

"Yeah. You love your mother."

"Yes, I love my mother, may she rest in peace." He crossed himself, then said nothing. He was kinda nodding, but not really looking at me.

"That's great," I said to fill the silence.

"Damn right it's great. It means this place is important to me. It means that my mother will never die as long as I am serving food in her honor."

"Cool," I said. His shirt was open at the collar and there was sweat in the black hairs curling there.

"Look, Eminem," he said, referring to my short blond hair. "Do you see what I'm saying? I run this place because I love my mother. And anyone that works here needs to love my mother too."

"Do all those guys love your mother?" I pointed to the guys setting the tables.

"Love, love, *love* her. They all do. Do you get it?"

"I think?"

"Okay, check it out, it's like this, do *you* love *your* mother?"

"No," I said, and when he heard me, he caught himself about to say something because he didn't expect me to say that. "Well, I *do*," I said. "But she doesn't love me."

I had been doing heroin for so many years I didn't know how normal people talked. I was being too honest.

"Your mother doesn't love you?"

"Well, no. I stole a bunch of crap from her and my dad...and yeah, I did bad stuff."

Then he was looking at me funny. I didn't like looking him in the eyes, so I was looking at the sweat on his chest and thinking about how those black hairs must be all in his ass crack too.

"What stuff did you do?" he said.

"Hungh? Oh, I just got arrested a bunch, and I almost killed a guy. But I'm getting better now. My sponsor Sonny says that I'm a selfish prick, but he also says I'm getting better. I don't do drugs anymore, you know?"

"No, I don't know. What are you asking like it's a question for?"

"No, I wasn't...what? Oh no, I wasn't, I was just asking it like, you know, like do you *understand* that I'm not like that anymore. That I'm clean and I don't drink and stuff. I mean, I *did*. I used to do it a lot. Like, before these past six months *all* I would *do* is heroin and shit, and it was all fucked up, but then I don't know, I just didn't want to do it anymore. Well, I hit a dog with my bike, and it died."

"You hit a dog with your motorcycle?"

"No, just a bike, like a bicycle. But yeah, I was high, and it was a little dog. A little white dog. I didn't see it walking behind its master, this lady, and I rode off the sidewalk curb right on its head."

"What did the lady do?"

"Oh, she turned back and screamed. That's when I realized that I had done something. I probably would have kept going, but she screamed, and oh shit, it was pretty sick. Half the face was smashed, like flat on the cement, but the rest of the body was still twitching, especially this one front paw that was pawing the air pretty fast. I got off the bike and walked back over and she was kneeling down at the dog and the little paw was still going, but slowing down. And when I looked at her there, kneeling and all religious looking, I realized that life was precious. I didn't want to do my thing anymore. I mean I didn't want to do drugs anymore."

I looked up from the chest hair and he was studying me again. I had laid a lot on him, but I thought maybe this is how job interviews go. I thought I might have a shot the way he was looking at me. He wasn't smiling, but it looked like he was about to smile, so then I started smiling, but then he definitely wasn't smiling.

He said, "So, you better get the fuck out of here before I call the cops." His voice was calm, but his eyes weren't.

"Wait, cops? For what? What's going on? I thought I was going to get the job."

"Are you out of your fucking mind? You thought a scumbag junkie like you was going to get the job? Really?"

"Well, that way you were smiling at me, and I was so honest with you, and I did say that I love your mother."

He stood up. "You have five seconds to get the fuck out of here before I break your faggot face."

"*Faggot?*"

He started counting. I got up and walked out. The Mexican guys had stopped setting the tables and everyone was watching me. The Chinese guy looked stoned standing there with a bunch of knives and forks.

I went around to all the restaurants in the area, but no one wanted me. Even when I kept the heroin stuff to myself, they still didn't want me.

One morning at the meeting, I told Sonny about everything that happened. I couldn't even look at him. I stared at the wall painting. The section next to our booth had a little Mexican man in a sombrero hunched over carrying something.

"That's bullshit," said Sonny.

"Some guy almost killed me."

"*Bullshit!* You're a selfish prick and you don't want to work. What a selfish prick." He was getting loud and disturbing the meeting. The guy that was sharing about raging at his wife at his kid's birthday party stopped talking for a second and looked over. I nodded an apology and he continued. I whispered to Sonny and he whispered back hotly.

"What do you mean? I *do* want to work. I'd sell my ass for work if it meant I didn't have to do drugs anymore."

"Bullshit, I don't believe you. You're just a selfish asshole prick. I bet you want to go get fucked up, don't you."

"No! What am I supposed to do? These nice restaurants don't want ex-junkies, I look like crap."

"What? Nice restaurants? Are you too good to work at McDonald's?" I didn't understand, but then I understood. I told him I wasn't too good for anything.

"Then go apply at McDonald's, motherfucker."

"Sonny, keep it down," said one of the other old-timers.

"Why don't you keep my cock down your throat?" All the guys laughed.

So I applied at McDonald's. It was near my place in Sherman Oaks on Ventura. There was a plastic play structure out front and a drive-thru. I went inside and I met the manager, Pat. She was white and had short hair and a wide middle. We sat at one of the plastic tables inside.

"Why do you want to work at McDonald's?"

"I think this place is fucking great."

"Why?"

"I like the fucking cheeseburgers. *Great* cheeseburgers. Better than Burger King. Burger King is shit. Their shit tastes burnt. Some people like burnt-tasting shit, but I like *your* shit. And I like your fries."

"Yes, we have good fries. And don't swear like that... Why do *you* want this job? I mean you'd be one of the only white guys I have, you know that, right?"

"That's cool. I hate white people."

"But, no, shut up, kid. What I'm saying is that we don't get guys like you in here, I mean *ever*. The only other white guy I have behind the counter is Dylan and he has some mental problems. I mean, he can sweep and clean the hot fudge sundae machine, but that's it. So what I'm asking is, *why?*"

"I just love your food. I love this place. I might not be the most educated person here, but I can work hard." I didn't mention the heroin this time.

"Don't worry, you're educated enough," she said, and shook my hand. I got the job right there. They needed someone for the drive-thru from 9 p.m. until 2 in the morning, five nights a week. I *was* the only white guy; everyone else was Mexican or South American. The ones that didn't speak English worked in the back and cooked the burgers. The ones that could speak English worked the registers. The nicest one was Marcia; she was tall and had a bunch of gold teeth like caramels. Juan worked the grill. He was shaped like a soft triangle with a huge bulging groin area and a super small head. His face was compact and smoothed over like a baby's. He spoke no English but I could tell from his little squeaks in Spanish that he was very stupid. He worked in the back, cooking the meat with all the smoke, and he was always smiling. Something was always pleasing his little dinosaur brain.

The drive-thru wasn't so bad. I just had to take orders on a little headset and then take the cash when the customers drove around. After 10 p.m., most people were quiet and just passed me the cash without a lot of talk. They were tucked in their cars waiting for their warm food. After the first week I got comfortable with everything, and I started talking to the customers. I would ask them how they were doing and try to draw them out a little; most didn't respond, but some talked to me.

"What the hell are *you* doing in there?"

"Just working," I'd say.

"You're the first white dude I've ever seen working in a McDonald's."

"Yup, that's me."

"Well, at least you can speak English."

"I try," I said.

But then I got into this thing of not being myself; I pretended to be people from different places, using different accents. I did this partly because I was warming to the actor idea. I had never taken an acting class, but I was trying to figure out what I was going to do with the rest of my life. But I partly did the accents because I was tired of being me.

"Hey, where you from kid? You from New York?"

"Yeah, Bensonhurst." I had never even been there; I just remembered it from *Do the Right Thing*.

"Hey, no shit, me too, which part?" This was a skinny black guy with a friendly face. He had ordered two Big Macs.

"Um, near the bridge."

"The bridge? The Narrows?"

"Yeah, yeah."

"Oh, that's Fort Greene."

"Yeah, exactly."

"All right kid, you hang in there."

It felt good when people believed my act, like I was accomplishing something. I would do Italian too. It was really bad, but maybe my ragged good looks helped people believe it. This blond girl came through and immediately started smiling when I talked to her with the Italian thing. She had a high laugh that sounded forced, but maybe it was real. She was really digging the Italian guy I was doing.

"You are so-a beautiful, sooooo-a beautiful-a! In all of Italy I never saw-a such-a beautiful girl-a. Oh mio, I love-a the beautiful girls like-a you."

She drove off laughing the high tingle, which felt good and lonely. But then five minutes later she came back, and over the speaker I knew it was her, because I heard the high laugh through the headset.

"Hi, *teeeeheeeee,* it's *me, teeeeheeeee,* the 'beautiful-a girl-a' from before."

"Oh, hi-a," I said through the intercom.

"Hi, I forgot something. I uhhh, I needed a . . . strawberry milk-shake. Small."

"O-kay, one-a strawberry milkshake-shake-a, small-a."

When she drove back around to my window she was smiling and

her face was splotchy with pink spots because she was embarrassed, but I could tell she was also pushing herself to be forward. One great thing about the accents is they helped me be more outgoing.

"So, you're from Italy? Why are you so blond?"

"There are tons of blond-a men in Italia."

"Oh, I've never been. Which part are you from?"

"I'm-a from Pisa."

"Like the leaning tower?"

"Yes-a, that was-a near my house-a."

"Do you teach lessons? Italian lessons. I studied it a little, but I would really love to learn it. I mean, if you speak it."

"Of course-a I speak it. I would love-a to give you lessons." She quickly wrote down her number because there were cars behind her and they started honking and another customer was yelling "hello" over and over in my headset.

The blond girl was pretty cute, but I could never call her because I could never give her Italian lessons.

One night there was a black guy in his thirties driving a car full of other good-looking thirty-year-olds, white and black, women and men.

"What the hell is that accent?" said the black dude.

"It's-a Italiano."

"*You're* from Italy? Bullshit."

"No, I'm-a from Italy, but I grew up-a here."

"Which part of Italy?" He was enjoying himself, the black guy.
"Pisa."

"Oh, yeah, I lived there. Which part of Pisa?"

"Near-a the tower?"

He started laughing and everyone else in the car started laughing.

"That's great, *Mario*. Where's Luigi?" he said. "So you're from Italy but you grew up here?"

"Si."

"*Si.* Shiiiiiit, so where did you go to school?"

"North-a Hollywood High." I handed him his change.

"Great, I'll know never to send my kids there, you fucking moron," he said, and he laughed and all the others laughed and they drove forward to get their food.

After that I stopped doing the Italian accent and I just focused on the Brooklyn accent. It worked better and I could talk about Bensonhurst a little because of what I saw in the Spike Lee movie. I would do the accent outside of work too, and I was getting a little better at it. Every once in a while someone on the street would ask if I was from Brooklyn or New York and I'd get to say yes, and it was kind of like I had a little bond with the person.

One night this other blond girl came through. She was driving a black Jetta. She had ordered a small fries and a small Diet Coke. She gave me two dollars and a quarter and I gave her eighteen cents and the receipt.

"There ya go," I said.

"Where is your accent from?"

"Brooklyn."

"Really? It doesn't sound like it."

"What's it sound like?"

"I don't know, Bugs Bunny or something."

"Thanks."

"I'm just kidding. Are you from around here?"

"No, I'm from Brooklyn, just out here trying to take care of my sick mother."

She was pretty. Her cheeks were smooth and her eyes looked like they knew things. When I said "my sick mother," she had laughed, which was strange, but then she said, "I'm Karen. Here, give me a call sometime if you want to do something fun." She wrote her number on the receipt and gave it back to me. "What's your name?"

"Jim," I said. I don't know why.

"Well, I'll see you later, Jimmy," she said and drove away smiling.

I kept going to the meeting every morning at El Jardin Encantado, even though it meant I'd only get four or five hours of sleep. The place was funny, a Mexican place in the middle of a wasteland. At night, I'm sure the place was full of show biz folk from all the studios. The interiors were painted with palm trees and exotic gardens; *jardin* meant garden and *encantado* meant enchanted. Because I went almost every morning, the guys in the meeting all knew me and nodded when they saw me, and some said hi. I had never talked in the meeting before, but the Brooklyn accent made it easier, so one morning I talked, using it.

"Yeah, and then I woke up that mornin' and this fuckin' lady was going crazy across the alley from me. She's like this fucking religious lady and she is always chanting on the rosary and praying to Mary and Jesus out loud in this hysterical kind of way, like a fuckin' nut or sumptin. And I was like comin' offa the shit, ya know? And I just couldn't take all the he-be-Jesus bullshit that mornin', ya know? So I opened my window and yelled, 'Hey lady, shut the fuck up!'"

Most of the guys in the meeting seemed to like that story, and they laughed, especially some of the older guys. It felt good to get that approval. But Sonny, my sponsor, didn't laugh. He was sitting across from me in the booth. When someone else started talking, he whispered to me, "What the fuck was that? From a movie or something? And what was that stupid accent, the Dead End Kids?"

That pissed me off because it *was* from a movie, the beginning of *The Basketball Diaries* with Leonardo DiCaprio, which I loved because it was all about heroin, and I would watch it all the time when I was high. I didn't say anything back to Sonny, and he kept going in the half-whisper, "What, you think you can pretend to be a New Yorker and forget about all that damage that you did as *yourself?*"

"No."

"Then what the fuck was that fucking charade? I'm serious. You need to be *honest*. You need to be honest with yourself most of all, and telling bullshit stories in here isn't going to get you anywhere. I don't care how funny they are. And that one wasn't even funny."

What he was saying pissed me off, partly because he was always telling unfunny stories that he thought were funny, but especially because what he was saying about me was true: I had stolen thousands of dollars from my family, and I had the two kids that I never saw, Caleb and John. They were five and six now. Now that I was working I could send a tiny bit of money; and I was planning on seeing them, which made me happy to think about, but it also reminded me how deep I was in. At the rate I was going I'd pay off the back child support in forty years.

Later that month, I started sending money to my ex, and as soon as I did she started asking for more. Years of nothing and then finally I can give something and she asks for more. But I did get to talk to the little guys on the phone, which was heaven, just to hear about kindergarten and their sports. About the fourth time we talked, Caleb told me about his mom's boyfriends, and I said, *Boyfriends, like there was more than one?* And he was like, yeah. And then I asked John, the older one, about it and he said she was getting drunk on weekends and maybe doing drugs. That's what the extra money was for, for sure. But what could I do?

At work I was putting in the hours and still doing the Brooklyn accent. Late one night, at 2 a.m., everyone was cleaning up. The drive-thru was closed, and I was helping Dylan, the only other white guy, clean the hot fudge sundae machine. It was one of his only jobs because he was slow and couldn't interact with the customers. We worked in silence. We had to take the nozzles off the dispenser part and clean those and wipe everything down. Juan came over from the back where he had been cleaning the grill. He leaned his huge hips against the counter and watched us, smiling an infant grin that stretched into his fat cheeks. I continued wiping. Dylan stopped and stood and stared at Juan until Juan stopped grinning and said something in Spanish and pointed at me.

Then Dylan said, "You shut up, Juan."

I had never seen Dylan get angry before. Juan was grinning again.

"You speak Spanish?" I asked Dylan. "What did he say?"

Dylan looked like he was struggling with his thoughts. Then he said, "You don't want to know."

"Yeah, I do, what did he say?"

Then Juan said something else in Spanish and made a gripping and stroking motion with his hand. Then he laughed.

"Shut up!" said Dylan. He tried to walk away. I held him by the shoulder.

"What did he say?" I said gently.

"He said he'll give you five dollars if you go in the bathroom and let him jerk you off."

I let Dylan walk away. Juan was smiling slyly now. His fat pelvis ballooned his pants so that all the contours of his body were visible through the fabric. One tiny baby's hand rested on this roundness. The little tapered fingers were sickening. He licked his top lip and then let his teeth rest in the flesh of his bottom lip. The teeth were small and sharp like he'd filed them.

I flashed both hands with all fingers flushed three times and said, "For thirty."

He let his teeth back into his mouth and said in his high voice, "Twenty-five." The words sounded like a ventriloquist was projecting the voice of a small Mexican girl into his mouth.

I said okay to the twenty-five and we walked around the counter to the bathroom at the back. No one was around and we went in. The bathroom door didn't lock so we went into one of the two stalls. There was writing all over the place, all in different pens and different colors. I locked the stall door. There wasn't much room in there with the two of us and the toilet. Juan didn't seem so confident anymore.

"Give me the money," I said.

"*¿Qué?*"

"You have to give me the money before I do anything." I made a gesture like I pulled my wallet out and then like I was counting money.

"Oh, *bien, aquí*." He reached into his pants pocket and pulled out a five and eight ones. "*Te voy a dar trece más tarde,*" he said, and made some gestures saying that he didn't have the rest but he would give it to me later. I said okay, and then we stood there waiting.

His eyes were a little watery and his mouth was wet at the corners with a little white mucus. I unzipped my fly and put his hand on my crotch. He wasn't doing much because I wasn't hard. I didn't like looking at him so I pulled him close to me. His face went into my shoulder. I could feel the fat of his pelvis against my thigh. His hand gripped tighter and pushed my limp dick forwards and back. I couldn't get hard. I was looking at the wall. There was a rough drawing of a girl's ass under a guy's ass and his dick was penetrating her. Underneath, it said, "Grimace and Ronald, hot sex!" There were other things written around the place like "McFaggot loves his meat" and

"Ronald is gay." I closed my eyes and tried to picture girls that I had been with, but there hadn't been one in a long time. I thought of the girl from the drive-thru, Karen. Her blond hair and the way that she blushed when I asked about guys. I could see that she had been hurt. I wanted to fill that place for her. Maybe I could be a different person with her. I would have to tell her that I wasn't from Brooklyn, but there was time. I could get to know her a little more and then when she felt comfortable with me, I would tell her that it had all been an act. She would understand. I kept thinking about her face and I felt myself get hard. For a little bit I could forget that I was there with Juan. He moved his head under my chin, his thick hair was in my mouth, and his lips were wet on my chest. But I could pretend that they were Karen's lips. For a while I thought about being in *The Basketball Diaries* and doing anything to get some smack and it made what I was doing seem cool. But it also made me go limp a little, so I just thought about Karen, and making love to her.

Then I came. It felt pretty good to come, like it always does, but it got on Juan's pants. He just stood there like he wasn't sure what he had just done. I zipped up my fly and took some toilet paper from the roll and wiped his pants off. I could see jizz on some of the papers on the floor.

Then he left. It wasn't so bad. His hands were soft. And I then had a little extra money that I could spend on a date with Karen. My kids needed money, but I needed a little too.

Made a list of actors our "character" had harmed
and became willing to make amends to them all.

⎯⎯⎯⎯⎯⎯⎯

Harry's Story

MY FIRST BRUSH WITH ACTING was when I was eight. I was in a play called *Caps for Sale: A Tale of a Peddler, Some Monkeys, and Their Monkey Business* based on a children's book by Esphyr Slobodkina. The story follows a cap salesman with a mustache who wears his entire stock of caps on his head—seventeen including his own cap. He travels from town to town yelling, "Caps! Caps for sale! Fifty cents a cap!" Then the cap seller takes a nap under a tree with all his caps on his head. When he wakes he realizes that a bunch of monkeys have stolen all the caps except his own. They all sit in the tree above him wearing the caps, and when he yells at them to return the caps, they imitate him; hilarity ensues. Finally the cap seller throws his cap on the ground in frustration and the monkeys imitate him by throwing their caps down at his feet; pleasantly surprised, he stacks the caps back on his head and leaves, calling, "Caps! Caps for sale! Fifty cents a cap!"

I played one of the monkeys. If I had been capable of such awareness, the monkey character was something that I should have paid close attention to because it was a role that suited me perfectly. If only I had known how apes would *become* my life. No doubt the seeds for many of my later issues were planted during the rehearsals and production of this play. You might focus on the thieving aspect of my role, but there was much more to that little monkey that has stayed with me. If my memory is correct, I played that monkey to perfection: mouth open, teeth bared, back arched, arms hanging relaxed, full of potential power, and my screeches were the loudest and shrillest. I was a primate natural.

Later, at summer camp, when I was eleven, my summer friends and I performed a lip-synched version of Michael Jackson's "Thriller" for the air bands show. I played the monster version of Michael. The idea was that one kid would play the *human* version of Michael at the beginning of the song and exit the stage under a cheap smoke effect and I would quickly change into his red leather jacket wearing a wolf's head; then I would enter the stage with the other zombies and monsters and the girl onstage would scream, then the other monsters and I would do our silly dance. This performance too did something to me, something I think was dark and damaging, but in the very least it revealed my penchant for transformation. I had never felt so exhilarated as when I had that mask on. It was the exhilaration of escape, escape from the self. I was no longer Harry, I was at the service of another consciousness. Maybe this "other" was something that had arisen from inside myself, but it was triggered by the change on the outside. The cheap scowling wolf mask gave me permission to do anything: I could easily be onstage in front of hundreds of people; I could *dance* when previously I had been paralyzed whenever the occasion for dancing had arisen; not only that, I was able to dance with an energetic flair I hardly knew I possessed; and most important, I was able to interact with the young actress in a way that was new. I was only eleven, but I had already had my share of fevers for young women, obsessions and pursuits all ending in rejection. But where my previous approaches to romance had always been of the sweet, demure style, I found that as the wolf I could approach the girl with aggression and panache; I could force myself into her consciousness without the trepidation of a courting poet, a permission-seeking wimp. I was restricted by the parameters of the performance: dancing with a high step and swaying, zombie-stiff arms in large circles, wrists bent. But I gave her meaningful looks from the eyeholes of my mask that I would have never dared before. My stare was the stare of an uncompromising carnivore that saw her young flesh as food; like Chaplin's companion in *The Gold Rush* who is transformed into a scrumptious chicken by the starving man's eyes, she turned into the Platonic form of the Female, a pinup's bent-over rump in a tingly blue G-string. She was only eleven, but I never broke my vampiric stare as I went through our moves with the other zombies.

At the end of the dance section, I was supposed to pursue her, and did I ever. I chased her from one end to the other, around the other kids in masks, knocking one frail zombie to the floor, until finally the girl ran behind the stage curtain and I tackled her into a pile of hay that was going to be used for an *Oklahoma* number. Snarling on top of her, I pressed the snout of the mask so forcefully into her cheek while attempting to kiss her, that when two counselors finally pulled me off there were three red streaks across her face that remained for a week. I avoided major punishment for my first assault charge because the performance onstage had been so great—everyone really got into the dance number, which won us the competition. I claimed that the mauling in the hay had been a result of going so deep into character. It worked. Thus, I learned that when my identity was concealed I had permission to be whoever I wanted and to do whatever I wanted. I also found that sexual energy was a great engine for performance: My lust had turned what would have been an otherwise bumbling adolescent attempt into a passionate and flowing rendition full of the requisite tight kicks and turns, drops and thrusts. My desire had turned my body into a voice, and the voice was saying: "I want to fuck, even if I don't know what that is yet." But I also learned—and this was an acquirement of dark knowledge, something out of Faust—that when I was performing, others gave me permission to be a madman. As long as it was part of the "performance" the audience would accept almost anything, in fact they *wanted* me to go beyond civilized bounds.

In sixth grade I played Tybalt in *Romeo and Juliet*. King of cats, indeed. I wasn't even sure what that meant, but it guided my performance. I had grown up with a cat in a neighborhood full of cats. One neighbor kept his cat on a small chain that was attached to a cement block. I have no idea why Mr. Johnson did this, because when he was home he would let the cat roam freely. The cat was called Gray. Gray was large and gray and had a boxy face, like a bulldog. Because the chain was attached to the block, Gray could move it incrementally, and over time he became very strong from pulling the cement block around, tight muscles under a silky gray coat. More than once I witnessed Gray stalk unsuspecting birds sitting on a high fence in the front of Mr. Johnson's yard. Believing themselves safely out of range of the cat, the birds chattered away, confident and stupid. Finally, after a slow ritual of low belly stalking and long stretchy steps, in a move that was both startling and sexual, Gray would leap with illogical power and pluck one of the birds off the fence. It was hard to perceive the moment of impact, but after the squawking explosion of birds toward the sky, Gray would land on the cement of Mr. Johnson's driveway with a wing-flapping bird in his mouth. The force with which he whipped them about in his jaws and then lay on his back and clawed their feathers from their breasts and wings with his hind legs was intoxicating. As a boy I too wanted to tear into birds until their heads detached and their blood smeared purple across my lips.

That is how I played Tybalt. I began the production with a quiet approach and proceeded with a slow accumulation of rage. I was in love with the girl playing Juliet, Elizabeth Gross, and I despised the faggot playing Romeo, Jesse Porge, pronounced *Por-hey*. Everyone called Elizabeth "Gross Lizard" because she wasn't the prettiest girl around and because of her name. To me she *was* the prettiest. She had large eyes and large cheeks and breasts just forming and legs smooth and thin. I called Jesse Porge "Pordge," pronouncing the *g* because he was a fucking pordge. He was a round-faced little tub of lard, a pudge with a butt-cut, and he thought he was the shit. He ate Romeo up, loved it like it was his life's purpose; he even wore his cape around school. I think he would have worn the tights too if it didn't mean that I and the rest of the class would have beaten the shit out of him.

We used to be friends, in fourth grade. He would be the game master when we all played the *Teenage Mutant Ninja Turtles* role-playing game. But that was two years before, and lots had changed.

At rehearsal, waiting to go on for the party scene:

"Hey, Pordge, why don't you go fuck yourself."

"It's Por-*hey,* and why don't *you* go fuck yourself, Harry? You're stupid enough."

"Oh, you think I'm stupid, eh?"

"I think you are one of the stupidest guys in class."

"Oh you do, hungh?"

"Yes, Harry, you're like a hairy ape."

"Oh, that's funny, Pordge, you roly-poly fucking *Pordge*."

"It's *Por-hey,* hairy *idiot*."

When he and Elizabeth kissed, it really killed me because I had hardly kissed anyone except for a game of spin the bottle at summer camp, and Pordge did it with so much feeling. I would stand offstage and watch them do the balcony scene with growing rage. He'd scamper up the little ladder that they disguised with vines and hold her cheek while he pressed his lips to hers. It was a fake kiss, an acting kiss, but it killed me every time. I knew she was acting, but it was like she wanted it: She'd close her eyes and lean into the kiss, blissful and sexual. It was a confusing moment. How could she do that, even if it was pretend, and not feel something? The way she closed her eyes, and leaned over the railing. It did something to me, lit something inside me, made me want to kill.

We did the play once for the school and it was a hit. Elizabeth and Pordge got the largest applause at the end, especially from the parents. It was stupid shit. I mean, so transparent, there is no way that they could have actually liked what Pordge was doing onstage, it was ridiculous. Sure, he said all the words clearly and did it with feeling, but the way he carried himself was all fake, and he spoke in a way that sounded phony. It was like he wanted everyone to know that he knew what he was saying, but it wasn't how people actually talk, nor was it even poetic talk, it was just a show for a bunch of wimpy teacher types who want to know that they are having some kind of influence on their students.

My friend Adam played Mercutio. After the show we snuck out and walked over behind the school library where there was a wooden bench stuck into the wall. It's where we used to play the *Teenage*

Mutant Ninja Turtles role-playing game back when I didn't mind Pordge.

Adam gave me a cigarette. "Try it."

"Tastes like shit." It was my first ever. He got them from his brother.

"Why are you so upset over those two?"

"Because I fucking love her."

"Gross Lizard?"

"Shut up. She's not gross, and she's not a lizard."

"Whatever, she looks like one, and anyone that wants to go out with Porgy is pretty gross."

"Wait, what?"

"What?"

"She's going out with Pordge?"

"Yes, you didn't know?"

I smoked the whole cigarette with Adam and I felt sick. I walked home because I didn't live far from the school. I was still in my red and gold tights, the Capulet colors. The air was chilly and my head and throat felt mushy and full of ash. Walking across the bike bridge I thought about murder. There was black water trickling in the darkness underneath, and I imagined Pordge's body splashing in it and floating down and away. How, how, how? How could she be with that guy? A fucking *butt-cut,* and he was so phony and so full of himself, and for no good reason because he was a roly-poly slug motherfucker. I walked home alone in the dark. Cats slunk about the dark houses looking for mice.

We took the show to a multischool event called Shake-Fest where each school presented two Shakespeare scenes. Our school decided to do the balcony scene and the sword-fighting scene because our teacher, Mrs. Young, was proud of the sword fighting that we had developed. We had choreographed the whole thing with the fourth-grade teacher, Mr. Aronson. I think I was the best at it—well, maybe Adam was the best, but he played Mercutio, so he couldn't show off his skills as much because he got killed right away. I'd always let him show off for a bit with a few spinning moves, but then I had to kill him. Then I always had to let Pordge kill me.

At Shake-Fest, the schools met in this auditorium, and each school would take turns doing their two scenes in the middle of all the others. There were five schools, and we went fourth. The first three were pretty bad. They did *A Midsummer Night's Dream*: a scene with the donkey head, which I liked, but they could have done it better. Another school did the scene from *Hamlet* where Hamlet tells Ophelia to get to a nunnery—the Ophelia tried to cry, but it was fake, and Hamlet was in black and stupid—and *Taming of the Shrew*, ha, well, *she* was a fucking *shrew*, that's for sure.

Then we got to our play. First they did the balcony scene. Because of the setup, Elizabeth had to stand on a ladder with cloth triangle cutouts on the sides with castle designs to disguise that it was a ladder. Elizabeth rested her arms on the top platform and looked out, and Jesse looked up at her and said his stupid lines. Elizabeth's father was actually the guy that stood in the center of the ladder to hold it steady. He was a supertall guy, with square shoulders and a square head and a brown mustache, and he made me think: American fireman. I think he had played in the NFL when he was younger. When they had been putting everything in place and her father climbed under the ladder, lots of people laughed because it was such a funny setup, and I heard someone whisper, "He's just *standing* there, for *so* long, that's like seven *million* years of bad luck."

Pordge and Elizabeth did their scene. It was pretty much how they had always done it, but a little different, and not just because of the ladder setup. Jesse was doing something else, something more than he usually did. I wasn't sure what it was until I heard another person whisper, *"He's crying."* I looked at his pig eyes and he *was* crying, there was wet below his deep-set sockets and a glistening snail trail down the pertly molded bubble of each cheek. The little fucker was showing off, and not the way he usually showed off by articulating and flinging the words about as if he owned them or had a special relationship with Shakespeare. There was something else going on:

> *Oh that I were a glove* [pronounced *glow-v*] *upon that hand,*
> *That I might touch that cheek!* [He always said this word
>   very quickly, as if he were saying *chick,* and he'd purse his
>   lips a little.]

His pronunciation and gesticulations made me want to smack him, but the tears on his face did something else to me: It cooked up in my chest a roiling, lustful rage. His tears were *my* tears, they were the outward signs of everything that I had felt for Elizabeth: her devastating beauty, her unattainability, the frustrations over being so young and not being able to do anything concrete. Once, on a special lunch outing with my mother, I had even asked my mom about getting married early. Elizabeth had been particularly nice to me at that time so I had naturally jumped to the idea of spending the rest of my life with her. My mom said that twelve was a little young to get married, so I cited a couple of young dancers that I had just read about who had been married at age fourteen with their parents' permission. My mom told me that we could revisit the idea in two years if I was still in love with her. Then she asked if Elizabeth was in love with me.

I cried at that lunch, just like Jesse was crying in the scene; his were *my* tears, because I knew that she *didn't* feel the same way about me, and I would never marry her, and we would grow up and she would live her life and I would live mine, and we would get old and ugly and the universe would die and none of it would matter. And here was Jesse delivering his fucking lines as if he *was* Romeo and not the pasty, pudgy, longhaired pompous fuck that I knew him to be. And he was *fooling* everyone. I heard someone whisper, "He's *really* good." I turned slightly and over my evil shoulder I saw that the tall, thin Ichabod Crane–looking woman that taught at one of the other schools was leaning slightly toward her friend Mrs. Young, our stout, powerful, black teacher. Mrs. Young nodded assent to Jesse's supposed skills in her self-assured way, full of pride for the simpering, overemotional turd in the middle of the crowd.

I could kill. He said everything that I wanted to say, in the way that I wanted to say it. Or so it seemed, but what I realized while watching helpless on the sideline was that it wasn't even the words themselves that got me worked up; it was the intimacy with which he interacted with Elizabeth and in front of everyone. He was pouring his heart out to her and being applauded for it; her goddamned *father* was standing underneath them, holding them up, as Jesse climbed the ladder and kissed her, multiple times. And for this performance he didn't hold back, no elementary school pecks for him, he was pressing himself against her with open lips and probably a froggy tongue hidden between. I was considered a freak whenever I showed affection for Elizabeth in life, but he was allowed to reveal his deepest feelings for her and in such a way that he was applauded for it: The more emotional he got, the more the audience was drawn into his performance. What fucking Romeo cries in the fucking balcony scene anyway?

A short digression: I had told her I loved her. After school one day, she was walking home with a couple friends, Rachel and Maggie: one tall with crossed eyes and blond hair, the other medium height, dark-haired, and tough. They walked home in the same direction as I did, across the bike bridge. When they were halfway across the bridge, I stopped them with my voice. Elizabeth and Jesse had been rehearsing the play for weeks at that point, and all of my desires—until then kept secret in my personal dream world of sunny fields and fluffy clouds—were being forced to the surface by the intimacy between her and Jesse that I was forced to watch. Until the rehearsals began for the play, I could bide my time and savor the unrealized plans I had for us, treating them as a fait accompli, without actually having to do anything to bring them about. It had been a relatively pleasant period when dreams ran free and defined my emotions in the slow moving days of elementary school. But the palpable intimacy developing, even in the early stages of rehearsal, had brought everything to a boil. I knew that if I didn't act soon, I would lose her to Jesse, and at that time, relationships seemed never-ending; if they did start going out, it would be interminable. She would be lost forever.

"Elizabeth!" The girls stopped like the Three Fates, one lovely, leading the way to paradise, the other two leading to boredom and misery. I was half a block behind them.

"Hi," Elizabeth said. I walked toward them. I realized that I had hardly ever spoken to her alone. My kneecaps turned to air and the back of my neck was wet and the crotches of my arms were wet. I was entering the scary zone, where physical things sucked away and my dreams came to the fore to be challenged, and everything that had been imagined and decided upon with assuring certainty in my head was now dragged out for inspection and judgment.

"Can I talk to you?" She didn't answer. "Alone?" Then she smiled and said something to the other two that I was still too far away to hear, and after giving me one more glance they walked on, leaving my beautiful lizard alone, caressed by a blanket of California sun that elevated the vision on the bridge to the heavenly. Once I passed the metal barrier and was on the bridge myself, I could see that the sun was playing a sparkly game in the trickle of green scummy water in the cement creek below, and for a second everything seemed perfect.

"How are you, cousin?" she said.

"Cousin?"

"Yeah, we're cousins, remember? Tybalt is Juliet's cousin?"

"Oh, right." I was standing next to her. She had her hand on the orange rail. There was a bit of graffiti carved into the paint, just by her large finger, but I couldn't read what it said. Down below, on the cement wall of the creek, there was a large bit of graffiti in spray paint that said LUST. It was suddenly hard to look at her, so I kept looking down at the water and at the mocking sun that jumped from the water into my eyes.

"How are you?" I said.

"Fine." Her voice…Then she said, "You wanted to talk?" There was really nothing else to say. I could tell her that I fantasized about marrying her, that I knew I would be someone special when I grew up, and that she could be part of that, that I would do anything for her, including fight someone, anyone, almost anyone, and I could tell her that Jesse was an idiot, a phony, and that I was the real Romeo, the Romeo of real life, or that Mrs. Young had turned us into star-crossed lovers, *real* star-crossed lovers, by forcing Jesse upon her in the play and trying to keep me from her by giving me the role of the cousin, but it didn't seem like any of that would serve my purposes. So instead I said, "I love you."

I wasn't looking at her so I didn't see her immediate reaction, but as I watched the reflection of the sun pirouette on a large ripple in the water, cable shaped, that was elevated from the normal plane of the water's surface, caused by a rupture in the cement, I heard a trickle of laughter that fused with the image of the sun-pumping ripple, and it shot terror into my black center, filling it with ripping, sinking meaninglessness. I looked to her; her face was kind but not emotional, not full of the same fervor that was consuming me.

"Harry," she said, as if she was trying to chide me into seriousness, as if I hadn't just confessed the most serious thing of my life. "You *don't* love me." She was still smiling, but in a kinder way. I could have jumped off the bridge. I wouldn't have died, but maybe I'd get a broken leg.

"Yes, I do. I love you, Elizabeth."

"Harry, stop it." She wasn't smiling anymore. The other girls, boring and tough, were a little way down the street, waiting. They were looking back like they could hear what we were saying, even though they couldn't.

It had happened. I had brought the dream out into reality and it had dissolved. It was just a dream and had found no purchase in the real world where it was dependent on other people for its realization. I wished that I could have sucked my words back inside where they had lived a colorful life of promise, had been nurtured by hope, and had never been tested. Now such sentiments would never be able to live without a forceful inner revision of the facts. Because it felt like someone had just taken a knife to a painting that I had spent three years composing, I decided to chuck the whole thing, and with the flourish of someone tossing a bucket of bloodred paint at a landscape full of lambs and shepherdesses, I said, almost in a yell, "Oh, so you love that motherfucker Pordge? Well, it serves you fucking right, you fucking Gross Lizard. I hope you fucking love each other in a great Gross Porgy lizard fucking mess."

She registered momentary shock, then said I was an asshole and walked off toward her two waiting maids who yelled back at me and also called me an asshole.

"Go fuck yourself, Harry asshole," said the tough one.

"You're a fucking Harry-monster," said the boring one. Elizabeth didn't even look back.

That bridge was then the loneliest place in the world.

So there I was in the middle of all those students from all those schools in my yellow and red tights and the stupid skirt they made me wear, full of the bile of jealousy and rage. Adam and I did our Tybalt/Mercutio bit; I killed him and then Romeo hit the scene. I dare say that the little fucker could see his fate in my eyes. We really didn't have many lines with each other, he said:

> *Now, Tybalt, take the villain back again,*
> *That late thou gavest me, for Mercutio's soul*
> *Is but a little way above our heads,*
> *Staying for thine to keep him company:*
> *Either thou, or I, or both, must go with him.*

And I said:

> *Thou, wretched boy, that didst consort him here,*
> *Shalt with him hence.*

And then he said,

> *This shall determine that.*

And then we were supposed to fight, and he was supposed to kill me. We had worked out the blocking for the sword fight, and had done it many times. He was supposed to thrust and I would parry, we would circle ninety degrees in one direction, I would strike and he would dodge, and then we would circle back in the other direction a full half circle where I would then strike at him, he would side step, and then bring his rapier up under my arm as if he had thrust it through me and I would act as if I was stabbed and fall. Well, we did all of that, albeit a little more slowly and deliberately that usual: The tension was so tight between us I was worried that someone would step in and stop us. When I made my strikes I did them with extra force, and when we circled, my eyes never broke from his. His eyes were full of weepy blue fear, although he tried to hide it, and I know that my eyes were full of the red fury of a devil scorned.

When we finally got to the death moves, I swung for him, and he sidestepped as he was supposed to do, but when he stepped in for the kill move, I didn't give him the open target that he expected. Instead I raised my rapier toward his torso as he thrust himself toward me. This move would have been bad enough on its own, but it was compounded by my malicious forethought: While he had been slipping Lizard the tongue at the top of the ladder, over her mustachioed father, I had removed the plastic cap at the tip of the sword. The tip wasn't pointed, but it was metal, and would do damage. And it did. At first no one knew what had happened, there was always a slight pause at that moment so that the deathblow could register with the audience before I made my dramatic fall backwards. But this time I didn't fall—he did, with my sword sticking out of his stomach.

Made direct amends to such "actors"
whenever possible, except when to do so
would injure them or other "actors."

—≈≈≈≈≈—

Dear Class

It is James Franco. I have had several conversations with
L_____, other faculty, and some of our classmates, and it
seems that my film at the second-year marathon has upset
some of you. It was not *The Clerk's Tale,* the film I made for
my second-year evaluation; it was *Masculinity and Me,* a project that I collaborated on for a class I took in the film studies
department called Film and the Body. In this class, we studied a variety of experimental, avant-garde, and medical films
that focused on representations of the human body. I understand that some of the material in my film (e.g., the close
up of an old man's penis in the act of urination) might have
been shocking, unpleasant, or distasteful, depending on your
perspective.

It was meant to be challenging, but not frivolous. We are in a fine arts program, so I felt free to work on this kind of material. It is hard for me to apologize for the content. I believe that most forms of expression should be allowed in an art program. But I can apologize for not warning anyone. Because I had planned to show a film other than my second-year film, I should have made people aware. I am sorry for not warning anyone about the content of the alternate film.

I understand that M_____ designed a precise schedule to create a smooth flow from film to film, and that my film may have damaged the presentation of T_____'s film, which was the film that came after mine. I have apologized to T_____ and offered to make reparations. Also, I was not at the screening because I had a documentary screening at the Tribeca Film Festival. I was very excited about the Tribeca screening, but I was excited about the marathon as well. I tried to make M_____ aware of the Tribeca screening, but I guess the message didn't reach him, because he scheduled my marathon slot the same time as the Tribeca screening. I was required to go to the Tribeca screening, otherwise my documentary would not have been shown, which is the only reason I wasn't at the marathon. I love being a part of the class and I would not have missed the marathon by choice.

I love NYU, and I love working with all of you. I have worked in film for a while, and I have been in several arts programs, so I know that NYU is special. It is hard to find a place like NYU that is at the same time instructive, supportive, rigorous, and innovative. I am writing this letter because I cherish the time I have spent learning with all of you. I know what we have is unique. I did not need to write this letter. I wrote it because I respect our class and the environment that we have established. Therefore, if I upset you, I am sorry.

Peace,
James Franco

*Continued to take our "character's" inventory and
when he was wrong, promptly admitted it.*

❯❯❯❯❯❯❯❯❯❯

Very Real

Int. Car—Night.

JERRY is in a car with VANCE. It rains outside.

*VANCE drives. He is forty-five. He is slightly overweight but virile. He
still acts as if he's twenty-five.*

They sit in silence.

VANCE: You know, I picked you up because I wanted a little company, but you're not really fulfilling your role, if you know what I'm saying.

JERRY: Oh.

VANCE: "Oh?"

JERRY: I don't know what to say. I thought you picked me up because my car was broken down in the middle of nowhere.

VANCE: Sheee-it. Well, the least you could do is talk a bit.

JERRY: ... Crazy weather, eh?

VANCE *[unimpressed by his attempt]*: Jesus. Yeah. It is. So where you from?

JERRY: Back there.

VANCE: Back there? What? That town? That little town?

JERRY: Yeah.

VANCE: They actually breed people back there?

JERRY: Yeah.

VANCE: You like it back there? Living back there?

JERRY: No. I hate it.

VANCE: Didn't make it very far, did ya?

JERRY *[says nothing]*

VANCE: Yeah, I guess you got pretty lucky I came along. You got lucky and I... got lucky.

[They sit in silence.]

VANCE: You get much pussy back there?

JERRY: Hungh?

VANCE: Pussy. You get much. You clip it often?

JERRY: Oh, uhh...no.

VANCE: No? I love pussy. Actually, no, I love ass. I don't do it in the pussy no more. Not since I was a kid. You ever do it in the ass? With a girl I mean?... You should try that shit. Totally psychological. Like they're just letting you in, you know what I'm saying? Not that I'm totally into a power struggle, I just like to know that they would let me in there, in that superprivate place. You know? The dark hole. You can get lost in there.

JERRY: You see that accident?

VANCE: Yup.

JERRY: Maybe we should stop.

VANCE: Yeah, and pick up another winner like you.

JERRY: I'm just saying maybe they're hurt.

VANCE: They have cell phones. It's the modern age. Everyone has cell phones.

JERRY: Well maybe we should at least call.

VANCE: Go ahead.

JERRY: I don't have a cell phone.

VANCE: Well, neither do I.

[Silence.]

VANCE: *So*, you don't like anal, huh?

JERRY: No.

VANCE: No? You crazy? I bet you never done it. I can tell. At least I know you haven't done it with a girl…Are you gay?

JERRY: No.

VANCE: You half a fag?

JERRY: What?

VANCE: It's okay. I got no problem with that. I mean ain't nothing gonna happen with us, you know what I'm sayin'? That's not why I picked you up. I'm just sayin' if you're half gay and like putting it in other men's assholes that's okay with me. I gotta lotta friends who are half fags. Ha ha.

JERRY: I think you should have stopped for those people.

VANCE: People? What the fuck you talking about, kid?

JERRY: Those people. They looked like they were in bad shape.

VANCE: You kidding me? I ain't going back there. I'm already late because of your ass. If you want get out and run back there it's fine with me, I'll slow down to ten miles per hour for ya.

JERRY *[to self]*: What the fuck? Crazy man.

VANCE: Crazy man? What, are you talking to yourself? Crazy?

JERRY: I think you're crazy. I think you're a fucking asshole.

VANCE *[laughs]*

JERRY: I mean who talks about anal sex to a total stranger? I mean what the heck? I don't want to hear about it, all right? And now you're just driving off and leaving those people back there! Where are you going that it's so important?

VANCE: You want to know?

JERRY: Yes.

VANCE: To beat on a guy.

JERRY: What?

VANCE: To punish this fucker for raping this guy's daughter.

JERRY: What?

VANCE: You know, rape? This frat boy faggot raped this girl so I'm gonna go punish him for it.

JERRY: What are you going to do?

VANCE: Beat him. Beat him with a pipe. Beat him till he's out. Maybe stick it up his ass.

JERRY: Are you serious?

VANCE: Yeah, why not? You think that guy deserves less?

JERRY: . . . Well, are you sure he raped her?

VANCE: No. I just do what the guy tells me. If Dad says frat fag raped her, then he raped her.

Ext. Café—Day

VANCE sits with SAUL, a middle-aged man. SAUL is nervous and VANCE is his regular self.

VANCE: So you liked it.

SAUL: Yeah, I mean, yeah, I liked it.

VANCE: So it was like the best script you've ever read.

SAUL: Well, that's a tall order. I mean I've read a lot of scripts.

VANCE: Yeah, but nothing like this. I mean honestly, name me one script you've read that's better.

SAUL: Well, in school we read *Chinatown,* so I guess technically I couldn't say it's the best script I've ever read.

VANCE: Okay, so second best.

SAUL: Well, we read *Casablanca* too. And *Citizen Kane* and...

VANCE: Okay, okay, so besides *Chinatown* and *Casablanca* and all that shit, it's pretty much the best script you've ever read.

SAUL: Well... it was very real.

VANCE: That's right, very real, very real. That's because it's my life. That's my life, sucka. Can you believe it?

SAUL: No, it's actually quite scary.

VANCE: It's not all real, I don't want to lie to ya. I mean, I didn't actually take down five cops like that with my bare hands, but the bit about getting sober is all real, of course...

SAUL: Of course.

VANCE: And when I slapped the shit out of my sister for dating that fucking Chinese motherfucker. And then how I slapped the shit out of his Peking duck ass and made him chew dog shit on our front lawn, that was all real.

SAUL: Wow.

VANCE: Oh that's nothing. I mean that was just kiddie shit. That script is just my twenties and thirties before I got sober. I'm thinking about writing a sequel for the sober years.

SAUL: You got worse when you got sober?

VANCE: Oh, hell yeah. That's when I really got into the cocaine smuggling thing in Florida. It was great, pre-9/11, we just smuggled that shit in through FedEx. I had this Brazilian buddy that was in with all the dealers over there; heh heh, they were all surfers. It was good times. That's when I met you, you know, before I went back to New York.

SAUL: I had no idea you were doing that when you were sober.

VANCE: Oh man, you had to have known, at least after we got caught. I came and made an amends to the meeting and everything. I mean I felt bad because I was acting like I was living a spiritual life but I guess really I wasn't.

SAUL: I guess I wasn't going to meetings for a while because I missed it.

VANCE: Yeah, everyone at the meeting was shocked, then they just ragged me about it. I turned state's witness on all those fuckers I was with, and had to set up a few sting operations for the cops, but then they let me get out of town for a while.

SAUL: So you snitched on your friends?

VANCE: On my brother.

SAUL: Your own brother?

VANCE: Yeah, I had to.

SAUL: Well, are you going to snitch on me?

VANCE: For what?

SAUL: For this thing.

VANCE: What? Oh *this* thing? Fuck no.

SAUL: Why not? I mean you snitched on your own...

VANCE: First of all, don't say *snitch,* it just, it just sounds silly. Second, I ain't going to say anything to anyone about this.

SAUL: But what if you get caught?

VANCE: Brother, listen, this shit is such small potatoes even if I did get caught the police wouldn't do shit.

SAUL: Vance, I mean you have a record...this kid is probably very rich...

VANCE: Listen, buddy, I ain't gonna rat you out, okay?

SAUL: You did it to your brother.

VANCE: Yeah, but he wasn't going to finance my movie, was he? I mean why would I turn you in and shoot us both in the foot like that? I'll tell you the truth, I'd rather go to jail for you if it came down to it. I mean that would be worth getting my film made. I mean I would, I would actually walk myself into prison if I knew that would get my movie made.

SAUL: Okay, Vance, but that wasn't part of the deal. When Joe Donuts said that you would come do this thing for me it never involved me trying to get financing for your movie.

VANCE: I know that. Sheee-it. Of course not. That's what I get the two grand for. No, we're just talking about the script because you seemed to respond to the idea when I brought it up on the phone, and you were the one who said "I'd love to read it sometime," I didn't push it on you. You were the one who said he wanted to read it and now since you've read it and loved it and thought it was the best script that you've ever read I figured that you would just be dying to make it.

SAUL: Well, we'll see. It's a complicated process.

VANCE: Sure, sure, I understand. Of course. But you'll make it happen right?

SAUL: Well… We'll see, I don't know, but we'll see.

*Sought through prayer and meditation to improve our
conscious contact with the Great Director, praying
only for knowledge of his will for us and the
power to carry out his direction.*

—————✦—————

McDonald's II

AFTER TWO MONTHS AT MCDONALD'S, things got into a routine. I worked nights from 9 till 2 in the morning. I would spend most of my days hanging out with my sobriety sponsor, Sonny. We'd watch old movies at his place or I would watch newer movies at my parents' place. Sometimes I would work out with weights in their garage.

The acting thing was growing on me too. Now that I wasn't using heroin, I thought about things that I wanted to do with my life. Acting and marriage seemed like good goals. I didn't know where to start with either of them but I thought about them a lot. I was twenty-seven and my time was running out.

I didn't feel like using heroin. There was a lot to live for. For extra money, I kept the handjob thing going with Juan. He could only afford to pay me the twenty-five bucks a week, but that was good enough for cigarettes. On payday, we'd go back to the bathroom and do it. But then, after the third time, he asked me to return the favor. But I told him he would then have to pay me *thirty*-five bucks. The next week he had thirty-five, so I did it.

We used the same position that we used when he would do it to me. I put my chest up against his and my cheek against his cheek so I wouldn't have to look at him. When he had done it to me I would close my eyes, but when I did it to him I kept my eyes open. I didn't want to imagine anything. I stared at the drawings on the stall wall. It seems like the same guy drew all the pictures in all the bathrooms in all the world. Sea slug dicks, and beanbag tits with perky nipples, and piggy asses. The drawings made me think of the church camps I went to when I was young, back when the pictures depicted things I hadn't done yet. While I worked on Juan, I stared at them and thought about childhood. Juan whispered in my ear, "Jesús. Jesús, Jesús. Shit, fuck, Jesús."

His belly pressed against my stomach; it was like a waterbed. Then when he came, it moved in quick spasms and jiggled all over me. The cum shot against the wall and we left it there.

During work hours, I hardly saw Juan because I was back in my little drive-thru area, but I'd see him when I passed the grill to go to the bathroom or when I'd go outside to smoke. He'd watch me walk by with his dumb animal eyes in his dumb baby face. If I looked he would smile a bat smile, his sharp baby teeth peeking over his bottom lip. I would give him my dead eyes. I didn't want him to think that our thing in the bathroom was anything more than a money thing. But I also didn't want to lose him.

I would work until 2 a.m. most nights, and then I would go home and sleep a bit, and then I would have to wake up for the daily meeting at El Jardin Encantado. I was always really tired, and Sonny would get on my case about paying attention in the meeting. I asked if I could go to other meetings, but Sonny told me I had to go to that meeting, the Valley Bucks men's meeting, because it was where I got clean and sober. I liked it because I liked all the guys, and I liked that we met at the Mexican place, but it was so early. One time, soon after I jerked off Juan, Sonny and I were sitting in our regular booth, the one next to the wall painting of the little Mexican in the sombrero, bent over carrying corn, and I put my head down sideways on the table, and then I was asleep.

"Wake the fuck up."

"Sorry, Sonny. I was just working late last night."

"First priority is your *sobriety*. *First* priority. If you don't have your sobriety you have nothing."

"I know, but I was *working*."

"*First* priority. That means before *everything*. Before work, before family, before sex, before *everything*."

"Okay, but you told me to get the job."

"Scan, don't be such a fucking idiot all the time, okay?"

"I'm trying not to be."

Then he told me a story. There was another guy sharing in the meeting about his wife, but Sonny talked over him. The guys at that meeting were used to private conversations during the meeting, but Sonny always spoke too loudly.

"You know, I had another sponsee about your age," he said. "He wanted to be an actor. They *all* want to be actors." This was funny coming from him because he was a failed actor himself. "And then this guy got a little job on a soap opera and he thought he was hot shit. *Hot* shit! And *then* he started falling asleep in the meetings because of *work*. And *then* he stopped *coming* to the meetings because he was so *busy*. And then you know what happened? He went out. Mister hot-shit hotshot started using drugs and then one day, you know what he did?" Sonny looked like he really wanted an answer.

"No."

"He took some *acid*. And he decided to jump off the back of a moving pickup truck because he thought he could fly. Well, he couldn't, and he knocked out all of his front teeth. Smile now, motherfucker. No more soap, no more hotshot."

"Was that in the nineteen-sixties?"

"Funny. I guess you're a *hotshot* too, hungh?"

"No, I won't do that stuff," I said.

"We'll see, you selfish prick. Keep it up Mr. McDonald's, coming in here and sleeping, and we'll see if you have any teeth to become a big actor."

"I'm just working at the job you told me to take."

"First priority means *first,* motherfucker."

Some of the other guys told Sonny to shut up because he was talking too loud. He told them to suck his cock, and everyone yukked.

Then I joined an acting class. I found one on Lankershim Boulevard, near Universal Studios called the Valley Playhouse. We met twice a week at noon. It was intense and good. My first scene was *A Hatful of Rain,* this play from the 1950s about a drug addict. Some of the dialogue was old-fashioned. I got matched up with this girl named Jeanette, who was nice but who wasn't right for the scene; she was too tense. She was supposed to be my wife, and I was supposed to feel guilty because I couldn't stop doing drugs and I was hiding it from her. It wasn't too far from what I had gone through with my real wife. But my real wife had been pretty and Jeanette wasn't pretty. So it was going to be hard to pretend that I was in love with her.

We had our first rehearsal over at her house near Pico Boulevard, all the way over the hill and on the other side of Hollywood, which meant that I had to drive a ways. She was married but didn't have any children. Her husband was a musician and a nice guy; he did the music for television shows. But I got the sense, just from the way she dressed and behaved, that one of the things Jeanette probably liked about acting was all the pretend romance and the excuse to kiss other guys. She did have a pretty good body, tall. At her house we decided to do an improvisation where we did the scene in our own words.

"Where have you been?"

"I was out," I mumbled.

"Out where?" She was doing the impoverished, pregnant wife thing.

"Just out."

"That's bullshit, Johnny! Fucking bullshit! You were with *her,* right? Right? Fucking answer me!"

"Yeah." I was supposed to pretend that I was having an affair because I didn't want her to know about my drug addiction.

"Okay. Well, I just can't do this anymore." She started crying, really working it. I let her go on for a bit because she seemed to relish it. Then I started in with my story, but in my own words.

"I don't know, babe. I just don't know about anything. I don't know what *home* is. Is *this* my home? I've had so many homes in all my life that I just don't know what to do anymore. I just roam these streets and I think of my childhood and I don't know who I am any-more." She had stopped sobbing to listen to my speech. I kept going and she started walking toward me, slowly. "I was just a kid playing marbles, trying to get by, just trying to be a *kid,* and then *bam,* I'm in the war and all my friends are being blown to bits, and then I'm in the war of life and *I'm* being blown to bits..." She was upon me.

"I think you're a fucking hero. Come home, Johnny. This is your home, come home." Then she kissed me, hard. Her tongue swished around on my teeth. I pulled her to me and tried to feel her good body against my body to make up for her bad face. It worked a little—her body felt great—so I forgot about what I was kissing up top for a second. But then I remembered that her husband was in the other room and we were just doing a scene. I pulled away and we ended the improvisation. Then we sat on the couch and talked about it.

"That was interesting," I said.

"I thought we got a lot out of that," she said.

"Yeah?"

"Well, I think maybe we cemented something solid about the relationship, so when things don't go well because of your drugs in the scene, we can feed on that."

"Cool." If she thought so, it was fine with me.

"Do you agree?"

"Sure," I said. And then, "Yeah, it reminds me of my wife and my kids."

"You're married?"

"Well, sort of. Not really, divorced. I don't see the kids much."

"Oh, why not?"

"Because I was a drug addict and then I left them and moved back in with my parents."

"You have two kids? You were young when you had them."

"Yeah, like twenty-one."

She didn't have much more to say to me after that.

On Friday night I was taking orders in the drive-thru. A girl's voice ordered a small french fries and a child-size Diet Coke, which wasn't much. When the car drove around to the window it was a black Jetta, and then I realized it was the blond girl that had come through before, Karen. It had been almost three weeks since I saw her. She looked good, but it looked like she had a bunch of makeup on. I took my headset and hat off so I didn't look like such an ass.

She handed me two dollars.

"*Hey,*" I said. "You look great."

"What happened to your accent?" I forgot that she thought I was from Brooklyn because I had been doing the accent with her before. I put on the accent again.

"*Wadda* you mean?" I said, overdoing it.

"Why didn't you call me?"

"I'm just shy, I guess."

"Bullshit, Jim, you should have called me." Then I remembered that she called me Jim. I gave her the change, which was like twenty-five cents.

"You didn't order much," I said.

"Because I didn't come for the food, I came here to see *you,* you goof."

"Oh, okay, that's nice."

"Yeah, because I *am* nice."

"Cool, me too. What would you like to do?"

"I want to see a movie with you."

"Fine, I'm off on Tuesday night, we could go then."

Then from the front, Marcia yelled back at me, "Sean, did you take your headset off?" I didn't want to answer because she said, Sean. "Sean!"

"Yeah, yeah, I'll put it on." Then to Karen, I said, "Well, I guess it's back to work."

"Is your name Sean?"

"Huh, oh, yeah, Jim-Sean, that's my full name. Well, whatever, I'll see you Tuesday?"

"Yes, give me *your* number because I don't trust your calling skills."

She was pretty and I was glad that she was so forward with me. I wrote my number on a napkin and I remembered to write "Jim" because that's what she thought my name was. Next to it I drew a little smiley face with a big nose. There was some soda on the part of the window ledge where I was drawing, so the face got wet.

At 2 a.m., when everyone else was cleaning up, Juan and I eyed each other and then met in the bathroom a few minutes later. We went into the stall and locked the door. He handed me the money and it was all there. I started unzipping his pants but he put his hand on mine. He couldn't speak English so he started gesturing. He pointed toward his mouth and then my mouth, then in English he said "blowjob."

"You want me to give you a blowjob?"

He nodded. He was so ugly when he was happy with his sharp teeth and his baby face on a fat man's body.

"Are you kidding? You want me to suck you?" I was pointing and gesturing so that he understood.

He understood and nodded energetically.

"No way, man, that will cost you like a *hundred* dollars."

He didn't understand, so I took the little wad out of my pocket and explained that it would cost him a lot more than he gave me.

He reached into his pants pocket and pulled out a twenty. I didn't take it. He held it there. Thirty-five plus twenty, it was a lot and also too little.

Then I took the twenty and put it on top of the rest and put the wad in my pants pocket. Then I undid his pants. I knew what his dick felt like from the handjobs, not very big, but I had never looked at it. It looked like a small tree root, a little torqued to the side.

I sunk down. I didn't want to go on my knees, so I squatted. And then I put it in my mouth all at once. I had tried to give myself blow-jobs when I was a teenager, on my back in bed, my asshole toward the ceiling; I had gotten as far as licking the tip, so I knew what that smooth feeling of the head was like. But now I had the whole thing in my mouth. I started working, just trying to get it done. I kept my eyes open and stared at his patchy black pubic hair coming in and out. Then I closed my eyes.

After a bit, the squat position wore me out so I went down on my knees. The ground was wet through my pants where the knees touched the tiles. I tried to keep a steady rhythm with my mouth while trying not to think about what I was doing. Then I tried to pretend I was doing it to someone else. It was tricky because I couldn't think about giving *Karen* a blowjob, so I thought about her giving *me* one. As if I was Karen, blowing myself. That worked for a little while, but I kept feeling the bumps on Juan's dick rubbing my bottom lip and I would be reminded of what I was doing. Then he came. Three big pulses. I kept it all in, I guess to be nice. Then I spit it all in the toilet. There was a turd in there.

The next day was Saturday. I went to the meeting at El Jardin. The meeting was always bigger and rowdier on the weekends. I usually didn't talk, especially when there were so many people. But I did that day. I said that I was so happy that I didn't have to do drugs anymore because of all the shit I had to go through when I was using. Then I told this story about having to suck dick when I was using, but really I was telling the story of Juan in the bathroom the night before.

"And I would go into *bathrooms* and get on my *knees* on the cold tile floor, and there was toilet paper all over the place and sometimes shit all over the place, and I would *do it,* I would *suck dick,* I would actually *do* that, just so I could get the *hundred* bucks, just so I could get some more shit."

All the guys in the meeting were quiet. Some of the guys had been through tough experiences. One of them had killed some people when he was younger, and one had been in the Mexican Mafia, but most were businessmen and film people. None of them had ever told a story like that. After I told that story, Sonny spoke to the meeting.

"It's crazy, the depths that we go to get our fix or a drink. *A hundred bucks.* That you would sell yourself for so little, on that cold floor with a dick in your mouth, and *still* not realizing the depths of your disease. It's incredible. But what is also incredible is the amount of your recovery. To go from *that* to become the responsible member of society that you are now, it's a fucking miracle. Finally paying for your kids, paying off your debt, and hell, you're even taking acting lessons. For me, there is no better example of God's grace."

After the meeting, guys came up to me and thanked me for being so honest. It felt good. I felt like I was more a part of the group, which was great.

Karen called my parents' house and my mom called me in from the garage where I was lifting weights, making myself look good. I took the phone into the bathroom and whispered the Brooklyn accent. Karen confirmed that we would meet the next night to see a movie. We decided to meet at the McDonald's parking lot at 7:30. That morning at the meeting, I told Sonny that I was going on my first date since I had been married. He told me to be myself. I tried to get together with Jeanette to rehearse *A Hatful of Rain,* but she couldn't because of some bullshit. She wanted to rehearse at night but I told her I couldn't until late, so she made me agree to a midnight rehearsal. I agreed because we were going to perform it in class the next day and I wanted it to be good.

At 6:30 I drove into the McDonald's parking lot and waited in my Ford Fairmont. I was an hour early because I didn't have anything else to do. While I waited, I threw all the papers and crap that was in the front seat into the backseat. There was even more crap back there, clothes and shit. Then I read over my scene from *A Hatful of Rain,* the one about feeling lost, about not feeling connected to the things I love, and then I waited. I had backed the car into the spot so that I was facing the McDonald's building. They made it so attractive with its slanted red eaves and bright yellow lettering. I thought of Juan's slanted dick, the smoothness of the head plugging into my tight mouth hole. Then I blocked it out and I just saw the building. Everybody I worked with was inside. In the drive-thru window I could see Jorge, my replacement. He was taking orders and making change like I did most nights. He was a young Mexican guy and I liked him because he would tell jokes. Some that I remember:

I knew a guy, he was so fat, when he steps on a scale it reads, "One at a time, please!" (I thought that was a good one for McDonald's.)

I tell you my wife's a lousy cook. After dinner I don't brush my teeth, I count them. (Hilarious.)

The driver's side window of the Fairmont didn't close all the way, and hot air trickled in through the space and over my forehead. At 7:30, Karen pulled up next to me in her black Jetta. I reminded myself to use the fake Brooklyn accent and then I got out of the car. The air was so warm it made me float.

"Hey, wadda ya know? *Karen,* good to see ya." I was being cute.

"No, let's take your car," she said. So I walked around and opened the door for her. We drove to the theater, which was just around the corner. She called me Jimmy the whole time, but it helped me believe I was someone else and not just shitty old me. On the way to the theater, I told her about my childhood. It was mostly truthful, but I pretended it all took place in Brooklyn.

"Yeah, so my dad was a priest out in Bensonhurst, which is something I take pretty seriously *now,* but when I was younger the whole church thing was a real drag." I tried not to swear. "I was more into playing basketball, and boy was I fucking good. I mean *really* good. I got on the team at college and I actually played for a bit. But then some bad things happened." She asked what the bad things were, but I didn't tell her. The drugs, and the kids and the ex-wife, and her fucking all those dudes, and all the money I owed, and sucking Juan's dick.

I offered to buy Karen whatever she wanted at the snack stand, but she didn't want anything. The movie started, *Titanic.* Leonardo DiCaprio was cool. I always liked him. Ever since *The Basketball Diaries.* I mean that was my story, heroin and basketball. He was good in *Titanic,* but I couldn't get into the movie itself. Lots of rich fuckers doing nothing. Halfway through, I reached over and held Karen's hand; it was sweaty but delicate. Then I got into the movie a little more. I thought about myself on that ship and I tried to think about which people in my life I would sacrifice myself for. My kids, definitely. I guess my parents. I held Karen's hand tighter and she squeezed back and I thought that maybe I'd do it for Karen too.

On the drive back to McDonald's, I asked Karen what she thought of the movie.

"I thought it was a shitty script," she said.

"Wadda you mean?" I was still doing the accent.

"Oh it's just James Cameron jerking off all over the place. There is that scene where Kate Winslet has some Picassos and her fiancé says they're trash? It's like James Cameron's saying *he* is the misunderstood artist, like Picasso! And then when the old lady throws the gem overboard at the end, it's like Cameron is saying *he* doesn't care about commercial success, that all he cares about is *art. Art!* Fucking *bull*. If that's his *art,* that bloated piece of shit that probably cost two hundred million dollars, he's in trouble."

"Wow. I didn't get any of that."

"It's just stuff I picked up."

I turned into the McDonald's parking lot and parked in the same spot, next to her Jetta, but this time I faced the car toward the street. She didn't get out. It was 11 p.m.

"I'd like to see you again," I said.

"It depends," she said.

"On what?"

"On if you kiss me."

She used a lot of tongue so I used a lot of tongue. At first it was violent and then she calmed down and just moved it around slowly in my mouth and it was really soft.

"You don't mind that I work at McDonald's?" I said close to her face.

"No. I *love* that you work at McDonald's. Obviously you're smarter than that place. You've got something else going on, Jimmy, I can tell. You don't have to tell me about it now, but I'm intrigued."

We kissed some more and then she got out. She kissed her fingers and then slapped them on the dirty window to say good-bye. I felt good. After her Jetta left, I drove around to the drive-thru. At the speaker I ordered a cheeseburger and a Diet Coke and then I drove up to the pay window. It was funny seeing it from that perspective. When I was working I had a whole world going on inside that little window, but I could only see a sliver of it from my car. Jorge was in there. I handed him a five and he didn't notice it was me.

"Hey, Hor," I said. He turned from the cash register and looked at me closely. He didn't like that nickname but when he saw it was me, he laughed.

"What's up, Sean? Your night off? Why don't you get the fuck out of here?"

"I *was* the fuck out of here. I went on a *date.*"

"A good one? Well maybe not, you're *here.*" He laughed at his joke.

"Funny, fucker. No, it was good. She's smart as fuck and she likes me."

"Why does she like *you?*"

"Because I'm fucking handsome and because I work at McDonald's."

"What?"

"I don't know, that's what she said."

"Sounds like she's crazy, bro." He laughed again.

"Fuck you," I said.

"Okay, okay, I got one," he said. "It's crazy, my wife likes to talk on the phone during sex. Really. She called me last night from Chicago."

"Ha, good one." I drove on to the next window and got my cheeseburger and drink. Marcia didn't notice it was me and I didn't say hi. Her gold teeth glinted as I drove off. I turned out of the lot onto Ventura Boulevard and unwrapped the burger as I drove. When I held the unwrapped burger I realized that Juan had made it. His baby-size hands had put that thing together. It tasted really good as I drove. I was driving toward Jeanette's house to rehearse *A Hatful of Rain.* I chewed and sipped from the soda. McDonald's burgers are really slim, but I like that. They're almost like eating air. Kind of like kissing Karen, it was there but also it wasn't. She thought I was a guy named Jim, from Brooklyn. Maybe I was. The streetlights on Ventura reflected off my windshield and made the burger taste like candy.

After our "character" has had a spiritual awakening as the result of these steps, we tried to carry this message to other actors and to practice these principles in all our scenes.

———⟨⟩———

The *Sass* Account

The following is an annotated fragment of an unpublished article about The Actor. The beginning of the article is extant but the rest is lost, although the annotations have been retained. Make what sense of it that you can.

I am staring at a photo of The Actor's backside. It's a nice backside, one that has been used with varying degrees of success in his films; sometimes it reveals character, sometimes it's just too much ass in the face. And, now that I mention it, it is an ass that has been speculated about more than most, the big question: Is it a gay ass or a straight ass? That's the funny thing about asses; they can be so ambiguous, a good ass is a good ass, straight or gay. Or as they say, "a hole is a hole." So, speaking of this ass, so often pondered, as I stare at it, I wonder why it is there. The editor in chief (EIC) wanted an arty spread, so we brought The Actor into the fold, into the cozy realms of the *Sass* office to discuss options, to make him a part. And this is what we get, *his* part. I feel that his ass has a brain, that it has been contemplating me as much as I contemplate it, that in fact it wants to fart in my face.[1]

---

1 *FART? How about SHIT on your face, you mealy-mouthed, sycophantic fucking pussy that kissed my ass every time I saw you? Were you one of the two fey blond dudes that sat in the corner while Manuel (the EIC as you like to call him) went off on his barely decipherable monologues about exactly NOTHING, revealing that all his loud talk is exactly that: a burst of igno-rance and fury signifying that you all are full of shit.*

Yeah, my ass would love to shit on you, especially because you begged me to have this fucking picture taken that wasn't my idea in the first place. Here's the goddamn email one of you sent when you thought that the shoot might not happen:

Hello,

I'm a bit confused by all this chaos. I think that Brad's [the pho-tographer] references were beautiful. Marina Abromavić is one of the world's most beautiful artists, and I think that a piece that ref-erences that should be quite good. Brad is one of my favorite art-ists, and has been for quite some time. I think that Brad's artwork is extremely, extremely successful from a critical and art historic standpoint. It is also very successful from a viewer's standpoint. I would hate to see what began as a collaboration between The Actor and Brad (Brad was the artist that James was most excited to work with in the original meeting, and I felt it was an excellent choice) turn into something that is lessened in any way for any reason. I think Brad's artwork is powerful, humorous, wonderful. I want this work in our fucking magazine.

If we can figure out a way to get Brad and The Actor together, I'm certain that we can work on it in a way that is befitting to The Actor's idea of collaboration, and to make him comfortable in every

How to relate myself to someone like The Actor? This was maybe the dilemma of my colleagues over at happy-go-lucky *Sass,* and especially the passionate and lovingly flamboyant EIC who lives for nothing except the expertly queer composition of each new issue. They brought The Actor into the inner circles of the herd, engaged in a wonderful (or so they must have thought) artistic colloquium about how to present that so slippery image of that amphibious being The Actor—Actor? It should be the "Annoying Dilletante." They should have just done it themselves, but instead they collaborated, and when you collaborate with an ass, you get an ass. Literally. So, *Sass,* knock off that opening sibilant, and take the crude result, you made your

---

way, and to allow him a piece of artwork that he can be extremely proud of, happy with, excited about—the ideas that arise, the open-endedness, the passion of the work, the thrill behind the piece, the celebration that it is, the artists that it evokes (Warhol, Abromavić, Mapplethorpe). It is The Actor's piece as well as Brad's and I think that that is a beautiful thing, because we all know that both of them can push each other beyond their comfort zones, and that's where the best work comes from! I know Brad felt very strongly about the piece, as we spoke on the phone about it being a conduit and an announcement of bigger plans and collaborations between Brad and James.

I have worked on covers with Richard Prince, Dan Colen, Terence Koh. I have worked with Mike Kelley, John Baldessari, Aaron Young…and *this* is the piece I am most excited about in the history of my entire career, as it is an extremely unlikely and awesome collaboration. I can imagine a very gallery (museum?) worthy piece, and I'd love to make this happen, from the perspective of a deep lover of contemporary art.

Love,
S.

bed, and this is what's in it, and it ain't pretty. I am about to be farted on, but it's fine, we are all farted on. And somehow it seems very relevant to the entire situation.[2] The Actor is resorting to his usual form, because we *assumed*, he made an *ass* out of *u* and *me*. *Sass* got the real ass end of it, didn't

[Here the article ends. It was torn. It's quite possible that The Actor ripped it in anger, if he is in fact the annotator. There are scraps of the article (see below) but for the most part the story is gone; all that remains are a series of annotations without a referent. They seem to be in The Actor's usual crazed scrawl, but maybe they were written in imitation.]

---

2 *It's not relevant because you're a fucking pussy who for some reason wants to vent about me. But it's fine, actually, it's nice to be disliked by a gaudy, tasteless, and obnoxious magazine like Sass; in fact, I prefer it. We tried to walk away so many times, motherfucker, and you are the desperate fucks that hung on. Let's read your side of the story and I'll chime in, okay piggy wiggly?*

3

4

5

6

---

3 *USUAL? What does that mean? I'm a great collaborator, so I don't know what you mean by USUAL? Have we ever worked together before? NO, and other people that work with me are very happy to work with me. Maybe you mean, it was <u>UN</u>USUAL, but necessary when I found out I was working with a bunch of tacky fucks that wanted nothing more than to get photos of me with my clothes off? And if anyone uses the word USUAL, it should be in this context, "as USUAL, Sass tried to get their male subject to take his clothes off for a bunch of boring and gratuitous photos."*

4 *OFF THE BACKLOT? Hmm, I guess, we tried to give you what YOU asked for, a shoot with a beatnik flair, that was YOUR fucking idea. And if anything, the beatnik inspiration photos you showed me were rougher and more "off the backlot" feeling than anything I sent to you.*

5 *I didn't ask for two covers! That was Sass's fucking idea. It didn't make any sense to me either. They wanted a regular cover and an ART cover. So don't act like I'm some big egotist that demands more than one cover, it had nothing to do with me, shitbag. Why not make some comments that have validity, you anonymous fuck face?*

6 *WHAT's your point here?*

7

8   9

10   11

---

7 *Um, no. That's not where it started. It started two years before with Manuel begging me to do the magazine and asking me to do the magazine every time he saw me over those two years, and my publicist, Cammie Dent, denying him because she thought the magazine was cheesy and that the editors were bad people. I wasn't sure why she thought this, but now I know. When Manuel called me while I was on a road trip he said, "Yesh, this vill be amazing, babee, amazing! We'll uze ur art, and you can write, and ve can do vatever you vant. It vill be super cool. And it doesn't need to be sexual, or anything, you already did that vif* SEXXX *Magazine, we can do something classy, you know?" I agreed to this, little did I know that it was mostly bullshit. I guess Cammie was right to steer me away from you fucks.*

8 *I wonder why you turned down Simon and asked for Tim? Maybe because you know he'd want to shoot me naked? NAKED, and go against what Manuel had said before. I have no problem with nudity, and in fact I did do another shoot with Simon A. Cramp that I was happy to go completely naked for, because he is classy and is a friend and not a fucking vampire pervert like the* Sass *editors.*

And don't act like you were excited about the Simon Cramp idea, you passed over him like soggy cereal, when actually Simon was the fresher idea. Sorry, Tim has shot tons of magazines, how fresh was that shoot going to be?

9 *Yeah, I did say sure. Brad is a friend and I like Tim's work. But the plan was that I would collaborate. That was the concept, BEFORE anyone else was hired. So, if Tim didn't like that idea, he shouldn't have accepted the job. Brad was fine with the idea.*

10 *MIGHT have been? Um, no,* definitely, *shitbag.*

11 *Sorry, this is false, you fucking slimeball. It was not a miscommunication,*

_____

what happened is that Manuel, the EIC, called me himself and said, "Tim said he wants to do you nude."

"Why?"

"Because he said it's the great next step for you." (This is the supposedly brilliant idea that every photographer has about me now. As if this most glorious light bulb went off in their amazingly artistic brains alone, and they thought, "Yes, an actor NAKED, that would be so cutting edge and artistic." Now I know how every actress feels when she has to deal with perverted producers and filmmakers who try to convince her a topless scene is essential to the artistry of the film).

"You said no nudity, Manuel."

"Yes, but it's Tim's idea. He said that if he has to do your idea of collaboration, then you need to do his idea."

[Yelling] "Then fire his fucking ass. Collaboration was part of the fucking package, if he doesn't like it, he can fuck off."

"Wait, my friend, chill out, dude."

Also, the representative you speak about tried to communicate with Manuel, who yelled like a baby and cursed him out. So, if there was any miscommunication, it was due to Manuel's tantrums, not mine. At least when I yell, people can understand me.

12

13

14

---

12 *I got rid of Tim because Manuel was using him as an excuse to get me* *nude. He then came to me with the Simon Cramp idea but he was too late, I* *shot with Simon for W. A GREAT shoot by the way. The* Craaazy Magazine *shoot was eight months old, but also great.*

13 *Barry told you fucks repeatedly that we wanted to pull out of the project* *and you wouldn't let it go. If anything you painted yourself into a corner by* *not letting me walk while you still had time to get a new cover subject. I really* *wanted out.*

14 *Duh? Why would I want you or your photographers around when I real-* *ize you're after one thing, and after I told you I didn't want to do the maga-* *zine? If you weren't okay with this situation why didn't you just drop me? I* *was willing to work with other photographers, but you rejected them. You're* *the ones that wanted me to use my collaborator, Brandy. She tried to give you* *your beatnik idea, and I think she did it well.*

15

16

17

18

———————

15 *Bruce loved the show. He didn't shut it down, not even close. What are your sources, dumbass? Bruce's studio got flooded, that's why we closed, bitch. And what do my films or* Soap Opera *have to do with this story anyway?*
16 *Yeah, it's called ____, motherfucker. And I'm in the PhD program, so I don't pay, they pay me. But I happily donate the money back so other students can benefit. Are you trying to denigrate my schooling? Because I don't see your point here. Yes, it does require weekly attendance. What do you do all week? Eat donuts and watch porn? Your writing shows it.*

> *HERE's the write-up YOU asked for:*
> *The Actor studied literature and creative writing at ____ with M___ S_____ and C__ B_____, and has MFAs from _____ University, ___ ____ University, and _____ College, where he studied with A__ H_____. His stories have also appeared in* Esquire, *and his collection _____ was published by _____ in 20__. He is now working on his PhD in literature at ____, a MFA in digital media at _____, and recently wrote and directed a film about the poet _____ called _____.*

17 *This sentence and metaphor are fucking retarded.*
18 *Yeah, it was the way Bannerson put it, that he was putting himself out by collaborating with me so I needed to do something for him. As if I was getting the privilege of working with him. It wasn't about the nudity, dumbass.*

19

20　　　　　　　21　　　　　　　　　　　22

23　　　　　　　　　　　　　　24

25

26

19　*Cute.*

20　*Then shut up, you fucking idiot. I was happy to collaborate, but not with people whose ideas suck.*

21　*You weren't played, Manuel, I tried to get out of this story so many times. You kept me in. I would be happy to have you at the shoot, where there was plenty of nudity, but not if you try to impose your perverted sensibilities on it.*

22　*Why? Let's hear it.*

23　*And why would you do that? The shots look exactly like the fucking beat-nik reference shots you showed me! Exactly! So why would you say stop? You don't give a reason. The pictures look great.*

24　*What does that mean? Not sure. Just meaningless stupidity, I guess. Or that I would influence you? Maybe so, you have no mind of your own and you're a liar.*

25　*Sorry,* Sass *is incapable of elevating me, the magazine is too scummy.*

26　*Manny isn't my collaborator. I'm not sure what you mean here. Just more stupidity, no doubt.*

27

---

27 *Actually, my work is very focused. If you took a second to read this fuck-ing thing you would see that. Why would you say it was done entirely through email when Manny SAYS that we met in person the day after the shoot? You didn't even read it? You're an idiot? You just want to be bitchy because I didn't want anything to do with your tacky, boring ass? Probably all of the above.*

I think the Q and A is pretty clear. I think Sass sucks ass. Yes, they're mad, but I don't care, I didn't want to work with them. I hope they feel good about themselves writing this stupid forward right when my father passed away.

Over and out, shitheads.

The Twelve Traditions of
Actors Anonymous

———❈———

TRADITION 1

*Our common cause (film) should come first; personal
achievement depends on the unity of the production.*

TRADITION 2

*For our film's purpose there is but one ultimate
authority—a kind and firm-handed "Director"
who guides according to the dictates of
collaboration. Our leaders are trusted
collaborators; they are not masters.*

TRADITION 3

*The only requirement for membership into
the acting fold is a desire for reality.*

TRADITION 4

Each film should be autonomous except in situations
where other films are involved (sequels, etc.).

TRADITION 5

Each film (or theatrical performance) has but
one primary purpose: to carry its message to
the public, to communicate.

TRADITION 6

A performer (or film) must never endorse, finance, or lend
its title to any related enterprise, lest problems of money,
property, and prestige divert us from our art.

TRADITION 7

Every film ought to be fully self-supporting,
declining outside financing.

TRADITION 8

We should remain forever artists, but
we can employ technical workers.

TRADITION 9

We should remain unorganized, but we may create
production companies in order to serve greater projects.

TRADITION 10

We should have no opinions on outside issues, hence the public life remains public and the private life is private.

TRADITION 11

Our public relations policy is based on attraction rather than promotion; we need always maintain personal anonymity at the level of press, radio, films, videos, video games, social networking, and otherwise.

TRADITION 12

Privacy and reality are the foundations of all our traditions, ever reminding us to place principles before personalities.

Our common cause (film) should come first; personal achievement depends on the unity of the production.

Film Is Life

I USED TO THINK it was all about me. I wanted to be something so badly I was blind to the art above everything.

Errol Flynn once owned a Gauguin painting, but he had to sell it when he became dissolute and was two million in debt. He said that we own a painting until we die and then the painting lives on.

If the painter's name lives on. Damn, there it goes popping up again: fame, pride, vanity. Do all artists just want to live on forever?

I can hear all the young actors saying in horrific unison, "Who is Errol Flynn?"

How long for Justin Bieber to fade? Is he about the art or about the ego?

This morning, a young actress asked me which actors I looked up to; I said, tossing off the obvious ones, Daniel Day-Lewis (even though I don't use his methods), Sean Penn, Jack Nicholson (I like his approach much more, the intelligent, self-within-the-character approach rather than the complete effacement of self behind character).

Then I said, almost obligatorily, Marlon Brando. She said, "Who?"

Daniel Day-Lewis just played Lincoln. He is so convincing. But while watching the film I was constantly thinking that he was the animatronic Lincoln from Disneyland come to life. Like I was watching an entertaining history lesson.

I once did a boxing movie for Disney. I thought I was in *Raging Bull* and I trained like I was in *Raging Bull,* but it was a Disney movie, so all my training was basically fool's work.

Imagine if Goofy tried to act in *Casablanca*. Would it be possible not to laugh? What if Elmer Fudd played Kurtz in *Apocalypse Now*?

When Brando tried to be funny in the Chaplin-directed *The Countess from Hong Kong,* the results were not great.

Although Brando was pretty damn funny in *The Island of Dr. Moreau.*

Anton LaVey was inspired by H. G. Wells's *Island of Dr. Moreau.* He had naked women with animal masks.

Masks can be great. When you act, essentially you're wearing a mask; it's liberating because *it's not you*. But wearing an actual mask can be even *more* liberating. You can take off all your clothes, or shove things in your ass and even though people know it's your body, you can still deny it.

Masks also put more emphasis on the body because the face is no longer expressive. They turn us into archetypes. Or bodies.

Sometimes it would be nice to wear a mask in the outside world. Just stay anonymous for a while.

Or maybe not anonymous? The mask that draws attention to itself; a dragon mask.

Mike Meyers was inspired by Brando's relationship with the little person in *Dr. Moreau*; it led to Dr. Evil and Mini-Me in *Austin Powers*.

Think of all the pieces that go into a movie. It's crazy to think that it's all about one person, an actor.

Although it can be deceiving because there are so many people working to make the actors look good. Makeup people, hair people, the lighting people, the props people, the effects people, the stunt people, the editor, the music people, the color correction people, and the director. It's as if everything is lined up to make the actors come off in the most interesting way possible. I guess that's from an actor's perspective.

Sometimes I like to forget about story and focus mainly on character. In that way it becomes more like life. Life is organized by character, not by story.

Then again, there are so many characters in life, it's a shame when you only think about *your* character.

But when we follow groups of characters we can lose sight of the human and think only in generalities.

I also hate the idea of the insiders, the ones who get the best parts and then continue to get the best parts. But I also know that I am an insider, maybe not *all the way inside,* but pretty far inside. So, I hate when it's just about me, me, me. But then again, I am pretty much about me.

Try to force yourself out of yourself. To teach. To give back. To give time, love, and money. The big picture is more important than you.

When I am the lead, I make sure that the character is well served, that his story is told with verisimilitude. That the supporting actors don't take away from his part in the film.

When I am a supporting character, I support. That's the best way to stand out as a supporting character: be supportive. I think of the supporting characters as good butlers: Just serve the main characters. It ain't your time to shine.

But of course, there are exceptions to all of these things, and sometimes you want to just screw the lead and chew the scenery. I guess in that scenario you don't care about the movie. But you don't need to care about every movie.

Life. You don't need to care about every experience in your life, but you should note them, even the boring ones. Life is the material for art, and when you cut down the barrier, life is art.

Art, when worked on too much, becomes too crystalized. It's too hard. It doesn't have the randomness of life, the little rough parts.

You need to know how to fit yourself to the film, to the other actors, to the flow of life.

There is a Great Director who is marshaling everything together, every little thing, but you just need to know how to follow your instincts in line with her direction.

What I mean is, get skilled, work hard, but then surrender to the world around you. And then, every once in a while, bite back.

Especially in art (art within life, not life as art). Art is where you can go crazy. But make it about the art, not about yourself.

We come together as a crew to make something together. Everyone does his little job. Think of acting as a craft, just like all the other crafts contributing to a film.

Sometimes it's hard to know what the tone of the film is; it's hard to slip in and be a part of, or to stand out in a good way, to feel like you're contributing something valuable. I suppose then it's about just doing your job as well as possible and not worrying about the glory.

The glory is nice, but the glory is fickle. And once you have the glory you need to spend all that time and energy trying to keep the glory.

Sometimes you can just let yourself go after you get the glory, but too many guys have done that for it to seem cool: Jack Kerouac, Charlie Sheen, Jim Morrison, Val Kilmer, Marlon Brando.

Sometimes you just quit midstride: J. D. Salinger, Rimbaud.

Also, don't get plastic surgery if you want to play natural-looking people. If you want to play people that have had plastic surgery, go for it.

Kazan said actors acquire the look of waxed fruit.

*For our film's purpose there is but one ultimate
authority—a kind and firm-handed "Director"
who guides according to the dictates of
collaboration. Our leaders are trusted
collaborators; they are not masters.*

Palace

HMMM. WELL, DOING THAT FILM introduced me to a lot. And
I think you could say that I probably wouldn't have been involved in
everything bad that happened after if I hadn't been in it. I mean, you
know, the public toilet thing, and, well, all the stuff they were saying
about my drug use, et cetera, which was kind of true, but not really
how they put it. But I'm not complaining. They didn't get it right, but
the *real* story is a whole lot worse than they said.

But it was the movie, I *know* it. I mean, at least it definitely had an
effect. Yeah, yeah, yeah, Eliot tried to make it okay for me because I
was only ten at the time and so he tried to make it seem like it was just
a regular movie and not about a molesting coach that gets his little
players to fist him. They actually went to a great deal of trouble to hide

it all from me. Like there was a completely different script just for me, a kiddie script, which didn't have *any* of the molester stuff written in it. Like in the scenes where we're in his kitchen, it would just describe everything up until the point where he blows me or whatever. As if the kid I was playing was just hanging out in Coach's house alone like two buddies and nothing else was going on. And then I guess when it got to the parts where he was supposed to be making moves on me they would just shoot it in close up bits and use a dummy when Coach had to kiss my stomach or whatever. When I eventually saw the movie, like four years later, I was pretty impressed with how they put it all together. It looked like Coach and I were really getting it on. I had no idea about any of it at the time.

But I *did* know. Seriously. I mean I had an idea that stuff wasn't right. Not with the movie, but with Eliot. I mean, my mom knew what the movie was about, she *had* to have known. And they had to have known what was going on with Eliot. I mean it was almost like with Coach in the movie! Like almost the same exact situation. My mom would take me to the Chateau Marmont. And it was like a routine: We would call Eliot's room, and then they would let us into the pool area where all the bungalow rooms are with all the palm trees and bushes and it's all lush and everything. And it was summer, so it was always nice back there. I remember that. The sun reflecting off the pool and sexy people lying about in their bathing suits. And my mom would go and wait by the pool and read magazines and I would go up and rehearse with Eliot in Room 89.

That's why hiding all the stuff from me in the script and on the set and everything else was just bullshit. I mean, it was like the *exact* same thing. It was like whatever they cut out of the script to make it seem like they were protecting me, that's *exactly* what Eliot and I did up in the room. *Everything.* Like the blowjobs where he would put everything in his mouth, my dick *and* balls at the same time. And the fisting. He would use Vaseline and go on all fours on the bed and tell me to do it. And if I got up to the elbow, then I got twenty bucks. I mean it was almost the script *exactly*. But I didn't know. I mean I didn't know it was bad. Well, I knew it was bad because I didn't tell my mom about it, I knew that much, but what I didn't know was that it would fuck me up.

That's what was going through my head when I finally saw the movie when I was like fourteen. My mom said it was okay for me to see it because it would *teach* me about child molesters and that it might be difficult material for a fourteen-year-old, but at least it would keep me from getting into situations like those in the movie. *Ha ha ha.* Oh shit, that just makes me laugh. *Ha ha ha.* I mean, not only because I had already lived through those *exact fucking circumstances,* but because when I actually saw the movie and *saw* what I had just lived through, it didn't *wise* me up, at least not the way my mom hoped. It made me into a madman. I swear. Maybe you want to blame my drugs and everything on the child-actor-growing-up thing, but that's bullshit. I didn't give a fuck about acting. *Really,* I *didn't.* That was my mom's thing, I mean that's why she let me go to Eliot's room alone, I'm sure of it. Even if she didn't *know* what was going on, she *knew* what was going on—I mean, who leaves their kid alone in a fucking dude's hotel room day after day after day? She wanted me to be a star so bad she was willing to prostitute me out, I swear to God. So, everything that happened after, it's not because I couldn't make it as an adult actor. It's because I *loved* what happened with Eliot.

Of course you all want to say it was wrong. And of course you want to blame the movie, and Eliot and my mom and gays and everything else. And I do too, and I think I *do* blame them. But on another level, I don't. I mean, I am almost *grateful* to Eliot. Okay, he introduced me to a whole bunch of shit way too early, and I shouldn't have been touching a grown man's balls at age ten, but then, on another level, Eliot gave me a lot of love. I mean he gave me attention. He called me "Superstar." That was my nickname, Superstar. And as stupid as that sounds now, it was more than my dad ever gave me. Eliot taught me about being an adult. You want to say that he fucked me up as an adult, that all my sexual experiences are a result of what he did to me. And maybe they *are,* but I'll tell you what, I bet you a million bucks right now that my sex life is better than yours.

Okay, the bathroom. Whatever. I lived near the beach, in Santa Monica. Me and Mom moved out there after the movie and after I did the television show, so yeah, it was on *my* money. And then after she met her boyfriend she moved to Burbank, but I stayed in Santa Monica. That's where I spent my late teens and early twenties. It was cool. I would boogie-board, hang out with friends, have parties, barbeques, go to clubs, whatever, I was your typical LA kid. But the fucking drugs were so good. Coke, and then crank, and then speed. And that was it, I was on fire. I would do crystal and I could fuck three guys in one night. And all the time I'd be thinking, okay, this is out of control, you're out of control, Corey, but I never really had a crash, you know. I felt like I was storing all these experiences up and someday I would stop, but until then, I would just do it *all,* ya know?

So it wasn't my idea, the bathroom. It started as a crazy discussion. Like what if you just fucked a bunch of strangers on the beach? Like my friends and I would go to Zuma or whatever and look for guys and there would be so many of them, and we just wanted all of them, so someone suggested a fuck-train in the bathroom. It was all a joke at first. But then I thought about it and I thought, why not? I kept seeing this image from the movie *The Doors,* where Ray Manzarek and Jim Morrison are on Venice Beach and they're talking about what to name their band, and there is this quote from William Blake about how if the doors of perception are cleansed then everything will appear as it really is, but I got the quote all mixed up with this other quote from Blake about how *the road of excess leads to the palace of wisdom.* And that is exactly what pounded in my head for weeks whenever I thought about the bathroom idea, until I finally said *Fuck it.*

I had my friend Dan set it up. We put the word out that there was going to be a big "sex event" on this one Saturday. We didn't know how else to do it. We just went around to all the beaches in the area and spread the word to anyone that we were interested in. Rollerbladers, volleyball dudes, sunbathers, lifeguards. We walked up and down the bike path that runs along all the beaches for about a week. All we told them was that it would be at the bathroom near the boardwalk, which was this horrible cement thing with steel toilets, graffiti, and dirty water on the floor, and rust everywhere.

That Saturday, wow. By noon, there must have been a hundred. Dan and I had planned for me to take all comers, but there were too many. I swear to God it was fucking Rome in there. I have images of asses, cocks, graffiti, green walls, grime, and cum. It was fucking amazing. And when someone was done, he would just run out across the hot sand and jump in the green ocean. I kept thinking about Blake's palace of wisdom and I knew that that cement bathroom was the palace of wisdom! You can call me fucking sick, and I know that the public loves to think about how I did that movie and then was caught with twenty other dudes in a public men's room, but I'll tell you something, that movie fucking *saved* me.

*The only requirement for membership into
the acting fold is a desire for reality.*

⋙⋘

The Memory of You

MANY OF US HAVE entered into this craft (amateurs as well as professionals) as a way to escape reality, but in fact reality is the only place in which to act.

We are all pieces on the board. Players. Players. Think about what you're playing for; extend your imagination into the future and see yourself getting everything that you want. What's there?

Once you extend your imagination into the future and see what you're doing it all for (fame, recognition, happiness, money, sex, enlightenment), you realize that there is nothing as meaningful as the process itself.

And once you realize that it's the process that is primary, you realize that it's the same for life. It's the living that is primary. The art of living. Your life is your finest performance.

The problem is that so many of these performances are forgotten (literally billions, trillions?) because they are not recorded. I like to think about how they're all recorded on the parchment of God, on the videotapes of heaven, on the databases of angels, and every performance, large and small, is appreciated by the Holy Spirit.

When you think about *all* the performances that have ever happened in life, it seems silly to worry about the ones shaped by movies. It seems like a whole lot of work for the very same thing that happens so easily in life. Like creating the intricacy and web of a single leaf using synthetic materials. Even if you did it and it felt and looked and smelled like the real thing, it wouldn't have the life of the real thing.

But then when you think that way it seems like the manufactured is better because it gets the spotlight. It is on a pedestal, it is raised to the rarefied level of art. It is inflected and framed.

Do you want to mix it up with life, or do you want to live in the cold museum halls of the precious and unapproachable?

I hate the deities of the cinema who stand apart, who hand down their wares from on high, who don't share the wisdom behind their endeavors. Hollywood has always been a private club. I open the gates. I say welcome. I say, *Look inside.*

In the golden age of film, Hollywood ruled the country; films were so pervasive Hollywood was a synecdoche for America. What happened in film captured the temper of the country; art was life and life was art.

In that sense, you could critique the country by critiquing Hollywood. This is what people like Nathanael West and Horace McCoy and F. Scott Fitzgerald tried to do. There is a frame within a frame that is framing the frame; it's like a four-dimensional object.

There will be people who tell you not to think this way, to think about film and performance as something separate from life, or that this kind of thinking is pretentious or that it has all been said before—and it is true, it has—but it doesn't mean that this kind of thinking isn't valuable.

Seeking your place, *that* is reality. Seek your purpose and how to best fulfill it. And if your place is not amongst the people of your time, then do your work for other times, for the times to come, or do your talking with your heroes of the past.

The sad thing about having the greats die is that it feels like you lose an appreciative audience. But then you think about Brando at the end—would he really care about a good performance? He got over acting a long time before. He just didn't give a fuck.

Or maybe he did. But does it matter? He was holed up in his house on Mulholland, living next to Jack Nicholson, not going anywhere. Would it have mattered if he appreciated a performance? Maybe.

So, that makes you realize that the main audience is an idealized audience. There will be some people that will appreciate greatness at some point, even if it's in a college classroom.

Freedom to make what we want. Do we have it? We need to take into consideration how things are made, the costs; these are things that can prevent something from being made. If you have money and backing, then you can make anything, at least once.

Think about your context, and if you fulfill the expectations of your context, then you can keep making. But you are also an artist, and an artist shouldn't seek to fulfill expectations but search for new ways, or turn the old ways into new ones. Politicians serve, artists lead. Athletes compete, artists reflect. Lawyers use the laws to make money; artists break the laws to find truth—or to make money.

Money says that something is valuable. Movies sell tickets, art sells objects, music sells units, writing sells mass produced objects. This means that these things are generally made with different ideas in mind.

Who says that a movie should be ninety to a hundred and twenty minutes? That idea is only in place because that's how theaters maximize their sales, so that they can get as many people into their doors as possible, so they can sell the most overpriced popcorn and soda as possible.

Think about the camera on you: You're on a set, there's a script, but there are no lines; you have a character, but that character can change; if you want, *you* can change your character; you can do things like cut her hair, or dress her differently, or put her through college, or have her sleep around, or have her be chaste, you can give her a new religion, etc.

Now think about the set and the apparatus falling away; the camera still follows you, but there is no crew; it's an invisible camera. It follows you everywhere; it records your every move.

The audience is there, but they too are invisible. Let's call them your conscience, let's call them *the memory of you,* let's call them everyone's idea of you.

To have an inside, there always needs to be an outside. The more elite the inside, the more people are on the outside. Get in there, but don't live in there. Be on both sides.

The problem is that once you're on the inside, people want to keep you on the inside, even if they hate you; they keep you behind the glass. You want to act humbly, but you are treated like royalty—especially on a film set. You can't act humble because they won't let you, so you need to act like a gracious knight.

The camera operators are the bishops, the director is the king, and you are the queen. The production assistants are the pawns; the wardrobe, makeup, and prop departments and the grips and electricians are the horses and rooks.

The queen is the tallest piece, the most conspicuous; you're moving about the board like you're the big cheese.

Everyone looks at the big cheese. They take pride in the big cheese. They all identify with the big cheese.

Sometimes I feel that making a movie is similar to a big fashion shoot. You get pampered and the shots are framed for maximum effect, and you're lit in the right way. What's the difference between this and a glamour shoot? In both, you just listen to the director.

But what is reality? When you go down to what Actors Anonymous calls the "veridic self," of what does that consist? We like to think we have core values and passions, but where do those come from but the culture around us? You are either drawn toward your parents' teachings or you are in revolt, but either way you have been shaped by them.

Genetics, okay, part of the character has been thrust upon us. Height, race, muscular build, sex: These things are harder to change in a character than worldview, cultural beliefs, religion, accent, education level, but they *can* be augmented. How many actors wear lifts, or change the appearance of their ethnicity, or have changed their sex?

The search for the real shows that there is no reality, not on the ground level. Think of the world as a grand set, think of all the designing and thought that has gone into that set. It's fucking amazing.

The reason I can read on-set—any old book—up to the moment they say "rolling" is that I don't need time to jump into character. I have played so many characters that acting is hardly different than living (or different than the book I was having a conversation with). Not only am I so used to being on sets—they are where I live half my life—I am used to the intensifying gaze of the camera.

Life before the camera is reality, the reality of performers acting out roles. Here existence is bracketed and highlighted. This is the way life works too: Life is choreographed, and we are subjected to invisible scripts imposed on us by family, school, and entertainment (movies, television, music, commercials, social networking, texts).

If everything is performance, maybe the most real performance is pornography. Two actors having sex on camera may be titillating an audience for pay, but they are still having sex. Their bodies are doing the act.

Something involuntary must be touched in them before they can come.

Maybe the search for the real is about playing the most roles and having the most sex.

TRADITION 4

Each film should be autonomous except in situations
where other films are involved (sequels, etc.).

〰〰✧〰〰

The Angel

SHE WAS THE ANGEL. The Actor's girlfriend. Think of all the best attributes that can be found in a young woman, and those are what she consisted of. Everything perfect. Of course…

(Section missing)[1]

---

1 This story is a compilation of various pages I found in **The Actor's** former Los Angeles apartment last summer. In July of this year I moved into _____ Havenhurst Drive, apartment #_____ , the unit **The Actor** used to rent. It is a fairly spacious one-bedroom in an old colonial style building. The apartment came furnished, and thus, I now lounge on the couches and sleep on the bed that **The Actor** once lounged and slept on. After living here for a week, I found several typed pages under one of the couches. There were coffee stains and other undefined markings on the papers. Some were torn, excising sequences in midsentence (as in the above sequence) and on further inspection, I found that, according to the

contingent on changing fashions over time; ever-varying opinions of how symmetrical or asymmetrical, large, round, slim, tall, or short one's face, breasts, waist, or ass should be. There is no need to codify a list in the vein of Edmund Burke, who ostensibly determined objective principles for beauty, basically what is smooth and various: "I do not now recollect anything beautiful that is not smooth." What is blindingly obvious to an enlightened twenty-first century reader of Burke's treatise, *On the Sublime and the Beautiful,* is that while some of us might be breast men like Mr. Burke:

> Observe that part of a beautiful woman where she is perhaps the most beautiful, about the neck and breasts; the smoothness; the softness; the easy and insensible swell; the variety of the surface, which is never for the smallest space the same;

there are others of us, such as Sir Mix-A-Lot, who "like big butts" and cannot lie: ass men. Earlier than Burke,[2] in the English Renaissance, it was believed that perfect female breasts resembled apples, but I for

---

interrupted chronology of page numbers, some pages were missing. In addition, some pages were numbered and others were not. I was not sure if everything was from the same story, but I tried to put everything back in as logical an order as I could manage.

2 I did some research, and I think The Actor is referencing Edmund Burke's *From a Philosophical Enquiry Into the Origin of Our Ideas of the Sublime and the Beautiful*. The quoted passage above continues, proving that Burke was an insatiable breast man:

> the deceitful maze, through which the unsteady eye slides giddily, without knowing where to fix or whither it is carried.

Meaning what? That he couldn't decide whether to look at the cleavage, the nipples, or the whole cup?

one have never said, when admiring breasts, "Look at those Granny Smiths!" Or, if we were to measure female physical perfection by artist's depictions, what could be said about Michelangelo's bodybuilding Sibyls, or the undulating fleshy folds of Rubens' Three Graces? I suppose today's subscribers to *Shemale* or *Big Beautiful Women (BBW)* magazines might find the living actualizations of the masters' depictions appealing, but I can't; I am not into chicks with dicks, and I admit that I get a little queasy when I see the bouncing cottage cheese on the back of Marilyn's legs as she runs into the ocean outside the Hotel Del Coronado in *Some Like It Hot*. Call me a pig. I am an ass man per se, but decidedly not a thick-ass man.

But the Angel was like none of this. She was small and blond, with large breasts (about the size of soft mangos) and a shapely ass, with no cottage cheese. She had a tight stomach, and a magic smile that tinkled and said *natural* and *friendly* and *pretty*. But this is all too specific; all that should be understood is that she was perfect. Whatever conception of that term might mean for your ideal composition, dear reader, conjure in your mind now. Be she (or he) black or white or Latino or Asian: perfection. Conjure it now, for this story is all of ours.

　　—This is ridikulus. I hate when peple list all the races like this and making generalizing so much that no one has any distinkt identity. They always say "purple" and "poka dotted" too when they make their lists. They want to show that even imposible races are ok too. So they kin say that no catergory should be beter than any other catagory. Unless you says "purple" and "poka dotted" are real races. this is third grade shit, to tak this ways about all the races.[3]

---

3 The above was written in a red scrawl on several of The Actor's pages. I have typed them out in the places they were written on the original sheets.

Let's begin this little anecdote: The Actor was in France for the summer, working on a small art film, the Angel was back in Los Angeles working on a shampoo commercial. There was a night in France...No, there were a few: young American exchange students...Hmmm, well, how do I begin? Let's see, okay, The Actor could be very charming if he wished. Well, no, he wasn't always charming. Actually, maybe he wasn't charming at all. When he was younger he had a difficult time talking to girls. In fact, he was very shy. Before he started acting, before he was The Actor, when everyone called him Shrimp, if a girl talked to him, it felt like his mouth was stuffed with a thick sock and he said nothing. It was only after he became recognizable from his movies that he became "charming." The fame allowed him to be as shy as he liked; his faltering speech was transformed into an attractive mysteriousness by the chameleon light of his celebrity. In actuality, he probably wasn't charming at all.

—That's right you wasn't. You was just a dopy fuck that won the dork lottery and became famous and you cashed in. Don't believe the hype little shit. And no more autobiografy! All you do is just write about yor conqests and pretend that that is litrature![4]

They looked something like an editor's notes, except for the poor spelling and diction. Later I found similar handwriting, jagged and broken, in the same waxy red ink in the bathroom behind the toilet.

4 I had just finished my business on the toilet, when I realized that the toilet paper on the dispenser was out. While staying seated on the toilet, I opened the cabinet under the sink and pulled out a fresh roll from the plastic bag. In the process, while trying to keep things from being smeared in my backside, I dropped the fresh roll. As I reached down for the dropped roll, you might imagine my surprise upon finding a message written on the wall in such a sequestered place. And being a message of intense declarative assurance, which, compounded by my being in a vul-

(I'm sick of it too, Shrimp. I mean I know you think it's innovative to do this split personality thing,[5] but I think it's just you covering because you can't write a straight story. It's like you can't tell a story from beginning to end, so you hide behind all this shit.

And please, we all get women, are we supposed to be impressed because you seduced a few American undergrads in France? Your alter ego, "The Devil"[6]

---

nerable, and I thought, until that moment, private position, with my pants down, so to speak, that I almost jumped (but didn't, I still hadn't wiped). The red scrawl's claim might be written off as a joke, like any scribbling on a bathroom wall, but something about it was different, and I took it seriously. For one, it was in my bathroom, and for two, three and four, I was bent over, scrambling for a clean roll of TP, my dirty asshole hanging above the dirty water, and thus, to be greeted by such an unexpected and personal message threw me. It said, "I SEE YOU."

5 I found this line particularly strange, because, as I said, the red portions which are typed out above, were originally in hand written red ink, and NOT in a different font. Was The Actor planning to type out the red lines in a different font, exactly like I have done? I don't know who this other voice is. I assume it was just The Actor writing as a different persona, as a way of criticizing himself. I have presented it as I found it.

6 This appellation is disturbing, especially after my experience with the scrawl in the bathroom. The bathroom writing was definitely in the same hand as the red ink written on the typed pages, which this italicized critic is now attributing to The Devil. Unsettling, to say the least.

After the message behind the toilet told me that I was being watched, I quickly picked up the fresh toilet paper that I had dropped. I pulled off the outer layers that had been exposed to the floor, and wiped myself. (I keep my bathroom clean, but I still hate the idea of all the bacteria on the floor *or whatever he may be, is dead on: This roman à clef is as transparent as fuck. Why are you writing about yourself? You're not that interesting! You're just a stupid actor that is taking advantage of these young girls, and then telling on yourself.)#*

———————————

infecting the paper and then being applied to my bare backside. This is the reason I don't have pets: they just walk around in shit all day and then walk upon the kitchen counter or jump on you for scratching love sessions). After flushing and pulling my pants back on, I washed my hands for a full minute, and then looked around the room to make sure no one could actually see me, as the scrawl declared. There was no one.

In the kitchen I retrieved some cleaning supplies. (These were my own addition to the apartment. As I said, I am a very clean person.) The scrawl behind the toilet would not come off. Using 409 for fifteen minutes with various rags didn't even smudge it. "The Devil" indeed. Eventually I painted over the disturbing message. Nevertheless, whenever I take a shit, I can't help but keep a constant lookout, to make sure there are no eyes in the walls.

In defense of myself, this is a piece of fiction. I know that my stories might sound like autobiography, and I am not making much of an effort to hide when I call my character "The Actor," but isn't fiction about writing what I know? If I wrote a science fiction piece about aliens on Mars, or a love story set during the Civil War, wouldn't I be criticized for my lack of knowledge in those areas? At least acting is something I know a little about.

I had discussed my plans to become a writer with a Distinguished UCLA English professor (who will go unnamed, as I met him in an addiction recovery program), and he said writing was a great idea, that I could chronicle the life of a film actor better than most. All the behind-the-scenes stuff and material like that. Well maybe I can. Not to say that any of The Actor's experiences are real, *they are not. It's just that I can* imagine *circumstances from an actor's perspective better than I can imagine electro beams or fixed bayonets.*[7]
7 The previous footnote is The Actor's own footnote. As you can see, I

Despite the angelic beauty of his girlfriend, the Angel, when she wasn't around, The Actor had an uncontrollable need to fuck every young thing he could. In France that summer, he fucked.

There was a tourist club on a barge called Concorde Atlantique, which was docked on the other side of the Seine from The Actor's rented flat. One evening, The Actor ate two cones of pistachio gelato, purchased from a stand down the street, and watched *Band of Outsiders* on his laptop. He then fell asleep watching *Weekend*. He woke up at one in the morning and caught the three-minute shot at the end, which follows some of the murder happy crew through the forest over to a man playing drums on the edge of a river, while a French narrator compares the ocean to hell. After watching the shot, The Actor pressed the space bar on his laptop and paused the film. He got up from the low French couch and went outside. He went down the dark circular stairwell to the street. The night was warm, and it was okay that he forgot to take his jacket. He lit a Parliament and walked to the footbridge, just across from the Louvre.

The bridge was filled with youths of all nationalities, sitting in the dark air on the wooden slats of the bridge, drinking wine and smoking. The river flowed wide and gaping below them. Lit cigarette ends moved around like glowing mites, and French laughter breathed out from the seated groupings. The Actor didn't stop; he crossed over to the Left Bank and walked north along the water. He passed a few drunken French people: a couple of twenty-something women in black skirts and spiderwebbed leggings, and a group of three loud, bald men, who thought they were clever, but The Actor couldn't understand what they said. One man pissed in the street with his pants down past his ass.

---

have presented all my own notes between brackets, in 10pt. Helvetica font. — TLNT (The Lonely New Tenant)

Just before the Musée d'Orsay, The Actor found himself at the Concorde Atlantique, the club-barge. For lack of anything better to do, he walked across the gangplank and paid the cover charge. The club was fairly empty. It was mid-July, and most young locals had left the city. On the top deck of the barge, a spattering of twentysome-things sat around small round tables. Mostly thin French guys with greasy hair, sitting amongst themselves without women. The Actor ordered a water from the bar at the capstan and sat down at an empty table on the side. He looked out over the river. It was romantic.

Soon after he sat down, a young American girl came up. She was not pretty. Brunette and chubby, with bad skin.

"Are you?" and she asked if The Actor was The Actor.

He said he was.

"I love your movies."

This was always embarrassing, because The Actor's movies were terrible.

He said thank you.

The ugly brunette asked, "Will you come sit with my friends and me? So we don't get harassed by the slimy French guys?"

The Actor joined their table. There were four of them, two ugly and two pretty. They were all sorority girls. They all knew who he was, and he didn't have to say much after that.

(Section missing)[8]

---

8 This page was torn off at the bottom. In the lower right corner, just above the tear, written in a blue ballpoint pen, there was handwriting, which I took to be The Actor's. It said, "die girls." On the back of the page, I found a phone number with an LA area code, written in the same hand-writing, with the same pen, as the writer of "die girls." Above the number was the single letter "D".

…ended up sleeping with the queen of the group, I'll call her "Diarrhea." She had a wonderful ass that he loved gripping while doing her from behind, despite the fact that she had let loose a loud spattering shit early one morning, after a long night of carousing in Spain.

This loud shit took place a week after the Concorde Atlantique meeting. The Actor, his friend, The Villain, and the four sorority girls were on a weekend trip to Pamplona to see the running of the bulls. After the first night, they all lay down to sleep at 10 a.m. The six of them shared the room: The Villain and three girls in the bed, and Diarrhea and The Actor on the floor. The curtains were closed, and the room was as dark as the bulls they had seen earlier that morning. Soon after everyone was settled and ostensibly asleep, Diarrhea went into the bathroom. The Actor tried not to listen, but the sound that followed was undeniable. Like a trash bag of wet guts being ripped open and dropped into a vat. The Actor and the four in the bed all pretended that they were asleep. But nobody was. After, Diarrhea came back and wrapped herself up with The Actor in the blanket on the floor. Then she gave him a blowjob.

—(Stupid idiot).[9]

---

9 After reading this, I put together the "D" written above the Los Angeles phone number, with "Diarrhea."

I don't know what possessed me, but I decided to call the number. I used the apartment line.

A perky female voice answered.

I was struck dumb, like there was a sock in my mouth.

Then the voice sounded scared. It asked who was calling.

I remained silent.

Then she said The Actor's name with a hesitant, worried inflection.

On instinct, I replied in the affirmative: a curt, and deep toned "yes,"

That famous shit, talked about endlessly by the five earwitnesses, was probably caused by the nine-hour drive from Paris to Pamplona, eleven hours of carousing, the rude ingestion of tapas, churros, and Alhambra beer, and watching Spaniards and tourists being gored under the rising sun. It made things especially uncomfortable for her and The Actor later when they spent an otherwise romantic day at the Pompidou and ended up watching Paul McCarthy and Mike Kelley's *Heidi House,* a video in which dolls were made to simulate prolonged shits into a bowl. While watching *Heidi House,* Diarrhea's squeamish reactions (fingernail biting and audible groans), might have seemed normal if she hadn't already proved herself to be the splatter queen of Spain. The Actor tried to ignore her reactions and pretended that the video was the most interesting thing he had ever seen, just as he tried to block out the memory of the echoing toilet sounds in Pamplona, which inevitably plagued him on a memory loop whenever he thrust into Diarrhea's beautifully sculpted backside. During sex he was never sure if the shit smell was psychosomatic or real.[10]

---

using an imitation of The Actor's voice, which I must have picked up from watching his films. It just came to me. I admit, as The Actor himself has admitted in this very story, that I think most of his movies are shit, but I must also confess a deep attraction to these horrible films. I watch them almost daily, usually with two cones of pistachio ice cream, which I get from an amazing place on Larchmont. It is a bit of a drive, but the smooth texture and rich flavor from the Larchmont vendor tastes like real Italian gelato, and it is usually just about to melt when I get back to the apartment and press play on my DVD player. There is something about watching The Actor's old films, in his old apartment, while eating his favorite food that makes me feel close to him.

10 I'll take this space to finish dictating my phone call with D.

It was very exciting to be "playing" The Actor in his old apartment, with

In addition to Diarrhea there was the smaller and less attractive "Cunty," another sorority girl who was not quite as pretty as Diarrhea, but was the daughter of the mayor of Cunt Point in Palos Verdes. She had no qualms about letting everyone know who her father was and what a special position she was in as the daughter of such an illustrious man. "My dad is the most connected man I know." Certainly, young Cunty.

Cunty was actually very good at French, and gave The Actor a few lessons in her room at the Hotel Excelsior Latin, where all the students stayed. After the lessons, The Actor would cuddle up with her on the

---

someone who was responding as if I was indeed The Actor. Everything was supporting my imaginary world.

I had said, yes, I was The Actor.

This was followed by a moment of silence, after which she said in a whisper, "I thought you were dead."

I wasn't sure if she was being literal or figurative.

In The Actor's voice, I responded with a short and frank, "no."

More silence, (considering, I guess), then she said, "I haven't heard from you since..."

"Yeah," I said gruffly.

She didn't say anything, but I thought I could hear telltale gasping sounds of someone holding back sobs. She was definitely no longer the perky person who had answered the phone. Yes, she was crying.

"Do you want to see me?" she said, now letting the sobs gush forth.

"Yeah," I said. "Tonight." I was feeling strangely confident about my impersonation of The Actor; he was flowing through me without any effort.

"Chateau?" she said.

I assumed that she meant the Chateau Marmont on Sunset, a half block down the street from the apartment.

I said, "Yeah, Chateau, midnight," and hung up. I didn't want to risk any more talking, in case I wasn't sounding as close to The Actor as I felt.

tiny cot provided in the cheap apartment-style accommodations. She was not great at much other than tutoring in French, but there was something nice about fooling around with her young body and having her say things like "You're fucking the mayor's daughter" over and over while they did it. Fucking her was also a turn-on because she was a friend of Diarrhea, and Cunty knew that The Actor was fucking Diarrhea too, so the late night French/sex sessions were an underhanded way for both of them to get back at the sorority queen. Get back at her for what was unclear, unless it was Diarrhea's sorority girl air of everything being perfect, when everyone in the Pamplona hotel room had heard her take the shit of the century, that soggy full-bodied alarum cautioning that all was not well in Pleasantville.[11]

---

11 After the phone call I was shivering with excitement. I couldn't believe how the situation had fallen into my lap. Of course, I would be discovered as soon as D set eyes on me, but I put that out of my head momentarily. I was too worked up over the possibility that I would be participating in The Actor's life, as *The Actor*. There is a particularly bad film that The Actor starred in where he plays a medieval star-crossed lover. He is kept from his true love because she is married to someone else. The film is full of clichés and flowery costumes, but I love it. Maybe *because* of the clichés and costumes.

I quickly drove to Larchmont and bought two scoops of pistachio ice cream. It was one of the few days of LA December rain. The LA drivers moved cautiously, but at least the gelato stayed cool in the chilly air.

I got back to the apartment, and watched The Actor's medieval love film for the two hundredth time. As I watched, I licked my gelato. I held one cone in each hand and alternated my licks from one to the other. I projected D and myself onto the roles in the film. But I didn't know what D looked like, other than having a well-sculpted, shit-projecting ass, (if D was in fact Diarrhea, and if Diarrhea actually existed outside of the ostensibly fictional story). Because of my unfamiliarity with D's looks, my pro-

But Diarrhea and Cunty were nothing; they were easy, compared to the crowning fuck of the France trip. Not to say that the crowning fuck wasn't easy, it was, but it was different in that the situation was unexpectedly, maliciously perfect. The crowning fuck involved a maneuver in which The Actor fucked the Angel's sister. He took her virginity, and did so without anyone finding out. It is almost too great to contemplate. A young blond virgin, out in Paris, late night, right on the Seine.

The Angel's sister was coincidentally studying French in France that summer. She came over to The Actor's flat one night, under the pretense of spending time with her sister's boyfriend. Maybe they would get some crepes or watch a movie in subtitles. The Actor knew that the sister (let's call her the Virgin) must have liked him for a while, as many girls must love their sister's boyfriends. The Angel had told him that the Virgin owned several of The Actor's films, her favorite being _____, a piece of romantic schlock, which was particularly popular with teenage girls.[12] The Actor knew when she agreed to come over that she was his. No matter how close the Virgin was to the Angel, how loving their family was, The Actor had the unbeatable charm of being a famous actor. The seduction of the Virgin was as smooth as a bullet through a birthday cake.

Within five minutes of the Virgin's arrival at the rented flat, the

---

jections eventually transformed into a new coupling: halfway through each glob of pistachio gelato, I began projecting myself into the role of the girl. I projected The Actor onto his role (easily), but it was different now because I was his beautiful blond lover.

12 Yes indeed, The Virgin and I share the same tastes in film. Romantic schlock popular with teenage girls, *and* twenty-something men that live in The Actor's old apartment. Heh.

crepes and the movie plans had evaporated into kissing on the low French couch. The Angel's sister wasn't a bad kisser. Her legs were tight and firm. The Actor gripped them while kissing her. Her thigh muscles were strong, and there were light blond hairs higher up where she didn't shave. The Actor slipped off her panties from under her dress and he put his face down there. Her pussy was hairy, like Courbet's *Origin of the World,* which he had recently seen in the Musée d'Orsay.

The Actor licked her hairy pussy for twenty minutes. It was hard to tell if it felt good or not because the Virgin gave little reaction. After twenty minutes, The Actor asked the Virgin if she had come, and she said that she had. He told her to hold him behind his neck, and when she did, he picked her up and carried her in front of him toward the dark bedroom. As he carried her, she wrapped her legs around his waist, and the slit in the back of her dress ripped upwards toward her back. He lay her down and unzipped the torn dress. Soon they were both naked.

He was looking down at her in the dark.

"Have you ever had sex before?" he asked. It took her a moment to answer, then she said no. She said that she never had the opportunity.

"What was the longest relationship that you've had?" he asked.

"Nine months."

"And you didn't have sex? Wow." They were speaking softly. The room was dark, he was on his side and his face was close to hers. It was the first virgin he had been with since...

(Section missing)[13]

---

13 The rest of The Virgin sequence was nowhere to be found. I searched

If my knowledge of The Actor's life story is accurate (I have read many magazine interviews with him),[14] the above sentence would have ended with something like, "the first virgin he had been with since his first girlfriend in high school." He told me all about it that night in Paris. His first girlfriend was named Ariel. He said he called her "my Little Mermaid." The Actor was never a regular devirginizer; he only started sleeping with women regularly after he became The Actor. But, unfortunately, he cannot tell you this, or finish this piece, because The Actor is dead. He was killed by a crazed fan on the UCLA campus. Well, she was not really a fan *anymore,* so much as a brokenhearted student whom The Actor slept

---

every corner of the apartment, but found nothing more than what I had found in my original search: two notes, a set of keys, and a pair of sunglasses.

One of these notes read:

"I love you Angel. You're the only one."

It was signed by The Actor.

I realized that the keys were in fact for the Chateau Marmont. There were two keys on the key chain and a one-inch square red cushion with tassels in each corner. The number 89 was embossed in black in the center of the cushion. I was familiar enough with the Chateau to know that Room 89 was a bungalow in a courtyard near the pool, separated from the main building of the hotel. (In the past, I had participated in my share of cocaine parties in this secluded bungalow area).

The other key must be for the secluded bungalow/pool area. I knew about a secret gate to this private area, hidden by overhanging shrubbery, just off Sunset. Needless to say, I had used this secret gate before.

14 [I too have read many magazine articles about The Actor, and she is pretty accurate here. I don't know about the whole murder though. Oh yeah, you haven't read this part yet. It was typed on a separate page in this **Comic Sans** font. You'll see what happens.]

with and then never spoke to again. She was nineteen years old; her name was Heart, *not* the Virgin! (*Anymore.*) The Actor was on campus; he was crossing the old quad, right in front of the library, on his way to the Humanities building to meet with his friend, distinguished professor of English, Professor Crane.[*] The Actor and Professor Crane were planning to go over Crane's notes on one of The Actor's recent stories. *This* story to be exact. Unfortunately, spurned and disgraced love stepped in the way and prevented The Actor from finishing his story (and his life). Never again would he get to write (or say) lines like, "You know, you are so special to me, Virgin. I just want to have sex because it would mean so much to both of us... The Angel? No, I love *you*... Yes, I *love* you."

Heart shot him with a .44 she got from a friend. Her friend's father was a retired UCLA history professor (all these professors!) who had ridden motorcycles with Steve McQueen. The bullet had sprayed chunks of The Actor's ribs through his back with such force that pieces can still be found speckled in the pillar to the left of the stairs leading up to Powell Library. Maybe tour guides will talk about it in the future.

---

[*] *Professor Crane wrote the foreword to The _____ Edition of* Macbeth. *In this foreword, he argues that large sections of* Macbeth, *in particular the weird sister scenes (particularly the anti-Semitic portions — "liver of blaspheming Jew" indeed) were not written by Shakespeare, but were added later by Jacobean playwright Thomas Middleton, who had his own play about witches called* The Witch. *Middleton took material from his less successful play and inserted it into Shakespeare's.*

"Life is but a walking shadow..."[15]

The previous section was written by the young woman that identifies herself as Heart. She is currently incarcerated at an undisclosed psychiatric facility somewhere in Malibu. The Actor is indeed dead, but under what circumstances is not certain. He might have been killed by the young woman that calls herself Heart, which is certainly not her true name, just as "The Actor" was not The Actor's name (nor was it really Shrimp).

I knew The Actor. He was my best friend. I went to Paris with him the last summer he was alive. (And yes, I heard Diarrhea's famous splattering shit in Pamplona. I was in the bed with the three other girls. In fact, I was actually having very slow sex with one of them, in order not to disturb the other two. I was having sex with one of the ugly ones. I think The Actor described her earlier as ugly and brunette, with bad skin.)

My name is The Villain. I put my name in red because when The Actor used to write about me, he always put my name in red. I am not sure what that says about me. I guess I might be a little sleazy, but not as sleazy as The Actor portrayed me. Granted, I am ten years older than him, and I was in Paris sleeping with college girls literally half my age, but underneath I have a good heart. Just as The Actor had a good heart. Which is why it is so tragic and ridicu-

---

15 This is around the place where the pages didn't have numbers. There were a bunch of different fonts, and it seemed like different writers. I assumed it was just The Actor writing in different voices, but I wasn't sure. I present them in the order that makes the most sense to the flow of the story. — TLNT

lous that some little cunt that calls herself Heart would be the one to destroy such a sensitive and unique soul as The Actor.

The Actor once told me that he hated every movie he had acted in. Even _____ , for which he gained a loyal following of teenage girls. I think he was an incredible actor; unfortunately, he never had a chance or role that allowed him to shine. I always felt like there was a glowing genius inside him, but it never got to come out.

I suppose that the Virgin had something to do with his death. I am not necessarily saying that the girl he deflowered in Paris is his murderer, as I do not want to give such a disturbed little bitch any more space, but I guess it was her.

I have done a little investigation of dates, and it seems that the UCLA professor that The Actor was so fond of referencing in his work (namely, me, Professor E. L. Crane, PhD)[16] actually emailed The Actor on the night that he devirginized the Virgin. Not that there is any mystery about what happened that night, it is pretty obvious: They fucked. But this little email exchange might shed some light on who The Actor was, or at least on some other dimension of his life.

The following was communicated through a brief exchange of emails between The Actor and myself. The Actor owned an iPhone and read the following email and wrote his response at 1:25 a.m. Paris time, apparently walking the streets of Paris:

---

16 Ah-ha, Professor Crane is the one writing in *italicized Courier*. Good to know.

On Wed, Jul 23, 2008 at 5:47 p.m. (Pacific Time),
Professor Crane wrote:

Shrimp,

I know you were a special friend of Joe Donuts
and would appreciate hearing his daughter's
account of his recent, quick death. (Read below.)
E.L.C.

On Wed, Jul 23, 2008 at 4:31 p.m. (Pacific Time), Sarah Donuts
wrote:

Ernie

I just wanted to let you know that my father died Sunday
at UCLA Medical Center. As you know he had been shot in
the head and was not in his right mind at the end. He had a
rapid decline after being taken to the emergency room, and
died six days after being administered. I saw him in the hospital on Saturday. This was the last day he recognized anyone.
The following Monday he was in critical condition and from
there I had a series of decisions to honor my father's wish for
no extraordinary measures. He kept calling me his angel, I
guess he was already on his way to heaven.

If you would please pass the word of his death. I would
appreciate it.

The service is this Saturday at 11 a.m. at St. Mary's in
Boston. I doubt anyone will travel, but that's the info for
anyone who asks. In lieu of flowers, anyone wishing to may
donate to the UCLA Rape Crisis Center.

Best,
Sarah

On Wed, Jul 23, 2008 at 4:39 p.m. (Pacific Time),
Professor Crane wrote:

Dear Sarah,

I'm sorry to hear about your father's death.
I think of him often, sometimes with fear,
often with a laugh. I am glad he didn't suf-
fer much and that the end came quickly. Joe
Donuts was one of our old men, one of our old-
timers, and was precious to lots of us. His
recent relapse into alcohol and drugs was disturbing, but it does nothing to supplant the
legacy of guidance and love he handed on to so
many. Unfortunately, many of us that go out
never come back. I know under normal circumstances Joe would have never been involved in
the kind of situation that ultimately took his
life, but that is where the disease can take
us. I loved Joe and remember crucial parts
of his life — the disastrous effect of reading
the Belgian mystery novelist Simenon. Rumi, an
ancient mystical poet he grew to love later,
was a much better choice for him. Please give
all my best wishes to your family, and let them
know he'll be remembered by some of us for a
long time. I'm glad to hear he was already with
the angels.

Yours,
E.L.C.

On Wed, Jul 24, 2008 at 1:25 a.m. (Paris time), The Actor wrote on his iPhone:

I am walking through Paris at 1:30 a.m. As I type, I am passing the Pompidou, which makes me think of the MoCA in downtown LA.

Joe and I used to go there when I first got sober and had no friends my age. (Before I was an actor, and was just a young fuck-up.) We'd look at the permanent collection (Pollock, Warhol), and then talk in the cafe. That was the best-tasting coffee I ever had.

He was so great with me. He treated me like a son and a brother. He was one of the people that made me excited about writing.

I loved the mix of experience, his hard edge, and Boston thug insouciance. He had no qualms about letting loud farts fly, and he loved to talk about women. Like they were life's big mystery. Those are thoughts that immediately come to mind.

I cried a little. He was really good to me. I'll miss him. Thanks for telling me.

How do I send a donation to the Rape Crisis Center?

As you can see, The Actor had a long night the night he took The Virgin's virginity. I assume he was walking by the Pompidou after seeing the young lady home. I was a friend and guide to The Actor as was the above-mentioned Joe Donuts.

Before Joe's demise, he and I took The Actor under our wings and helped him put his life together. Joe and I did encourage him to start writing because we thought it would be a good outlet for The Devil inside him. The Actor was definitely tormented.

Unfortunately, I don't think his writing is up to scratch. His intention was stronger than the result. He turned in several stories that were basically admissions of all his shameful acts. Although I think these stories served a purgative function, I don't think they are fit for public consumption. For several reasons. I have told him this on many occasions. I would have told him one final time at our last meeting, but he was killed. It was sad to lose Joe and The Actor so close to each other. An older rogue and a young, confused miscreant.

I have nothing to do but turn to the master, William S. for guidance. He always teaches the way.

"They are the abstract and brief chronicles of the time: After your death you were better have a bad epitaph than their ill report while you live."

17

!!!!!(This is the real E. L. Crane! Shrimp, I don't appreciate you putting me in this story and using me as a mouthpiece to praise your own tattered glory. Besides, the fact that what you have written sounds

---

17 [Here is where it gets a little confusing. I guess someone else (The Actor?) was impersonating Professor Crane? Well here is *another* Crane. Did Joe Donuts really exist/die? I'll have to look it up somehow.]

nothing like me! Aside from the very personal emails that you have taken the liberty of inserting whole, I sound nothing like a distinguished professor of English. I sound like you, a vulgar, uneducated mouther of other people's lines, namely an actor!

I have several issues with the use of the emails, that I hope you will seriously consider before using them as fodder: 1) It is an infringement on my privacy, and on Sarah Donut's privacy, and an abasement of Joe Donut's memory. The man died! And what? You just want to throw it in your story because you think it's dramatic? Fuck that. 2) Addiction recovery is <u>*anonymous*</u> *for a fucking reason! Don't put it in your stories. That is real-life shit that goes on in those meetings, and if you treat it lightly, it will come back and bite you. Joe went out. That is real; you saw what happened to him, a quick downward spiral. I strongly suggest you check your priorities, messing with your sobriety is not worth writing a piece of shit, melodramatic story. You are supposed to be living a spiritual life.*

In addition (these are the notes I would have given you had you shown up to our meeting): I HATE that The Actor dies. What a silly end to the story. Why do you kill off your character like this? To avoid having to write the rest of the Virgin scene?

James, I am going to be as frank as I can be:

Stop writing. You don't have the facility for it. You have the love, but not the skill. As I have said innumerable times, you throw in a lot of flash, to hide a lack of substance. I think this comes from your deep fear that readers won't accept you as an actor and a writer. Well, if you continue writing about a character called "The Actor," of course they won't accept you as a writer!

You need to either buckle down and learn to tell a story, or just stop writing. This material is like a combination of National Enquirer *gossip, MTV-style quick cuts, and experimental fiction schlock. Of course I am a scholar of the English Renaissance, and you could say I know nothing about what is current, but I also know that Shakespeare has been read for 400 years. Can you see this mess being read even two weeks from now?*

Basically, don't kill The Actor in your story. But more than that, don't write this story. Just write about people with regular names (no "The Actor," "the Virgin," "diarrhea," etc.), and then reveal a few artistic truths for us, instead of showing us your (and Joe's!) dirty laundry. If you can't do that, just stop.

(Final sections)[18]

---

18 [Here is another hodgepodge of stuff that I found. I tried my best to put it in an order that makes sense. (On another note, after the movie, before I met D {Diarrhea?} at the Chateau, I smoked a bunch of The Actor's cigarette butts {Parliaments} that I had found around the apartment. Then

When the Angel was eighteen, before she knew The Actor, she was raped. She had been a freshman at Ohio University and one night she got drunk. Her small frame could not handle much alcohol, and because she didn't drink much in high school, she didn't know her limit. She had passed out on a bed at a party, and when she woke up, she was being fucked by a boy from her dorm. She knew him a little; we'll call him Ben. He was a foolish boy who was in a fraternity at the time—he was later expelled from the frat for undisclosed reasons and moved to LA to try his hand at acting. When the Angel woke and realized what was happening, she just lay there. She was too scared. She let him do it.

After, she didn't tell anyone because she was afraid that she would be blamed for being drunk. She dropped out of school at the end of the year and moved back to LA.

After she had been dating The Actor for two years, she told him the story of her rape while sitting in his car in the ArcLight parking lot, after going to see *There Will Be Blood*. She cried through the whole telling.

Up to that point, The Actor had been a good boyfriend, to the Angel and all his previous girlfriends. He had had several long-term relationships, beginning with his high-school girlfriend, Ariel, and had been faithful to all of them. Learning that the Angel had been raped was a heavy blow. And the fact that it had happened two years prior made revenge less tangible, while the pain was hot and present. Even though she had kept it inside, the rape was old news for the

---

I took my clothes off and jumped on all the couches and the bed. Odd behavior for a man in his late twenties, I know. —TLNT]

Angel and Ben the rapist, but for The Actor, it was like it had happened the day before.

The Actor didn't know what to do, so he went to his addiction recovery friend, Joe Donuts, for advice. Joe was in his fifties. When he was younger, he did muscle work for Irish heavies in Boston in order to support his drug habit. He got cleaned up when he was forty-two and moved to LA. In LA, he did extra work in films and occasionally got a small speaking role. Eventually he got in with the Teamsters and made his way to the top. He had been sober for fifteen years and was a mentor to many young men trying to get clean, especially the ones that were rough around the edges. He always had good advice for The Actor, and kept him diligent about his commitment to recovery and living sober.

The day after watching *There Will Be Blood* and hearing the rape story in the parking lot, The Actor met Joe Donuts at the Griddle on Sunset, and told him about the Angel's rape. Joe was usually very collected, cool and unshakeable. But after hearing the rape story, he showed a new side. He was no longer the calm, grounded Joe; he was the old Joe. His eyes got teary and his mouth flattened into a hard straight line. Joe told The Actor what they were going to do.

Joe was going to call a guy he knew in Boston named Vance. Vance would drive out to Ohio and wait outside the _____ fraternity for Ben to come out and then kick the shit out of him. The Actor told him that Ben had moved to LA to be an actor. Even better, Vance would drive to LA and do the job; all they had to do was find him. The Actor told him that he knew Ben was enrolled at his old acting school, Valley Playhouse. Perfect, Vance would get him there. There would be no connection to The Actor, and Ben would get what he deserved. He certainly wouldn't have a chance at a career after Vance got through with his face; it was the least he deserved after mangling the Angel's life.

This part is all real. It was so disturbing that The Actor had to write a play about it.[19]

[Note: Sorry for leaving the footnotes momentarily and intruding on the main body of the text here, but I need to set up the scene you're about to read. Here is the scene from The Actor's play that Missy gave me. Just pretend that that character "Saul" isn't an old man talking about his daughter, but is actually The Actor talking about the Angel. I changed the name of the other guy to "Donuts" so we could all understand the connections to The Actor's life better. (His name wasn't Donuts in the original script)]:

Ext. (The Griddle)[20] Café
[Two men sit at a table outside and talk in confidence. They are SAUL and DONUTS. Saul is in his sixties. Donuts is in his fifties.]

---

19 Okay, I wrote the part you just read. I had come to the end of the material that I had found under The Actor's couch. I had searched for more; all closets, behind all appliances and under every piece of furniture for more pages, but there was nothing, not even any red scribbles.

I have a friend, Missy, who took a playwriting class with The Actor through UCLA Extension. She gave me a scene from a play that The Actor had written for class. The play was about this father whose daughter gets raped and he tries to get revenge.

I made up that stuff above about the Angel being raped, because it seemed so close to the play that The Actor wrote. I don't know if the Angel was raped or not or if any guy named Ben had moved to LA or went to the Valley Playhouse — which is indeed The Actor's old school.

Missy would only give me one scene from the play, and she made me promise not to show anyone.

Who knows, maybe I'm right, maybe the Angel was raped.
20 I added that.

SAUL: I don't know how to thank you, Donuts.

DONUTS: It's fine.

SAUL: I can't say it made anything better, but it is still somewhat satisfying.

DONUTS: Well, he deserved it.

SAUL: And Vance made it back all right?

DONUTS: Yeah, Vance's fine. Called me from Boston. I'm telling you, he's a guy who enjoys that sort of thing. He's got a lot of anger, you know?

SAUL: I hope doing all this was okay for you. I know we're supposed to be sober and spiritual and not do this kind of thing.

DONUTS: Hey, yeah, it's part of my old life. I don't like to do that sort of thing anymore; I'm just an actor now. But that kid deserved to get a message.

SAUL: Yeah... Yeah he did.

[They eat for a second.]

DONUTS: You know he's been in a coma for three days.

SAUL: What?

DONUTS: They had a story in the paper yesterday.

SAUL: Fuck!

DONUTS: I don't think it's going to turn out well.

SAUL: What do you mean?

DONUTS: He's either going to die or he'll wake up a vegetable or some shit.

[End of Scene][21]

---

21 That's all that my friend Missy would give me. I begged her for more of The Actor's scenes, but she wouldn't give them to me. She said I was too

obsessed. I could have killed her. Doesn't she know what love is? I could feel The Actor's pain, anger and helpless despair seeping through the lines of his play.

The Actor wrote the play because he couldn't avenge the Angel. What happened in the play was wishful thinking; it's not what really happened.

How was The Actor supposed to deal with such feelings of inadequacy? He couldn't assault Ben himself because he would be arrested and it would be all over the papers, and he couldn't call the police or tell the school because it was the Angel's word against Ben's, and nothing could be proved. In addition, it had happened two years prior, and she had been drunk.

In real life, The Actor had chickened out on Joe Donuts' offer to fly his thug friend out from Boston, and all he could do was write a scene for a UCLA Extension class. The rape and his inability to rectify it drove his friend Joe Donuts crazy. Joe, that ex-con who had seen so much bad happen to so many people, couldn't let the rape go. It was the injustice of it, and that it happened to the girlfriend of The Actor, whom he considered a son. When The Actor didn't take him up on his offer for revenge, Joe had to anesthetize the pain that the rape had caused to his own soul. He went out and started using heroin again. He would never have been at the drug deal that ended with a bullet in his head if The Actor hadn't told him about the rape.

Missy said that The Actor had been extremely serious when he read this scene in class; he wasn't crying, but almost. Missy said the teacher, Ms. Prism, loved the scene. Ms. Prism *had* cried. I said that Ms. Prism had probably been raped when she was younger. Missy didn't like that.

I begged Missy for more scenes, and just before I was about to resort to stealing her computer, she gave me an additional snippet from The Actor's play. It's a speech; Saul, the father character, is speaking again:

SAUL: When I think about that night, I can't help but wonder if she called out for me. And if not aloud, was she thinking of me while it happened? And if she did, was she hoping that I would come save her, or was she thinking that she was shaming me?

She didn't tell me it happened. I had to hear it from her mother.

One night out of the half million in human history. One girl out of millions who have been raped. It's a small blip on the great radar. But down here on earth, the imprint of this act has been pressed upon my family and me. Somehow, the course of human actions brought her to that room on that night, the molecular balance of that boy mixed with his temperament and the physical disparity between him and my daughter was forced closed. Something that can never be erased.

Somewhere on the scrolls of history, this act is recorded. Now the only thing in question is if the act will be answered.

This kind of thing will never end.

It's a little melodramatic, but can you blame him? The poor Actor was trying to process his pain and impotence. Of course when we read about a rape, it sounds cliché and overdone, but does that mean that it isn't fresh and painful for those involved? Ever since Daphne, Leda, and Persephone, women have been raped in literature. Sure, we're sick of it. But how does a young man get over it? A young artist? What can he do?

I'll tell you what he did. He slept with every young girl that he could find. He wanted to take Ben's place. He couldn't stand that someone had taken advantage of his lover, so he was going to take advantage of everyone he could find. But he didn't have to rape, he was The Actor, he had the charm, he could have as many girls as he wanted freely.

And I'll tell you what else happened (I figured all of this out as I donned The Actor's sunglasses I had found, left in the apartment, and walked down to the street through the rain to the secret Sunset gate; it was getting late): After The Actor had slept with many women, before France and in France, while the Angel was busy doing her shampoo commercial, he got caught.

It wasn't the Angel's sister, the Virgin (or Heart as she likes to call herself) that exposed him, (and she certainly didn't kill him); it was Diarrhea. The little anecdote about The Actor being murdered on the UCLA campus was just another attempt by The Actor to purge himself of guilt, to expose himself for the chickenhearted cheater that he was. What the UCLA murder scene was covering was the very real, (but narratively uninteresting) break-up of The Actor and the Angel. You see, Diarrhea had found out that Cunty had been sleeping with The Actor in France.

This was months after Paris, when they had all returned to LA. Cunty and Diarrhea were at UCLA and The Actor was shooting another movie. The Actor would meet Diarrhea at the Chateau Marmont bungalow he kept for assignations, number 89. They would meet there in secret and relive their times in Paris.

The Actor couldn't stop. He had to be Ben. He had to fuck young girls. He had to own the rape.

During winter break, Diarrhea was visiting Cunty at the Mayor's house in Cunt Point, Palos Verdes. They stayed up late one night and got drunk on the Mayor's liquor, and Cunty let slip that she had been sleeping with The Actor in Paris. The girls got into a fight.

But it wasn't The Actor's infidelity that pushed Diarrhea over the edge; it was Cunty's revelation that she, and The Actor, and everyone else who had been in the Pamplona hotel room had been laughing for months behind Diarrhea's back about her record-breaking shit. The Actor had even turned it into an art video with a real asshole propelling real shit.

Diarrhea was devastated. She promptly called The Actor's apartment, got the Angel on the phone and told her she had been fucking The Actor since France.

I now understood the second crumpled note written in The Actor's hand that I had found at the apartment. It read:

"I'm a fool"

No one saw me as I approached the secret gate. I hoped the glasses would be enough of a disguise in case I did come across anyone.

To my great joy, one of the keys on the chain opened the secret gate. I slipped inside to the brick-paved patio area; thick, exotic shrubbery, heavy with rain, surrounded me.

I saw no one. I quickly crossed the patio to number 89. (I instinctually knew where to go).

The second key on the chain worked in the door.

Inside, I was quick about my movements. It was almost midnight.

The lights were off and I kept them off. I left the door open a crack and made my way to the kitchen. Somehow, I knew where it was in the dark.

In the kitchen, I found two small bottles of gin and quickly swallowed both. They burned. Then I opened a drawer where a knife would be. In fact, there was a knife there. I picked it up. It was a small steak knife. A knife that The Actor had used many times to cut the juicy Chateau steaks.

I took the knife, went to the bedroom, and slipped off my clothes, except for the sunglasses, and waited under the covers. The knife was under the covers too.

me is he   him am I   see will you?   reversed actor   the avenge to
want

...smeared ben like walls on it smear and blood diareahs take   want i

me c u   u c i   toilet   the behind   devil of writing   red, red   write will
i

anymore angel? no and love? no and acting no and hiding? no and end? No

*Each film (or theatrical performance) has but
one primary purpose... to carry its message to
the public, to communicate.*

—————〰〰〰—————

Tristan

"You have to do this."

"But this director sucks...He sucks."

"Doesn't matter."

"Doesn't matter? It does matter. He did *Robin Hood,* he did fucking *Robin Hood,* he sucks, he's terrible."

"This movie is a movie that Brando would do, okay? This is a role that a young Brando would do."

"Ummmm..."

"I'm serious. You don't see roles like this anymore. *Heroic* roles, especially for young people. You just don't see it."

"I don't know."

"Of course you don't. The actor *never* knows. That's why the studio system was so great, the actors were told which roles to play and someone who was smart and knew what the people wanted put the actors in the right roles."

Silence.

Teacher again. "The actor *never* knows. Trust me."

"But…"

"*Trust* me. Okay? Trust me. You will have a sword, the girl, this script, you don't know what this script is, this script is something that just isn't made in Hollywood anymore. You don't know how deep this script is. This is a very smart writer, *very* smart. This character, I'm telling you, the depth of a young Brando or an Olivier."

I should have known. I should have known.

A performer (or film) must never endorse, finance, or lend its title to any related enterprise, lest problems of money, property, and prestige divert us from our art.

1. Tell a Lie

MY FATHER JUST PASSED AWAY. He died of a heart attack two days ago. Despite being educated at Stanford and Harvard, he hadn't had regular employment for fifteen years. He and my mother had moved back to Palo Alto, California, after finishing business school in Boston because he had liked it while attending Stanford. He worked in telecommunications in Silicon Valley, at Rakem, IBM, and ROLM. When I was about to graduate high school, he tried to start his own company, some product that would help companies electronically organize their inventory. He was so excited and confident about this company; he would tell all his friends and family to invest in the company, not because he needed funding but for their sakes because he was so sure that this would be a huge success. Then, at the last minute, one of the major investors pulled out and the company folded and the technology was developed by another company and my father had nothing.

That seemed like the end for him. He had many other ideas after that. He tried to open a restaurant with a friend from recovery and a coffee shop with an Afghan refugee he had befriended, but those fell apart due to personality issues. He went back to school and took science classes because he believed there are gold particles in rivers and that there was a way to pull them out. He did experiments in the backyard, little containers of river water that we weren't allowed to talk about with our friends. He was an alchemist. He did math problems that he claimed to work on for years, on notepads and napkins and then, once he had the answer, he would say that it was obvious all along and he needed a new problem. He would ask for arcane math books at Christmas, but I am not sure if he ever read them. He meditated a lot and got my brother into it, and now my brother works at an ashram.

My father helped with charities to give relief to Afghanistan and Iraq; he even traveled there during wartime. But when he got grants for these companies, he didn't receive any operating fees. He made no money. I helped my parents keep their house in Palo Alto. I paid for Christmas presents and dental work and my brothers' college educations and I don't know what else. I felt like I became the father.

At the end, my dad was very sweet. He was supportive of my film career, and he even started saying good things about the roles I played and the films I directed. The last time I saw him was at a screening for my film about Hart Crane, *The Broken Tower*, at the Los Angeles Film Festival. At one time in his life, my father had wanted to be a poet and had actually gone to Stanford to study with Hart Crane's old friend, Yvor Winters, but the year my father arrived was the year Yvor left (or died, can't remember) and Ken Fields took over. I also knew that my father enjoyed the art films of Antonioni and Bergman and Kurasawa, and I think he saw me aiming for the greatness and austerity of those directors with my film. My mother said he was very moved by *The Broken Tower*. In it, I play Hart Crane, and I cast my real mother as Hart's mother. Hart's father was a millionaire, but he never gave Hart any real support, and then when Hart's father died Hart expected a huge inheritance, and when it didn't come he jumped off a boat and killed himself (there were probably many reasons he did this, not just the money). There were a few scenes where Hart argues with his father about following a career in poetry and his father tells him to be practical. I turned out better than Hart: I don't have an addiction and I am able to support myself financially. I will not kill myself now that my father has died, and I don't expect anything of his money.

But when I went home to arrange the funeral with my mother and my two brothers, my meditator brother told us that my father told him to burn all his journals. My father has hundreds of journals in which he worked out his problems using the I Ching. I guess my brother was closer to my father, and maybe there is some dark stuff in those journals—my father was involved in some weird things when he was a young man at Stanford—but by God, I want those fucking journals.

2. Tell the Truth

I wanted to tell the truth all the time. I wanted to use my life as a model for my work. I thought that I was interesting enough that this would translate, truth = interesting stuff that people want to read. I could go around to everyone and say only true things, but would that mean anything? When would it get interesting? Who would I have to tell the *truth* to for it to be art, when would people begin to notice that I was doing something artful? I suppose I realized that it was the press that wasn't used to people being honest, not that people always lied when they spoke to them, but the big celebrities were good at not revealing too much—K____ E_____ doesn't sleep with tons of women, and M_____ P_____ has never done drugs—and sometimes when celebrities *did* reveal too much they were crucified for it: Look at Tom Cruise jumping on Oprah's couch because he was so in love. It's the snarky little fuckers that write for *South Park* or *Family Guy* and hide behind cartoons that get revered. They are honest, but honest about everyone else, not about themselves.

But I couldn't get the truth out, unadulterated. Everyone had a way they wanted me to talk about things, and even when I did speak the truth in full, these shows would cut up what I said and put it into a package that served what they wanted to say. And, in addition, what could I tell the truth about? What did I have knowledge of that was valuable if it was known? All I could do was reveal things the way they were; I had an insider's knowledge of how things worked and from the inside I could begin to peek out to the outside and say, "Hey, look, this is what it's really like, not like they show on TMZ or on Paris Hilton's reality show."

So, yes, I did it. I had lots of sex. Lots. Most actors seem to do it, capitalize on their celebrity appeal. It's funny, lots of guys that become actors were shy or nerdy or sensitive when they were younger, so when they become famous they really cash in to make up for those years when they were overlooked and rejected. S_____ N_____ was one that cleaned up, man, he slept with (big time actress), really, and (big time pop star). A_____ A_____, N_____ D_____, S_____ M_____, ha, not only did these dudes have girls on the side, they also went out with the celebrity girls of their

day. V_____ R_____, II_____ P_____. M_____
P_____ had models (all ages), politicians, and actresses.

I had something going with most of my female costars and worked up a routine so that I could see someone every night. One of my favorite approaches was to ask the young girls that requested to take a photo with me to email me a copy of the photo; that way I can give them my info very quickly in front of a crowd of fans and later work out a way to see them. Usually this happens at an event, which means I am usually away from home, so I have girls I can see all over the world. Usually they are ready when I go back to that city, whether it is Rome, Portland, New York, Los Angeles, San Francisco, Detroit, Asheville, or D.C.

So I was in Toronto: It was 2010; we premiered *127 Hours;* a person fainted during the arm amputation scene, then another one fainted before the movie ended. Ambulances were called. It was the first time we screened it for an audience, so we were not used to that kind of reaction, something that would become more common as we screened it more often. Danny and I went up onstage with Aaron Ralston and gave a Q and A. That was during the day. That night, we screened it again. As we entered, a girl, okay-looking, stepped out of the crowd and asked for a picture. I asked her to email it to me. We watched the film and a couple people passed out. Later, at the end of the festival, the girl emailed me the picture, but it was too late to see her in Toronto where she was going to school, and I had already spent the night with a Princeton student who was volunteering at the festival. But, as luck would have it, I kept in touch with both of them—in addition to a Berkeley student that gave me her info in front of a crowd that had gathered to listen to me talk to Peter Sellars—and the Toronto girl, Barbara, eventually came to New York to visit her grandmother. Well, in the intervening months she had sent me plenty of photos of her body and especially her ass bent over in a G-string, so when she arrived at my Lower East Side apartment, I was ready and she was ready. Not only did she allow me to do everything I wanted to her, she let me film it on my phone.

Every film ought to be fully self-supporting,
declining outside financing.

~~~~~~~~

Faith & Victory

THE ONE THING I HAD going for me was that I wasn't an actor. Thomas and I were friends and I went to the clubs where all the actors were, but at least I wasn't one of them. Going to acting class, doing scenes about abortions and being gay, going on auditions, thinking about yourself all the time, trying to be pretty, going to the gym, doing your hair, taking headshots, being vacuous and insecure, fuck that.

I drove through Silver Lake. Long streets of single-story buildings. Strange offices, acting schools, video stores, bars with old world signs, and new age coffee shops. Debris and graffiti. Everything was run down.

I was a volunteer at Faith & Victory Church, an orphanage/hospital for "retards," way way west on Sunset, deep in the funky part of town, where paper and trash floated in the air and stuck to the bushes and scuttled on the sidewalks next to the cement embankments.

I worked with the retards because it made me feel good. Actually, I usually just worked with one of them, Miles. I didn't like working with the others because they were too busted up. Most were missing their throats or pieces of their brains or their limbs so that they were just writhing things in messy sheets. They lay around and drooled out of deformed orifices and made disgusting wet noises that made no sense. It was stupid to talk to the ones that were that far gone. You could stand there and be a warm loving body for only so long. After a while you started to feel like a retard yourself.

But Miles had a working mind and was actually pretty funny. He was fourteen and told me he was banging the two good-look-ing Filipino nurses, Maria and Angela. He wasn't. Miles had a mouth that looked like a ragged anus because his father and stepmother had abused him when he was a young child. Most of his teeth had been knocked out by a stick that was shoved in his throat and his stomach was messed up too.

The kids at Faith & Victory were all way gone mentally, and either their families couldn't provide for their needs or didn't want to. Lots of actors and agents volunteered at the hospital and did art with the kids. It was through a program called CALove. I suppose, like me, they all wanted to feel better about themselves. I wasn't an actor, but my friend Thomas was an actor, pretty successful, and he told me about the place when he heard I was feeling bad.

Thomas used to party with me back when I was working as a production assistant on big movies, about five years ago. Monday through Thursday I would work on sets in the day, bringing actors coffee and shit, and then at night Thomas and I would go to the clubs.

Then on weekends we would do speed and watch three or four movies in a row, in the theater and at his house. We watched so many
movies. Mostly action shit, but we were into comedies, and sci-fi, and
old foreign stuff too. But suddenly after a couple years of this, Thomas
stopped, he told me it was over, and then he started trying to do good
things. I didn't.

Time passed. Then when Thomas called and told me he heard I was
feeling bad, I hadn't talked to him in a couple years. He was right,
I *was* feeling bad. I hadn't done any drugs in four months, so I felt
like shit. I just lay around the apartment and watched television, and
smoked cigarettes, and sometimes I would go to the shitty golf course
and play a little. I used to hang around the Starbucks near UCLA and
look for girls, but it stopped working after I let my beard grow. So I
was at the apartment most days.

When Thomas told me about the volunteer work, I told him I was
busy.

After his call I stared at my carpet for three days. It was beige and
there were patterns that spoke to me. After that, I called Thomas. The
next day I went to Faith & Victory Church for the first time.

Thomas was working on his TV show that day, so he didn't come with
me. There was one other newcomer that day, a tall and handsome
blond guy in shorts who I hated immediately and didn't want to look
at. And there was Casey, a famous actress. She was probably twenty-
four. She wasn't the best actress, but she was hip and was not bad-
looking. I used to see her around the clubs when she was eighteen or
nineteen. She was always drunk back then. But here she was. It wasn't
her first time at Faith & Victory Church; apparently she volunteered
all the time. We were briefed in the hospital lobby by a woman from

Alabama. She was about twenty-eight and had started the CALove program. She and Casey were good friends.

Be loving and don't be shocked by anything you see, the Alabama woman told us. The main thing was to just be available for the kids. They didn't get any love in their lives, so just our presence was helpful. And be prepared, our clothes might get ruined.

Then Casey chimed in. She gave me and Blondie a serious look and said, "It can get pretty intense in there."

"I bet," said Blondie, as if he knew all about servicing retards.

"What do you mean intense?" I said. I stared hard at Casey. I was trying hard to pretend I was in the lobby with only Casey and the Alabama lady and tried to block out Blondie. He was part Swedish or something. He made me think of candy canes stuck in people's asses, and gray rooms where people said nothing but inanities. Whenever I looked at him I started hating myself, and I would chant "suicide" in my head over and over; just a little whisper in my head. But when I tried hard, I could block him out pretty well.

Casey said, "The kids are so beautiful here. But it's *intense*, that's all."

That didn't explain things for me, but I didn't ask any more questions. The Alabama woman went back to arrange things and we waited. I looked at the wall and tried to think about nothing. Blondie and Casey chatted a bit about acting schools and mutual friends, and smiled politely.

I thought about knives crossing my veins. I was nothing, I was resigned to it. I was just an empty organism using resources until I died. Their little chat buzzing in my ears made me think about mass murder, and I tried my hardest to concentrate on a photograph of a little brown barn in an idyllic snowy landscape.

Then Alabama came back and we all walked down the hall past a bunch of orderlies and nurses and into a community room full of broken toys and painting supplies and stench. We stood in silence, and a minute later they brought the kids in. Misshapen heads and broken bodies with limbs too long or short, walleyed, all hobbling like goblins.

I saw the blond fucker, Christopher, light up like it was a real treat to see such distorted kids.

Alabama directed us toward the kids. She introduced me to a little Asian girl named Kim. I sat down in a children's chair, my knees up at my chin. Kim stood beside me. She couldn't speak. Her mouth was pulled back on one side exposing stubby, jagged teeth stained by plaque. In the pulled-back corner of her mouth, there was white-yellow crust and it was in the inside of her eyes and her eyelashes too. And her face was wet from the constant drool that she would smear about with the back of her hand over her cheeks and eyes. There were large wet spots on her My Little Pony T-shirt.

I sat there and she gripped my forearm with both hands and twisted and regripped and twisted and did it again. She was pretty strong. Then she held my wrist to her face. At first I didn't know what she was doing, but she kept doing it. She liked to feel the blood pumping against her face. A few times she tried to pull my shirt up so that she could get at my heart, but Alabama or the nurses would stop her. Then she started drawing on her arms with the markers and then my arms and then my shirt. They didn't make her stop doing that.

I spent an hour like that and that was it. When I drove away, it felt good. Driving back down Sunset, Silver Lake looked better. The McDonald's arches were a glowing symbol, and I took its meaning like sunlight into my smiling face as I drove by.

When I got home I watched *L'avventura*. It was the third time I had tried. This time I finally got into it and it paid off. I liked how guilty and empty everyone was. At 1 a.m. I walked down Sunset to Hyde to see what was there. The usual was there. I sat in a booth with some people I knew. We sat and looked at each other and didn't say anything good. I drank a few things and looked around the place. I couldn't work up the energy to meet anyone new. Then I thought a little about the Asian girl, Kim, and the power was still there.

I liked that day.

A week later I went back to Faith & Victory Church and met Miles. He had been at school the time before. He went to a regular high school with nonretards. Miles was different from all the others at Faith & Victory because he wasn't retarded; he was just damaged. He was one year old when his mom died and his father and stepmother started torturing him. Eventually they were caught and went to prison for a year, and Miles was left with an amorphous hole in a chinless sackhead. His teeth were sporadic and jutted outward. When he spoke, saliva sputtered and ran at the sides, slicking the neck folds beneath, which pumped when he spoke.

When they had stirred Miles's face into mush, they had also fed him insecticides to make him shut up. His stomach was ripped apart and he needed special medical care. He only ate mush food and special shakes.

Miles's uncle had a hard time paying bills. He said he couldn't pay for the private attention Miles would need if he lived at home, so that's why Miles was at the hospital. Miles thought he was going back home someday, as soon as his uncle got it together. But Miles had been at Faith & Victory for the past ten years.

That second day at Faith & Victory, Miles came right up to me.

His mouth was scary, but I followed instructions and didn't get disturbed. But I kept staring.

"I'm Miles. I rule this place."

"That's cool," I said. "You must be proud."

"No, it's boring. But sometimes I fuck the nurses."

"Oh yeah? You think those nurses are pretty?" The nurses were not pretty. They were mostly short and wide.

"I think they are ugly, except for Maria and Angela. They're hot. And I fuck them both all the time. *Doggy* style!"

"They're not bad. Good work," I said. Even Maria and Angela were not that pretty, but.

A single hair was growing out of the corroded surface below his bottom lip, pubic and violating. No human would ever kiss those lips.

"I'm going to fuck Casey next," he said. I looked around. Casey, the blond actress, was on the other side of the community room working with Kim. Kim had her head against Casey's chest, listening to her heart. Casey was laughing, a rare thing for her.

"Good luck," I said to Miles. "That would be great."

"I'm gonna get in there," he said. "Actresses love me."

"Yeah? That would be pretty great. What's your trick?"

"It's easy," he said. "I pretend to be all helpless, and then when they treat me like a little baby, I make my move."

"Easy as that, huh?"

"Yeah, easy as that," he said, and he was smiling, but his mouth didn't really smile. It just went up at the sides, and showed all his bad teeth framed by the broken flesh of his lips.

I started going to Faith & Victory once a week, usually on Thursday afternoons because that was when Casey went. I know I was there to help the kids, and that is what made me feel better, but I also liked being around Casey. She really was hot still, even though she was hotter back when she was eighteen, when she was doing all the vampire films.

One day I said, "I loved you as a vampire."

She turned from the coloring book she was working on with a boy whose head was larger than his whole desiccated body. For five full seconds she looked at me with those heavy-lidded eyes. She looked like a vampire right then. Then she said, "We're here for the kids."

Right, we were there for the kids. Casey turned back to the coloring book, where the big-headed boy was drawing a mess. There were clouds of scribbles all over the page. Nothing stayed between the lines of Spider-man's face.

I noticed the blond fucker, Christopher, looking over at me like he had been listening. I caught his eye and he turned back to his retard. It looked like he was laughing but I couldn't tell because he was talking to his kid.

He looked up again, smiling like he was such a nice guy. "How are you, Mike?"

"Oh, I'm fine, Christopher," I said, smiling back. I put on a phony German accent. "*Dah, dah,* everything ez goot." He made a face like I made no sense because he didn't have an accent, but he knew what was up. Casey looked up at me and then at Christopher, and they both started laughing.

"Okay, Mike, whatever you say," Christopher said, still laughing. Then he looked back to his retard, some kid that couldn't speak with long arms that draped like vines.

Christopher had started showing up on Thursdays as well. I'm sure it was because of Casey. He was an actor too. He wasn't as successful, but he liked to talk as if he was. If someone got him going, he could talk about acting all day.

Most Thursdays I would arrive around 3 p.m., when Miles was getting back from school.

"How was school?"

"Fine."

"Any fuckers pick on you?"

"Yeah."

"What did they call you?"

"'Asshole face.'"

"Fuck those guys."

"Yeah fuck them." He liked saying "fuck."

"What do you want to do about them?"

"I want to kill them?"

"Okay, I'll fucking help," I said.

Then we started working on a film project. It was just a little kid project, but it was fun for both of us. Miles wanted to be a director when he grew up, so we decided to make a movie.

The movie was called *Murder Hospital*. It was all Miles's idea. He wanted me to play this murderer that was loose in the hospital killing all the retarded patients, and nurses and doctors. We pretended that Casey was the head nurse and Christopher was the head doctor. The climax of the movie would be when I tried to kill Casey and Christopher. Miles was the detective that was trying to solve the crimes. The story was that he would follow the clues of my murder trail and then stop me just in time before I killed Casey.

We started filming with a little video camera that I had. The great thing about the camera was that it was small and had a really long zoom, so we could film people from across the room without them knowing. We would huddle together in the corner and giggle as I filmed Casey's face and Miles watched on the LCD flip screen. Then we would film Christopher working with his kids. This would all be establishment stuff in the movie, the "doctor" and "nurse" at work before the murders started happening.

We got a lot of good material one day when Christopher was working with Kim. He was talking to her and she was gripping his arm. Then she started pulling his hand under her shirt.

"No, don't do that, Kim, no, no."

Kim was grunting and crying like she was upset, but there were no nurses around to help Christopher. Then Kim put her head against his chest and was holding tight around his neck. Christopher was pushing her off and she grunted louder and squealed and started trying to bite him. Miles and I were recording it all in our corner. We had to control ourselves because we were laughing so hard.

"Kim," Christopher said. "Kim, please get off my neck. Kim!" He was trying to say it in a nice tone but it was obvious that he was getting upset, and her grip was strong so he was having a really hard time getting her off. She grunted and slobbered and bit him.

"Goddammit!" Christopher yelled. And Miles and I almost fell over, but I controlled myself because I wanted to get it all on camera. When I watched the tape back later a lot of the material was jiggly because of all the laughing. Then Miles was laughing out loud and I put my hand over his mouth. It felt hard and craggy and wet.

Finally, two nurses came in and ran over and helped Christopher get away from Kim. He was still trying to be composed and dashing and pretend that he was a nice guy but I could tell he was embarrassed, especially because Casey was there. Then it got really bad because Kim started punching herself really hard in the face and the nurses were trying to restrain her, but Kim was actually really strong, and when the nurse would grab her she would bite the nurse. So Christopher tried to help again and he ended up ripping Kim's shirt down the front so that her nipple was showing. The nurses yelled at Christopher to get away. It looked like Christopher was going to cry. In the end, two more orderlies came in and carried Kim out, grunting and thrashing, flat young chest exposed for all to see.

After they left the room with Kim, Christopher walked out. I think he really was crying.

Casey turned to us. "You two idiots can stop laughing in the corner. There is nothing funny going on." I filmed her saying that too, which was good because it was *real,* even if it didn't fit into the movie.

It was a good day of movie making.

On other days, after we got a lot of stuff on Casey and Christopher and some of the nurses, we started going into the rooms where the kids were bedridden and we started filming them. We would film the kids from my POV, as if it was the POV of the murderer. I would creep the camera through the door and slowly walk up on the beds and then over the kids, who would look up with large dumb cow eyes. Then I would push the camera down toward them as if the murderer was getting really close. None of them cried, they just lay there like dumb ugly things.

Then one day, around Halloween, I bought a fake rubber knife from a costume shop. We did some more of the murder scenes, and I had Miles work the camera so he could record me as the murderer. We took one of the lab coats from the doctors' lounge, and we turned my murderer character into a murdering doctor.

No one really knew what we were doing in our little movie, but everyone kept telling me, "We've never seen Miles so happy. I don't know what you're doing with him, but it's *really* working."

Our new thing was that Miles would go into one of the rooms where there were a couple of bedridden kids. Miles would face the door with the camera and whisper "action," and then I would come in with the lab coat on and the collar turned up, very arch, acting like I was sneaky. I was a real vaudeville villain. Looking back at the tapes, I saw that I was a horrible actor, but there was also something really scary about the whole thing. I suppose because the retards we were pretending to kill weren't *acting*, they were just being themselves: retarded. And they were so helpless. We could have really killed them if we wanted to.

After I swung into the room, I would whip out the rubber knife and hold it above my head as I descended on the latest victim. I would stand over the kid and Miles would get closer to me with the camera. Then I would let out a cackle like I was a madman and really enjoyed killing. Sometimes Miles would laugh during this part, because he was enjoying it so much—probably not the killing part of it so much as the satisfaction of capturing his vision. Then I would bring the knife down really fast toward the kid's face, like I was hacking him, like in *Psycho*. I would come really close. One time one of them *did* start crying, loud, but he couldn't cry properly so it came out blubbery and wet, like a seal's bark. Miles and I ran before anyone came in. Miles had left the camera on when we ran out and when I watched the footage later it was just a blurry hallway and feet. I could hear us both laughing like little girls as we ran.

We filmed one scene with Miles as the detective. I brought him one of my suit jackets and a Sherlock Holmes hat with bills in the front and the back, and I even brought him a fake pipe. But the hat couldn't hide Miles's face and as soon as I handed him the pipe I realized what a stupid idea it was. Miles couldn't close his lips all the way, and he couldn't hold the stem in his ragged teeth. I took the pipe back and said pipes were for idiots and he didn't need one. Then we filmed some simple stuff, just him walking down the hall looking for clues.

Immediately after, he insisted on rewinding the tape in the camera and looking at what we shot. He looked like he normally looked: busted. But it was worse, because it was on camera, so it was emphasized. When I was with him normally I could almost forget all the fucked up stuff about his face, but when it was on camera there was no fooling anyone.

Miles said, "I think the detective is stupid."

We didn't film him anymore. We decided we didn't need the detective character. So then *Murder Hospital* was all about me. It was a story about the murderer and his victims after that; there was no detective anymore.

So the murderer never gets caught.

Thomas let me go to his house in the hills to edit the stuff on his computer. I'd digitize the tapes and edit them on Final Cut. It was pretty easy once he showed me the basics. The film was terrible. Shaky shots of me acting like a psychotic moron and retarded kids stuck inside their stymied brains, confined to their beds, rolling their animal eyes. But it was frightening because of all that. Because of the retards, and because I was set free in that place. Set free by Miles, the kid that wasn't retarded, but was put in that place because someone had tried to actually murder him. I watched his one scene as the detective over and over. The poor asshole face walking down the hall "looking for clues" about the murders. But he was looking in all the wrong places; the clues were all over his face.

We filmed a ton of stuff, and we almost had a whole movie. But then we needed the climax, the scene where I killed Casey and Christopher. We had stuff of them working with the kids, but to do the killing scenes we would need their cooperation.

"I don't want to be any part of whatever you sickos are filming," Casey said.

"But it's for Miles, it's not for me."

"Bullshit. I know what you two are doing. Sick shit. Everyone is so happy because they think you're helping him, but you're not, you're just making it worse. You're feeding into whatever is dark inside him."

"We're just making a *movie*. What's wrong with that? He wants to be a director."

Then she spoke to me in a quiet steady voice, like she was trying to penetrate something, "Mike, you're a moron. You don't know what you're doing. I know that you think you're doing good, but you aren't. If you hurt Miles or anyone else here, I am going to make sure that *you* get hurt." Then she walked away.

Casey wasn't going to be in our movie. *Her* movie about the princess had just come out in theaters, and it had bombed. I actually liked it, but I was in the minority. Her little lecture probably had more to do with the princess movie bombing than with Miles's film. Plus, she was just a moody person. Thomas, my actor friend, had fucked her a few times a couple years before and said she was very needy and emotional, and if he wasn't around when she needed him then she would have a fit.

Miles was very disappointed that we couldn't get her for *Murder Hospital*. I felt even worse because I didn't want to ask Christopher to be in it. I would have rather murdered him for real than ask him for help. Miles and I couldn't finish our movie. All we had were the murders of the retards.

I stopped going to Faith & Victory Church for a while.

In December I went to Vegas three times, on three consecutive weekends. The first two times were with Thomas. After Thomas had cleaned up, he had started trying to *do* things, productive things. One of these things was learning to fly planes.

"You should really try it, Mike, it's great. I got this great guy, he trained Tom Cruise out at Santa Monica."

He said all this like I was an actor on a TV show and could afford lessons. Really, I had no job, and was scraping by on what my parents and grandmother sent me each month.

To get his pilot's license, Thomas had to do a series of tests. One of them was a cross-country trip with his flight instructor. Which meant he had to fly somewhere two hours away. The instructor, Skip, had the bright idea that they fly to Vegas at 11 p.m. when there was no air traffic. Then they could hang out in Vegas for a bit and then fly back at 3 or 4 in the morning. Thomas invited me along.

We met at Van Nuys airport at 10:30. I hung out in the lounge as they got ready. Then we got in the little plane on the dark runway. I sat in the back seat of the old Cessna and Thomas and Skip sat up front with their huge headsets. They talked into the mikes and played with the gauges and buttons that were lit up in the dark. The takeoff was much rougher than a commercial flight, but it was fine. We went up and got beyond the lights of the runway and then the outlying city, and we were in blackness above the hills. I lay back, listening to the whir of air in the joints of the aircraft, the sound of the propeller. The air was chilly, but I was comfortable. I fell asleep thinking about horses and parks, and the sun on the surface of a lake, and Casey, in a place where she was in love with me, and where I was a good person.

When I woke up the guys were talking to the control tower in Vegas. We landed and the place was empty except for a few people in uniform that stood about the runway. There was a nice car service that met us at the airplane door and drove us straight to the Hard Rock Hotel and Casino. The Hard Rock was the newest place in town and Thomas wanted to see it. Everyone was gambling and drinking, and when you looked close, everything was ugly. The patrons were fat and the cocktail waitresses were worn down and saggy.

We took in a burlesque show at 40 Deuce and Thomas paid $500 for a table and a bottle of vodka. As far as I knew, Thomas had been sober for years, but he started drinking the vodka, so I joined in. The show was horrible. The girls didn't even strip all the way, they came out for fifteen minutes and twirled their pasties a bit and left. Then there was nothing to do but sit around and finish the bottle. Thomas and I drank. Skip, the instructor, said that he would fly us back. Thomas drank a lot.

"How the fuck is it volunteering with Casey?" he said. He was pretty drunk.

"Fine. She's not that into me, but whatever."

"She's not into *any*one but herself. That girl is *fucked up*. I mean what the fuck, *what the fuck?*"

"Yeah," I said, but I didn't really know what he meant.

"If I was a dude, which I am"—he was really gone—"I would tell that bitch a thing or two about not being a bitch. And I did."

"What do you mean?" I said.

"When we were fucking. I *told* her. I told her she was just a shallow little actress and that she was fucked up because acting is all she knew. Because she's been *doing* it since she was three or something. How are you going to be a whole human being with that kind of upbringing?"

"Yeah," I said.

"Stage moms and agents and money and fame and everything all wrapped up together, and it's just all fucked up."

"Sure," I said. "Who needs her?"

"And her movies suck now."

"Yeah," I said.

We stayed a little longer. I got a buzz on and chatted up one of the waitresses. Melanie was her name. She was blonde and busty and dumb, and she said that she was a med student.

Then it was 3 a.m. and Thomas was so drunk he was falling asleep at the table. We had to go back; Skip was getting tired.

We got a cab to the private airport and Skip and I helped Thomas into the back of the Cessna. I wasn't really that drunk. I guess I was surprised that Thomas had drunk so much, so I held back. After we took off, Skip asked if I wanted to try flying. He said it was easy, like a video game. I took the controls and it was pretty easy. The plane just coasted on the air.

There were no other planes around so Skip asked the control tower for permission to fly over the main strip with all the casinos. They said it was fine and I turned the plane in that direction.

"Aim it toward the Luxor light."

The Luxor light was a blue beam that shot out of a fake pyramid straight up in the air. They said it was so bright you could see it from space. I turned the plane toward the light. Skip was letting me do all the steering, although he was doing something with the pedals at his feet that was helping.

"Let's fly through it," he said.

I was on course for the light. I looked back quickly and Thomas was asleep with his mouth open.

I kept the plane steady and we coasted through the beam of blue light, and it felt like something special was going to happen. The underside of the wings lit up bright blue. I thought of tractor beams and teleportation devices. We were in a place that few people had ever been. One special place in all the well-traversed globe. I thought about how maybe there were still a few other places in this world that were undiscovered and maybe I could find them. Maybe there was still something to life. And then it was over.

We flew out from the blue light and beyond the lights of the strip to the lightless desert. There was nothing to see. Skip told me to keep flying. He checked the gauges and electronic maps, and I just kept it steady in the direction he told me. About an hour into the flight, my mind shut down. I told Skip I was falling asleep but he said I would be all right.

But I really was falling asleep and then I did. I caught myself once and my head jerked back up, as it used to do when I dozed off in class, but then it happened again and I didn't wake until we were on the ground in Van Nuys. I guess Skip had taken the controls. Skip didn't talk to me as he taxied down the runway. He backed the plane into its spot and told me to drive Thomas home. It was 5 in the morning.

Thomas and I went back to Vegas the next weekend because this club was opening and Thomas got invited as a celebrity guest with a bunch of other actors. He took me and we and all the other celebrity guests went on a private jet.

That night they took us to dinner at a Thai place that was connected to the club, and Thomas had to have pictures taken to promote the opening. Then at about midnight we went to the club, and there were strippers dancing on platforms, and strippers in bathtubs full of rose petals, and Paris Hilton was there. It was so loud that there was no talking, but we all danced together in a little VIP area. Paris's handler gave her a joint, and she, Thomas and I, and some of the other actors smoked it on the dance floor.

At about 3 a.m., Paris left with someone. I couldn't find Thomas so I left the club and took a cab over to the Hard Rock. I went to the 40 Deuce and found Melanie, the blond waitress. She was happy to see me. She said she got off at 4, and I told her to meet me at the blackjack tables in the Venetian, because that was where we were staying.

I never gambled, but at the Venetian I played blackjack and I did really well. I started with $300, and by the time Melanie found me I had $6,000. We wanted to celebrate but there was nothing else to do in Vegas, so we went back to the room. I was sharing the room with Thomas but he wasn't there. We ordered two omelets and sat and talked. She told me about growing up in Virginia and her two younger brothers, who were in college but they weren't really good students. One had just gotten out of jail; he had been caught selling speed. Her father and her grandfather were both doctors, and she had studied pre-med in Virginia but hadn't continued to medical school. So she wasn't really a student like she had said the first night but she was *thinking* about it. I told her about Faith & Victory Church and Miles and how his mother had tried to kill him and how I liked to help the retards and I even told her about the movie Miles and I had made.

"Isn't that a little violent for those kinds of kids?"

"Well, yeah. I mean, yes. But Miles isn't like them, he's not retarded, and none of the kids knew that we were pretending to kill them in the movie. They don't even know what's happening to them."

"Oh. Well, it still doesn't seem right."

"It's fine. Casey Deems volunteers there too. We're pretty close."

"Really? I liked her in that vampire movie."

"Yeah. She was great."

"The princess one sucked though."

"I thought it was pretty good," I said.

"It was terrible!"

"Why do you say that?"

"Because it was stupid. A princess wandering around a castle? She's sad because she's so rich and isolated? Boo hoo. Give *me* that fucking money, bitch, *I'll* be happy. Know what I mean?"

I felt myself getting a little mad, but I didn't let it out because I wanted to fuck her. And I did, although it took a little while because I didn't exactly feel comfortable with her after she was criticizing my movie and Casey. But then I felt fine once I got into it. Her boobs were fake and I worried about how hard to squeeze them.

We didn't go to sleep. After the sex, we watched *Spider-man 2* on pay-per-view, and then Melanie left at 7. Thomas never came up. I went downstairs at 8:30 and met everyone and Thomas was there and we all got on the plane. Melanie had depressed me a little with her brothers and all that, but I felt good about the $6,000 I had won. Paris was on the plane and she had a duffle bag full of money. She had won $100,000 at blackjack. I stopped bragging about my $6,000.

Then, the next week, Thomas got invited back to Vegas for the opening of the Playboy club in the Palms hotel. We joked about how we were Vegas regulars and how sick we were of Vegas, but we decided to go anyway. It was the same kind of deal: Thomas and I and a bunch of other guests took a private jet and Thomas took some pictures on the red carpet and did some interviews, and then we went into the club.

Thomas went off somewhere and I played some more blackjack, but I wasn't as lucky as I was when I played at the Venetian. I quickly lost $300 and stopped playing.

Everyone involved with the opening ended up in a huge suite that was called the Hugh Hefner Suite. Hef had been at the club but had flown back to LA earlier that night, so his suite was full of Playboy models and actors. I was pretty drunk at that point, and I saw Thomas. He was drunk too, and it was still weird to see him like that because he had been sober for a year.

"What is your problem, Thomas?"

"What do you mean, asshole?" He actually seemed mad.

"I just mean that I thought you stopped drinking."

"I do whatever I want, and you're only here because I brought you."

"I know. I'm not doing anything. I'm just asking. As a friend."

"Well, you're not my friend, okay?" He said. "Okay?"

"Okay." I said. His eyes floated in milky fluid.

"You just follow me the fuck around, *everywhere*. Vegas, LA, you even follow me to Faith & Victory Church. I mean, what the fuck?" He was really drunk.

"You *told* me to go there."

"Fuck you, Mike. You just want to fuck Casey, don't you?"

"No."

"You just want to fuck her like all guys want to fuck her. Well she's fucked up! Okay? She's fucked up. She is a fucking head case. She got raped and everything, so now she is all fucked up, so fuck her, and fuck you."

Thomas swayed and leaned on Hugh Hefner's bar.

"I really don't know what you're talking about, Thomas, but I'll leave you alone." I was mad at first but then I was just sad, in a weird way. I spent the rest of the night drinking free drinks. I saw Paris Hilton dancing with some guys.

When I woke I was on a circular bed. It was rotating. There was a man in a black uniform above me. He was telling me to get up.

"This is Mr. Hefner's suite," he said. "You can't sleep here."

"Okay," I said, and lumbered up from the bed. He stood and watched as I moved toward the door. There were empty glasses all around the place. The sun was coming through the windows. Way down below, Vegas was a field of warehouses. The guy strode past me and opened the door, then made sure I walked down the hall.

It was only 7 a.m., so I sat in a café and had some black coffee until 8:30. Then I met everyone to get on the plane. I saw Thomas, but we sat far apart, and in Burbank I took a cab alone to my place.

On Monday I took what was left of the $6,000, which was about five and a half, and I mailed it in a large brown envelope to the UCLA Rape Crisis Center.

The next Thursday I went back to Faith & Victory Church. I hadn't been there for weeks. I told Miles I went to the Playboy Club in Vegas. He loved that.

"Did you bang?"

"I banged two of them at the same time. One was high on speed and we did it all night in Hugh Hefner's circular bed. The bed rotated while we did it."

"Awesome!"

I had my video camera and I told him that we were going to finish *Murder Hospital* that day.

"Awesome!" said the asshole mouth, but it came out like there was a *th* in it.

Miles and I went into the community room where Casey and Christopher and some nurses were with the kids. Most of them were coloring. Christopher was actually playing an acoustic guitar and singing "He's Got the Whole World in His Hands" to a few kids sitting on the floor.

I positioned Miles with the camera in our usual spying spot in the corner. I told him that once we started not to turn it off and to record everything, no matter what. I put on the lab coat and turned up the collar. In the pocket I felt the rubber knife.

"Okay, you ready?" I whispered to Miles.

"Ready," he whispered and I reached over and pressed record on the camera.

I started walking toward Casey like I was creeping. Then when I got close I stood over her and started cackling, first softly, and then really loudly. Casey looked back at me. She was sitting in a little chair so she had to look up to see my face. I was holding the knife high above her.

Through the cackling I could hear her say, "What the fuck are you doing?" Then her eyes looked scared. Before I could bring the knife down to pretend to kill her for the film, I saw Christopher out of the corner of my eye running toward me with the guitar in his hand. I was ready for that Swiss faggot. I smiled a murderous smile.

Miles recorded it all.

We should remain forever artists, but
we can employ technical workers.

$\approx\!\!\!\sim\!\!\!\sim\!\!\!\sim$

Back to Bataan

I WAS IN A FILM about the Bataan Death March. The real death march happened soon after the day of infamy, December 7, 1941. When the Japanese attacked Pearl Harbor, they also attacked American bases in the Philippines, which had been stationed there since the Spanish–American War. These bases had been low-priority outposts and were not prepared for such an attack. It was the "country club" base, and most of the equipment and weapons had not been updated since WWI. The US army was not prepared for immediate response to the attacks, especially after suffering such a blow to its fleet in Pearl Harbor. So, soon after the Japanese attack on the Philippine bases, 75,000 US and Filipino troops, under the command of General King, surrendered. This was the largest US surrender in history.

The Japanese had been expecting only a third of the number of POWs and were unprepared to accommodate the actual number. In addition, the Samurai code of Bushido determined that surrender was a dishonor, and therefore prisoners were below contempt. The Japanese forced their staggering number of prisoners on a sixty-mile death march to various prison camps in the region. There was little water or food, many prisoners were infected with malaria, and if anyone faltered they were bayoneted or shot.

Three years later, when the United States was able to focus its military energies on the Pacific, there were only about three hundred US soldiers still alive. They had been so mistreated and subjected to such deprivations that they resembled Holocaust victims. If these soldiers were rescued, they would do nothing to contribute to the war effort, but their rescue was deemed a sentimental mission and necessary to make up for the lack of US support earlier in the war. The assignment was handed to an inactive unit of army rangers led by Colonel Mucci. The mission, planned by Captain Robert Prince, was ultimately a success that saved all the POWs, and resulted in only one US casualty.

In 2003 I acted in a movie about the death march and the rescue mission called *The Great Raid*. It was produced by Miramax and directed by John Dahl. Benjamin Bratt played Colonel Mucci, and I played Captain Prince. We filmed for five months near Brisbane, Australia, because terrorist activities had made the Philippines too dangerous to use as a location. I stayed in a garish apartment on the beach in a city called Surfer's Paradise. Whenever I mention this city to any Australians, I get a lot of eye-rolling and disclaimers about how the quality of that cheap casino/tourist city does not reflect the rest of Australia. But it was fine. I stayed inside most of the time that I wasn't shooting. I had hundreds of books to read, and I didn't dare venture into the undiluted, ozone-less sun.

Since Oliver Stone made *Platoon* in 1986, it has become a trend for war movies to put the actors portraying soldiers through an abbreviated boot camp. This boot camp crucible has been all but codified since *Saving Private Ryan,* where the depiction of the D-Day beach landings set a new standard for filmic immersion in a historic war zone. The man who was responsible for training the actors for *Platoon* and *Private Ryan,* Captain Dale Dye, was the military advisor on our film. Our boot camp was almost two weeks long in the wilds of Australia, the longest actor boot camp he had ever conducted. And also the largest. In addition to the principal actors (who are usually the only people in actor boot camp), we had sixty background players who, unlike most background performers, would be with us for the entire shoot. They would portray the rest of the ranger battalion.

As I was the captain in the film, I was regarded as a captain during boot camp. I gave orders and I planned the missions (with Captain Dye's help) against the other camp full of Japanese actors who were going to portray our enemies in the film. We all had real M-1 rifles and BARs and sub-machine guns. Only the bullets were blanks. Dale Dye had us run reconnaissance missions on the surrounding farmhouses in the area. These were real farms. I don't know what they would have thought if they saw young men in army greens with guns, sneaking around their property at night. But they didn't see us; they were just watching TV.

One night at 2 a.m., we all lay in the dirt under bushes and waited to ambush the Japanese actor/soldiers. It was all set up. Captain Dye had told the advisor for the Japanese actors to send them toward our camp at a certain time. We lay in the dirt for two hours. Finally we heard them. The poor Japanese actors thought they were going to be sneaking into our camp, but as they crept by at the appointed time, we got 'em! We fired hundreds of blanks at them before they fled, defeated. We won the war game, even though it had been set up.

Then one of our guys was bitten on the neck by a spider. The spider bite was real. Australia has some of the most poisonous spiders and snakes in the world. He was sent to the hospital.

One night at midnight, Dale Dye took the whole company on a stealth raid on the Japanese camp. We took the wrong route and went by a cattle farm. I was at the front of the long column of actor/soldiers with Captain Dye and Benjamin Bratt. We were halted by a grunting man in the dark. He was about a hundred feet in front of us. It was hard to determine what he was saying, but the grunts had a thick Australian accent. Captain Dye whispered that I should hold the company back, and then approached the thickset, grunting man in the dark. The light from his farmhouse was orange in the haze. Then we saw that the farmer was holding a shotgun. *His* gun was real and, I'm sure, loaded. Then I could make out some words, something along the lines of "Get the fuck out of here."

But Captain Dye was already trotting back to us, head ducked, in case there was any shotgun spray following him.

"Move Captain Prince, move!" whispered Dye. He always called me by my character name. In fact, we were not even allowed to mention that we were making a movie. We *were* in boot camp. I quickly gave the order to turn the company around and retreat. All seventy of us turned and ran. I had never seen Dale Dye scared, except for that time, his gooseneck stretched in panic, running from a potential firefight that he had entered with fake bullets.

When the boot camp was over, we had a little ceremony. I looked each actor/soldier in the eye and congratulated him. It was funny looking eye to eye with these guys. We had accomplished something, we were definitely better at pretending to be soldiers, and the movie would benefit from our training, but for whom were we pretending at this ceremony? We were still just actors, not trained killers. There was one guy, I'll call him Chucky, who had asymmetrical eyes—we all do, just take a photo of one half of your face, and then duplicate it, and flip it, and put it together, and you'll see a very different person. But Chucky's asymmetry was pronounced. One eye was at least an inch below the other. I really noticed this when staring into them at the ceremony.

Chucky was just an extra, but he was a hard worker. He was a local. He didn't say much, but during the boot camp and the shooting he proved himself to be someone that could be depended on to fill in for whatever was needed. He rode a motorcycle, and one evening after shooting, about two months into the shoot, he crashed and killed himself. We were shooting out in some cane fields, and there were many kangaroos in the area. Apparently one jumped out in front of Chucky, and Chucky, being a skilled motorcyclist, swerved around it. Right into an oncoming car.

I had already left the set by the time Chucky had his accident, but some of the other actors were still there. The car was on the side of the road; Chucky's motorcycle was on its side, next to his body, and his head, still in the helmet, was on the other side of the road.

We had a memorial for Chucky. Before the funeral, Captain Dye met with the company—he still considered us a company—and called us all by our character names. He told us that he wanted us to wear our military costumes to the funeral. Captain Dye was used to ritual, and he knew how to put large numbers of young men through tough group experiences, to make them cohere as a unit. Our group was bonded by the mission of the film, so wearing the uniforms wasn't as crazy an idea as it sounds. But nobody did it. Everyone wore his real-world clothes.

At the funeral, Chucky's friends and family said nice things about him. They said the movie had been very important to him. He had been very into athletics and extreme sports such as skydiving and rock climbing, but the movie had opened up the idea of more possibilities. He had wanted to go to Hollywood.

In the final film, I don't think you can even see Chucky. He is just another guy in green in the background. It is hard to make out individuals other than the main actors. In the film we go on the raid, massacre a bunch of evil Japanese guys, and save the POWs. The film took about a year and a half to edit, for no good reason that I could discern. Finally, in 2005, there was a big premiere in Washington, D.C. Harvey Weinstein, the original president of Miramax, was a friend of Hillary Clinton. She and John McCain both came to the premier and sat together. Weinstein introduced them as the future presidential candidates. I spoke to Hillary—she and Bill are big film aficionados, always renting DVDs out in Connecticut. McCain didn't say much to me; he looked catatonic.

When it was released in theaters the next week, the movie was a bomb. It was the last Miramax release before Disney kicked the Weinstein brothers out of their own company. So there was no money put into the advertising. It's not a bad movie. Looks nice, at least. And I read a lot of books in Australia. It's not the worst movie I ever did, but I wish I could forget most of it.

We should remain unorganized, but we may create
production companies in order to serve greater projects.

—∾∾∿∿∾∾—

Power of the Image

POWER OF THE IMAGE. Power of information. Power of flow. The power of the image can create flow; it can attract and bring attention to whatever it wants. This is why celebrities are a big part of presidential elections. This is why celebrities get paid millions of dollars for their books. This is why companies want celebrities to endorse hair products.

Camera people, sound people, production designers: Get them to make your work look good. Sometimes the difference between a movie star and a soap opera actor is the lighting.

Of course there is the script, and the way it's edited, and the subject matter. But if you shot *The Godfather,* shot for shot, on a soap opera soundstage, with soap actors, don't you think it would seem silly?

Or, let's say you shoot it on all the original sets they used with all the same actors they used, even Brando, but they lit it like a soap opera—it would change everything. The acting would suddenly look bad.

When I direct, I am often more interested in the technical sides of things. It's hard for me to allow much time for lighting because I often find the payoff to be incommensurate with the time spent. But I like to think about framing and camera movement as much as I do the acting. The camera movement combined with the editing is the grammar of film.

The grammar of film is more complex than the grammar of text.

Within each shot are innumerable variables: Who has been cast, how those actors play their parts—do they use accents? Do they transform themselves physically? How are those actors presented in individual shots—close-ups? Tracking shots? Zooms? How are those shots edited together—jump cuts? Minimal cuts? Constant cutting? Tracking shots leading to static shots? Who and what are the scenes focused on? What is made primary? Are there filters used? Is there background music? Special effects? On and on.

Now, of course, there are some conventions. We are used to watching films on the big screen and television shows in the comfort of our homes. And of course movies all end up on the smaller screens as well.

There are conventions of duration, usually ninety to a hundred and twenty minutes for a film and thirty to sixty minutes for a television program.

There are actor types that are often used. This is a tricky thing to define, but there are certainly trends. Asian, Latino, Black, Middle Eastern, and Jewish actors generally get the shaft as far as the types of roles being offered. Oh yeah, and women too.

There are genre conventions. Action movies. Gangster movies. Cop shows. Vampires. Teen shows. Reality shows about the trashy little pockets of our country, trashy in an interesting way. These shows have some of the more original characters around.

There are conventions about material that is accepted: Violence is more acceptable than sex. Straight sex is much more acceptable than gay sex. In comedy you can get away with subject matter like mastur- bation, rape, and death much easier than in dramas where the mate- rial is used for its disturbing aspects.

Because film and acting are so technical, they can be learned like a science. Of course, on top of the technical aspects, or nested within them, are the artistic considerations. I've been on sets where I look around and see all these adults focused on putting something together, all these professionals, good at what they do, and what they're making is the most puerile crap ever.

It makes you wonder why everyone does it. If so many people feel like they're stuck doing material they hate, why do they all do it? And what is the way out? It seems like one way is to work with the great directors. Every actor says he wants to work with Scorsese, and I'm sure it's the same for the below-the-line positions as well. But why are we all sitting around waiting for Scorsese? Why not be your own Scorsese? And even if you can't make movies like him, the power of creation is enough. If you work on your own projects, the projects you believe in, then you have the power of making a Scorsese film.

I hate the guys who are held up like gods because they make big movies. This is the whole reason for this testimony. To show that they are not born into those positions. We are all capable of making something. You can be the director and actor of your own life.

But you usually need to collaborate. That's the catch. It's hard to create a great life without other actors, without people helping with the visual aspects, and the audio aspects, without a good soundtrack. It can be done—look at *127 Hours*—but still, being alone for so long? That's no kind of life.

In life we all want to get along; in art we want to be defiant. In design we want pleasing things; in art we want pieces that become tools to pry underneath the surface, to rip through the façade.

You want the crew to be amicable, especially if you're making something disturbing. Every kind of subject should be fun to make; the participants should enjoy doing it. Bergman acknowledged that he made films about tough subjects, but it was not masochistic because he was transforming the material into art, the painful parts were purged by the art.

I used to spend tons of energy and time getting emotionally prepared on set, but now I can turn it on much faster. If you believe in the scene you don't need to emotionally prepare much: The situation will present itself to you as reality, and you will react. It just requires the imagination to take you there.

Think about how few crying scenes there are in any given film. Think about how many scenes there are with your clothes off. We often spend so much time preparing for these kinds of scenes (emotional self-torture, time in the gym) for so little payoff.

Be an acting animal. Breathe acting so that you don't have to think about it much. Let the material shape you, let the imaginary circumstances shape you. Let the character be born. Don't put too much of your own spin on it, let it arise naturally from everything around you.

And if you're the lead of a film—or a supporting character—know how to ride the production so it does half of the work for you. Meaning, you don't need to show some things through the character if the set, or lighting, or special effects are doing much of the work for you.

We should have no opinions on outside issues, hence the
public life remains public and the private life is private.

From the Foreword to
the Second Edition

FRIDAY, 1 A.M.

During this time I listened to a lot of Motown. There was a song in
the Ryan Gosling/Michelle Williams movie *Blue Valentine* that was
supposed to be *their song*. It was this obscure Motown song by someone called Penny and the Cents, or something like that. They used
the song in the film because no one else used it as *their song* because
it was so obscure. But after it was put it in the film, it became known.

What does fame get one?

The picture of me sleeping with my mouth open next to a bunch of
attentive students says a thousand words. But it says the wrong words,
or it says the words that TMZ wants it to say. It doesn't say: *This*

photo was taken at 10 p.m. during an optional guest lecture by William Kentridge, hosted by the graduate art school. James wasn't even in the Columbia art department but he went to their visiting artist lectures anyway, even though he was in four other graduate programs at the time and working on the film Howl *and hosting* Saturday Night Live, *and a bunch of other things. Like many students do, he fell asleep in class.*

But beside fame, what does putting on a persona get one?

We all have masks. Often, I like to write about young people, because it's a time when they are still sculpting their masks.

When we get older, after years of use, the masks meld with our faces. Yes, there are little tweaks here and there, but the mask is reinforced by response. We wear the mask and people respond to the mask and the mask becomes us, the outside response from others nails it down tight.

James used to try to buy all the new albums. He had over 500,000 songs on iTunes. It was a bit of an addiction. Just click "$9.99 Buy," and then "you might also like these Genius Recommendations." But the drive crashed and he has never recovered his half a million dollars worth of music.

I like when the press presents me as dumb. It sure takes the pressure off.

Natalie Portman went to Harvard. She's even mentioned in *The Social Network*. She is tied to Harvard. It gives her a lot of intellectual capital in the press. But in person, she doesn't act like an intellectual.

But she is smart; she spends more time listening than talking.

This is the testimony of someone who wears masks for a living. Whenever he wears a mask in front of the camera and thousands of people see it, it remains with him a little bit.

Is there a veridic self underneath?

Or are the surfaces what rule?

Some people, mostly creative people, don't like scholars because they look at art from the outside but know nothing about the actual making of art.

Facebook.

I think it's nice to have a mix of everything. Some critical writing is better than fiction. Most critical writing is better than fiction.

Twitter.

Google.

Instagram.

James would listen to Motown because it meant he didn't need to keep up on the next big thing. There was an established body of work that he could explore without worrying about keeping up with its expansion.

After he lost his iTunes music, James just plugged "You and Me" by Penny and the Quarters—the *Quarters* not the *Cents*—into Pandora and got a bunch of other obscure Motown songs.

Perez Hilton.

B____ slowly kisses her way along my stomach. I'm used to it. Sometimes twice a day. Sometimes four in a day.

The Atlantic Wire.

On the show *Entourage,* the main character played by Adrian Grenier does things to the extreme. I want to think that it's over the top, but actually, it might be less extreme than what actually happens in Hollywood.

Gawker.

Once, when someone asked Elvis about the Vietnam War, he said, "I'm just an entertainer."

Kenneth Anger.

I hate the idea of not being able to talk about something if I want to.

Lindsay Lohan.

There is nothing tinnier than obvious fake laughter, when one person in the crowd is laughing louder than the rest, to be heard above the rest, as if she is saying, "I'm in on the jokes, and I appreciate James. *I'm his ultimate fan!*"

Paris Hilton.

But sometimes I think that the politicians have no more right to be politicians than I do. Ronald Reagan? Arnold Schwarzenegger? You just need the right advisors.

Anne Hathaway.

Sarah Palin. Okay, she was dumb, we get it. But we're all actors now, aren't we? Some actors are smarter than others.

Christian Bale.

I met B_____ in Morningside Heights, near Columbia. She was work- ing the desk in the student exhibition hall, reading Kafka. She had a cool demeanor, but it was more like she couldn't get her words out so easily, so she covered everything with an icy smile.

Some people smell when you bend them over.

Ryan Phillippe.

During breaks, M_____ and I would meet sometimes in the _____ building. She made it easy. Third floor, one of the empty rooms. I'd hold the door shut because there was no lock.

I'd spend at least one of my twice-weekly nights up at Columbia with B_____. She lived on Amsterdam, in some old church property that Lucien Carr lived in, Ginsberg's buddy when he was at Columbia, the one that killed their other buddy. Young Kerouac helped him hide the murder weapon and then they went to see a film.

At 1 a.m. I'd finish writing and walk from Dodge Hall, where Berryman, Trilling, and Van Doren all had been—I think—across the boulevard and up the hill to her old building and to her room with the mattress on the floor and the art theory books stacked around.

The boys—Kerouac, Ginsberg, Burroughs, Carr—used to have arguments about Thomas Wolfe in these parts. Night of the Wolfians, they called it.

I had no wolf pack. I was a lone wolf.

Michael Fassbender.

Ryan Gosling.

Alexander Skarsgård.

Jonah Hill.

Balthazar Getty.

Michelle Williams.

Katie Holmes.

Jack Nicholson.

Adam Sandler.

Columbia's Butler Library, the place where they filmed the beginning of *Ghostbusters*. The Slimer part. This girl came up to me as I was writing this and just started talking. She was eighteen I guess, a freshman and an art history student. She just wanted to talk to me, and so she did. And she was tired of trying to study, and it was 2:30 in the morning, and she didn't think that either of us should be studying anymore. And I asked her what she suggested that we do, and she said that we should just sit there and talk, talk, talk, and it didn't matter what we said, but that we should just talk *at* each other and then we would get to know each other, and we would share our souls with each other.

I looked at her and I thought she was crazy, but she was also very cute, and I wouldn't mind getting to know her soul for a minute. Her talking-at-each-other plan actually had some structure. It was more like an improv game.

"So how do we do it?" I said. "I want to get to know your soul."

"Easy, it's easy," she said. "You say something, and then I say something, and then you, and then I, and we just keep going and going, and we'll get closer and closer to each other, okay?"

"Uh, okay, so, uh, I'll go," I said. "I'm Japanese," I said, even though I am not Japanese. But she didn't flinch. "I have eaten my panties," she said.

"I have eaten dog shit," I said.

"I have eaten dog," she said.

"I killed a dog."

"I dated a sociopath, and he killed a person."

"It was my dad," I said.

"The person was a baby," she said.

"My dad was a baby," I said.

"You are a baby," she said.

"I'm retarded," I said.

"You know nothing,"

"I know something."

"And so do I, you're going to die," she said.

"I hope so," I said.

"When I shit, it is roses," she said.

"Your asshole is a rose garden," I said.

"Your dickhole is a guppy."

"Big vaginas have teeth," I said.

"I am a shark," she said.

"I am death," I said.

"Death the dork," she said.

"Time."

"Air."

"Blood."

"Wind."

"Gas."

"Explosion."

"Love."

Our public relations policy is based on attraction rather than promotion; we need always maintain personal anonymity at the level of press, radio, films, videos, video games, social networking, and otherwise.

Luciernaga

I LEAVE THE MEETING EARLY and make my way over to S_____'s, my realtor's house. She wants to give me a present for the loft, even though she found it for us a year ago.

S_____ is pretty insane. She wants to fuck. But that means I have to put up with superlong text messages about her strange adventures in Africa. I never take the bait, but she likes to hint that she is involved in international espionage and that she uses sex to lure her subjects. I'm not kidding.

I still have a bunch of her text messages on my phone:

Hey I won't bug u but if u were serious, text me if u want to get together sometime when u're back in town. I have an insatiable brain and u do too I know it ;)

... Brilliant; then I will too. Happy Christmas ;-)
(I guess these are the older ones).

Hope to get to know you ;-) Just to let you know, I'm going to South Africa for 3 weeks at the end of the month but not until after the 20th.

Btw, been meaning to tell you, I like your stories. Have lots of ideas about them.

You were in my dream yest + I considered mentioning it to u but thought better of it ;-). See u soon.

Why not tell me???

Well apparently, you already think I'm weird, so nothing to lose there, I suppose...

I had a dream about you.

You were back in Palo Alto and you were talking w/one of my greatest heroes (in real life) who runs a shelter for homeless vets w/addiction probs. Anyway, after u were done talking alone w/him, he told me he thought u were a special guy. I said I didn't know how I could ever trust u, but he said it'd be ok.

I wrote: My dream was a little different.

I was going to say, then it got erotic but we'll leave that up to the imagination for the moment. Unless of course you feel like sharing?

You me and the vet guy got down, then I kicked him out. We were at the Franco complex in the LES. Was amazing.

Aww I think you're underestimating the prowess of the vet guy. Wartime craving, deprivation + all that. Did u really have a dream about me or were u just saying?

Lots of dreams.

Too bad I'm not that kind of girl, then, hmm. You intrigue me luciernaga (sic; autocorrect for "Mr. Franco"?), but not for the reasons you think.

: (

…Oh dear, it's about the biggest compliment I could give, silly. Of course you're attractive to me physically, but I'm more of a heart and mind kind of girl. U seem to embody both. I'm not capable of sex for the sake of it. Anyway, you could get that anywhere. Not that you've offered! Ha, I overthink everything. I would really like to get to know you. We would hit it off.

…Yes! I hope you like a couple of the places we saw today and yest. Closer to NYU and nice space. Anyway, looking frwd to seeing you.

I was reading one of your stories last night + I came across the part where a character u call Roberto meets 2 girls, gets really high w/them, then finds out one is Vietnamese and adopted and just after we are reminded how high he is, he says, 'I love adoption.' I laughed loudly, for like 10 mins. No need to write back just thought it might make u chuckle.

I think I had a typo earlier, that she was 'adopted' but you get the idea. Anyway just felt like sharing xo.

Hey if you're in town on Thurs and have 10 minutes, I'll give you a killer birthday present. First I'll read you my favorite Henry Miller excerpt and follow it w/one big passionate kiss. I could meet you wherever's convenient. One time offer. Oh and I'm a really good kisser for birthdays...

I guess these texts go a little past the Oscar period, but we'll just shove them in to give a sense of things.

Her place is cozy. Faded white paint on the outside, crinkling, and inside, wood floors, Indian rugs, and a fireplace. I open her present. It's a huge framed picture of a white bunny in the snow.

A housewarming gift.

I just wrote a poem that worked out in my head that I'm too vulnerable to hang w/you right now. Much as I'd love to give u your b-day special-i just can't be one of 'them'. If u knew me at all it'd be diff't and I'd love to get to know you but any other agenda will just wreck me right now. The past 6 weeks of travel, my assignment and what I saw...so many women in Thailand prostituting themselves b/c their fisherman husbands were killed in the tsunami and they have 5 mouths to feed after all this time. Nothing sacred left. I can't go there. What i need is to talk and that was not my proposition. So I don't see why you would come.

Unless you actually care to get to know me, I've got nothing for you. You don't know my other job, but suffice it to say, I'm not all I seem. You're a busy guy and I don't want to waste your time. I can't give you what you want; you can't give me what I need.

What do you say to a rain check? I hope you have a memorable birthday, my dear. Now you're Jesus's age when he died. Could be something special in that! Sorry to be a drag, but truth is truth. So there it is. Hope you understand. XO

G-string. I was supposed to be here last night, but I was at B_____'s.

I haven't yet done anything with S_____, meaning this is the first time (and the only time). I guess that's why I'm doing the early morning thing. Get in and out, don't have to spend too much time with the overromanticized version of her life.

Lovely. Trevi fountain's pretty at night. I'm going to Darfur for a story. I know I may not make it back. Just in case, I wish u all the best, love light peace

I just go for it.

She squirms like crazy. Makes it really fucking hard to lick properly.

Pretty early for all this.

She sits up and is ready to do it for me, but I'm not in the mood anymore. Sometimes it's difficult the first time with a new person.

She pulls a decorative pillow tight to cover her waist.

She wants to be a journalist. She wants to write.

She has written stories about her uncle, a drunk who raised her. A Massachusetts upbringing.

I'm sorry if I offended you.
Please don't be offended. It has little to do w/u. You are who you are (not that I really know who that is). I guess I wanted to be 'that girl' but when it comes down to it, I'm not. I wish u lots of birthday blessings and hope there's no hard feelings. XO

It's fine but I hope you heard what I said. I'm really serious. Also, you could get interrogated just for corresponding w/me, did u know that? Esp since I just got back. And not by the cops, man. Nothing illegal but I'm into some corporate political shit. You should know that w/your career and all. You most likely won't be bothered b/c I'm pretty well protected but it's only fair to tell u. Anyway, I SUPPOSE I'll acquiesce to tmrw at 8:45ish since u twisted my arm. Let's just keep in touch.

Soon after this, S_____ learned that her uncle was dying of cancer.

So, here's an honest question for you. No judgment-just asking. Why do you bother w/me, answering my texts, sometimes sending them, etc? Is it just that you find me attractive and want to keep the option open for a potential sex buddy in NYC? You must have plenty of others. You hardly know me at all, so that's it right?

No, I tried to tell you I'm not just what you think I am. I may be cool and nice and cute or whatever, but I'm fierce and intelligent and demanding, too. I can be tough to deal with. You may not want all that bullshit.

But I'm really fun and don't get attracted to people until I know them. So that's where I was coming from.

Btw I'm putting caramel flavored calcium supplements on the giant cookie…

My theory is that most women bore you other than for sex, that you keep pretty closed and trust only a few people, and that as brilliant as you are, to some extent you hide in your literature. Maybe I'm way off but I have put thought into you and your ways and what it must be like to be you.

You're so bright and talented. What are you looking for in a woman? Don't you want a challenge or at least an equal? Someone w/some guts and experience, creativity and brains? Maybe you already have it. Anyway, I'm a fireball. If you're ever feeling adventurous, you know where to look. I'm not going to keep bugging you.

Really? That surprises me. Why else would you want…well anyway, I'm trying to get to know you obviously, w/minimal resources. I guess you want and need low maintenance right now. That makes sense. There must be plenty around. I'm not high maintenance b/c I do my own thing including lots of travel and whatever. I just want real. Are real and serious the same thing? Plus don't you want a lover who's smart and interesting to talk to?

At the very least, wouldn't the sex be way better? Ok, I feel like I'm way out in left field, taking your time, and not your type of gal. It's time for me to leave you alone. I'm going to delete your number from my phone so I don't be stupid and hit you up at a weak moment. You know how to find me. XXOO-S

Hey sorry about being all over the place last night. Guess w/my uncle close to dying I'm having a hard time and I'm already at the bus to head to visit him. I really will leave u be. Just was reaching out for support and connection last night in my own f'd up way. Hope u don't hold it against me. Good luck w/your career. I'm rooting for u always.

Thanks. I'm all a mess b/c he raised me and then didn't talk to me for years and now there's all this unfinished business which he won't talk about. Anyway, thx for understanding. I'm a cool person just going through a thing. Sorry you are there for it. He's an alc and smoker so kind of did it to himself which is why I don't really drink. Anyway it's morning so now I see more clearly and I'm sorry for in some way dragging u into my emotional unrest. I'd hate to never talk to you again but I understand if it's time to cut it off. Obv I didn't delete your # yet :)

Privacy and reality are the foundations of
all our traditions, ever reminding us to
place principles before personalities.

The Spider-Man Journals

THE ACTOR'S JOURNALS, if they can be called that—actually a binder of sketchbook pages full of text (written backward) and attempts at portraiture in the style of the Old Masters, obliterated by angry, childlike scratches—have come to be called *The Spider-Man Journals,* because of the obfuscated subject that peeps through the ragged effacement. Close study will reveal that the effaced depictions are limited to the eponymous hero of the *Spider-Man* films, and possibly something of The Actor's own involvement with said subject.

They were found in May 2007 underneath the couch of a Great Western star trailer by an actress, who we will call Cent. She was occupying the trailer at the time for her services on *Day's End,* a film about teenage vampires. One might ask how an unknown actress like Cent, on a relatively low-budget production like *Day's End,* might come to occupy a trailer of the size usually relegated to someone of

The Actor's stature when acting in a movie the size of *Spider-Man 3* (the most expensive movie ever made), and the answer, to be frank, is that Cent, although all of seventeen, was screwing the thirty-eight-year-old producer, Marc Steely.

One spring day on the Sony lot, Cent was doing green-screen shots on Stage 19. After all the post-production work, these green-screen shots would eventually portray Cent's character, Brie, in a pine tree high above a forest with her character's new paramour Zed (played by Zack Needly), who was a vampire and, as a result, a cool outsider at the local high school. Between the long lighting setups for these shots, Cent would go back to her large trailer and watch episodes of *Lost* on DVD, talk on the phone, or read. She was reading *The Brothers Karamazov*, and she was proud of the fact; she fancied herself a smart, hip girl. During one particularly long lighting setup—they usually take two hours—she was lying on the carpeted trailer floor, casually chatting with her mother. Her mother lived in Austin, and being very religious, had not been informed by Cent of her budding affair with the producer twenty-one years her senior, Marc Steely. Cent looked over and saw a large sketchbook lodged underneath the low couch. Her mother droned on about Cent's younger brother, Butch, who was once again in trouble with the local authorities—he'd been caught performing some sort of Satanic ritual at midnight at Austin High, involving the immolation of two rabbits. Cent retrieved the sketchbook from under the couch. On the phone she heard pieces of her brother's story. The cops had been abusive and called him a faggot. He had convinced Cent's mother to fight the burglary, animal cruelty, and public endangerment charges on account of police brutality. But Cent was too busy examining the sketchbook to respond. Then in the middle of her mother's monologue, Cent said, "It's like Leonardo."

"What is?"

"Nothing, Mom. I'm going to have to call you back, they're calling me to set."

Cent hung up and continued perusing the sketchbook. She handled it gently, as it was loosely connected in places. At first it was difficult to decipher anything in the scribbled mess: She could see that there were drawings beneath the scribbles, and there was mirror writing in the manner of Da Vinci's sketchbooks, albeit in much cruder letters than the master's elegant reversed Florentine script. After poring through the twenty-six pages of violent scribbles, Cent took the sketchbook into the trailer's small bathroom (small, but larger than the one she would have had had she not been involved with the thirty-eight-year old, balding Marc Steely) and held the first page up to the vanity. Even when the script was oriented to read left to right, it was difficult to make sense of. The individual letters were barbed and broken, and the lines were irregularly slanted and often obscured by the aggressive scribbles that shot across the page in great jagged arcs that spun into intense vortices. The easiest line to make out was on the first page. It was repeated three times, in three different sizes, in hot blue ink. It was the old Greek imperative, exploited by Freud, and known to Cent through the howling Doors anthem "The End," which she had heard while watching *Apocalypse Now* repeatedly with her dad as a child, before he skipped town for good.

Kill the Father, it said.

Beneath the violent refrain were less discernable lines, as well as the remnants of a portrait, almost totally obscured by the scribbling. All she could make out was the chin, the left nostril, and the outside corner of the left eye.

Later that day, Cent told Marc Steely about the sketchbook. Being the ever-paranoid older lover, Marc was immediately suspicious of the sketchbook. He asked to see it, and on the first page he saw the triply stated imperative written in reverse, *Kill the Father*.

That couldn't be good in any context, but especially not with the accompaniment of psychotic scrawls. And written in reverse! That was the way that the devil wrote. When Marc asked for the pages, Cent refused.

Marc Steely went to the head teamster, Joe Donuts, and found out that the star trailer Cent occupied had indeed been used on the *Spider-Man 3* production and had belonged to The Actor. The journals were undoubtedly the work of The Actor, a not particularly talented but fairly attractive actor in his late twenties. He wasn't sure why Cent's discovery upset him so much, but it undoubtedly did.

It was hard being a balding producer with a hot young girlfriend. Usually Cent stayed at Marc's house in Beverly Hills, but that night Cent told him that she wanted to stay at her own apartment. Another disturbing turn of events.

The following morning Marc knocked on her Great Western trailer door at 8 a.m.

"Come in," Cent said.

She said it without knowing it was Marc. She could have said it to anyone. If it had been her young costar Zack Needly or even The Actor, she would have said the same thing. Very disturbing.

When Marc entered, she was sitting on the carpeted floor, smoking, looking at the journals. He couldn't be sure, but it looked like she wiped a tear from her eye. She didn't look up.

"You just say 'Come in,' without knowing who it is?"

Cent looked up at him.

"Oh, good morning." She definitely had been crying.

"What's wrong? Are you crying?"

She looked back at the violent drawings.

"No. I just…my brother is in trouble with the police again, and my mom is being so crazy."

"*That's* why you're crying?"

"I'm *not* crying. I'm just pissed at the whole situation. That Butch doesn't have a dad, because our dad ran off when he was like two, and he's just so fucked up."

"I thought you didn't care about your family."

"Why would you say that?" She looked up at him again.

"I don't know. That's what I thought. So, you're not crying over those sketches?"

"Why would I be crying over the sketches?"

"I don't know, just a question." He was standing against the wall by the door. For some reason he didn't feel like he could get close to her. "You know they belong to The Actor."

She didn't say anything. She just took a long drag from her cigarette.

"I thought you were going to stop smoking."

"Oh, God. Are *you* going to be my dad now?"

"Did you hear what I said? Those drawings belong to The Actor."

Cent turned over one of the pages, very gently.

"I already knew," she said, without looking up. It looked like she was crying again.

"Do you know him?" said Marc.

"Who? The Actor? No."

"Are you, like, in love with him?"

She looked up at him.

"What? Jesus. No! What is your problem this morning? I'm sorry I didn't stay over last night. Do I have to like, be with you every second for you not to be a total asshole?"

"No. I'm just wondering why you're crying about those stupid pictures."

"I'm *not* crying! God. And they're not stupid. Will you just get out of here, please? I can't deal with you being like this right now, I have to get ready for work. You *do* want me to be good in this movie, don't you?"

Marc left and got himself a cup of coffee with two packets of Splenda from the craft service truck. He definitely didn't like this business with The Actor's sketches.

He finished his coffee, had another, and then ate half a breakfast burrito with turkey bacon, when his stomach started to hurt. He tossed the other half of the burrito and decided to contact The Actor directly. He was a producer; that's what producers did, they contacted actors. It would be no big deal. He would just tell The Actor to come pick up his sketches, and he would be done with them. He could have his regular loving, nonsmoking Cent back.

Marc called Endeavor and was connected to The Actor's tough-talking female agent. She said that The Actor was currently not working. When Marc said that he had something that belonged to The Actor, the agent told him that he should keep it. When Marc asked if it was possible to get a contact number, the agent said it was impossible and hung up.

Marc had the impulse to contact the head of the agency and have the agent fired, but he didn't call. He wasn't sure if he had that kind of power, but he didn't try. Instead, he called a club promoter friend, Sasha Apple. Sasha was pushing forty-one, but she knew all the young actors in LA. She was at the center of every hip gathering and had slept with half the guys in town under twenty-five.

At 9:30, Marc got her voice mail. He called several more times that morning, but couldn't reach her. He wandered around the lot, thinking of people to call. He couldn't focus. It was strange how worked up he was getting, but he couldn't help it. He stayed away from the set of *Day's End,* even though he was one of the producers. He knew that seeing Cent would only upset him, and he didn't want to do anything that might ruin her performance. She was doing very well in the movie, and there was the potential for her career to really take off. The prospect made Marc proud but also paranoid. More paranoid than proud. He thought of all those young actors that she would be kissing in all those future movies. Not good.

He contemplated sneaking into Cent's trailer and stealing the sketchbooks, but there were a bunch of PAs around and he would be seen.

By noon there was still no call from Sasha Apple, so he went to his office in the Thalberg Building and googled The Actor. He found a bunch of fan sites and some news items about The Actor's drug addiction, but those were all from three years ago. The most recent items were about the death of The Actor's father. They said he was shot in his Palo Alto home last Christmas. Some of the less reputable outlets linked The Actor to the murder. One of them said that The Actor was currently at an undisclosed institution.

After learning this information, Marc decided it was his *duty* to go into Cent's trailer and confiscate the sketchbook. If The Actor's father had been murdered, it was probably not a good thing for Cent to be holding onto a sketchbook that said *Kill the Father* three times.

Marc made sure that Cent was shooting on-set, waited for the PAs to clear, and then went into her trailer. If anyone caught him, he would just say he was doing producer things.

The sketchbook was gone. Marc searched the whole trailer, but it was obvious that Cent had taken it.

Marc stormed out of the trailer and slammed the door, no longer concerned about who saw him. He paced around. He was very upset. She was choosing the sketchbook over him. Marc bummed a cigarette from one of the grips, even though he didn't smoke. The cigarette made his head light and his throat hurt. It was his third cigarette ever.

Finally, at 1:30, Sasha Apple called back. Her voice was always gravelly, but it was extra gravelly that afternoon. She talked quickly.

"Marc? Sorry, I had a long night last night. We just opened a new place on La Cienega. You and that new little cutie should come by. Oh, wait, you're keeping this one a secret aren't you?"

"Sasha, shut up for a second. Do you know The Actor?"

There was a pause. Then she said, "Yeah. Everyone knows The Actor. He used to go out a lot."

"He used to?"

Another pause, then, "He doesn't anymore. I don't know where he is."

"Is there like some big secret I don't know about? Why is everyone being so fucking crazy about this guy? His fucking agent hung up on me!"

Sasha was silent again. This was the most quiet she had ever been. Usually one had to force words through her endless barrage of talk.

"Sasha? What the fuck? What is going on with this Actor guy?"

"I don't know. Maybe you should ask someone else."

"Tell me!" A few grips walking by looked over. Marc lowered his voice. "Fucking tell me now, Sasha."

"I don't know," she said. "I think his dad was murdered or something. Then he just disappeared. I haven't seen him in months. I swear to God, that's all I know."

"Do you have his number?"

"Marc, I…"

"Give me his fucking number, or I swear to God, Sasha, I am going to have your new place shut down for serving minors and cocaine use and for being a fucking whorehouse! I swear to fucking Christ!"

"Jesus, Marc. What is your problem? I've never heard you like this, except when you were on coke. I don't have his number, all I have is an email."

"Give it to me!"

Marc was so intent on getting The Actor's contact info that he found himself suddenly unsure about what to do with it once he got it. He could write to The Actor and tell him to come and pick up his sketchpad, but in light of his father's recent murder, this track seemed unwise. He looked at the ripped piece of the day's shooting schedule where he had written the email address:

moc.theactor@rotcaeht.com

A palindrome. What did it mean? "Mock The Actor"? "Rot California 80"? "Rot cat"?

Instead of writing to The Actor, Marc called his friend Ty. Ty was an editing teacher at a third-rate film school in the Valley called Encino Film School. It was right next to a drug rehabilitation center called the Warm Heart Treatment Center, which specialized in a ninety-day detox program. Because the two facilities were separated by a chain-link fence, the film students and drug addicts often mingled during smoke breaks, and more than one addict had pursued a relationship with a film student after his treatment ended. Marc Steely knew Ty from college and often went to him with computer questions.

"Ty, how are you?" Ty was never good. He hated his students.

"As fine as can be, over in hell."

"What happened? Another film student/addict romance?"

"What? No, we have plenty of those. No, one of the kids had the great idea to film one of the addicts shooting up into his dick."

"Oh, fuck."

"It was just water in the syringe, just to make it look like heroin, but his dick got infected and had to get cut off. Now, the treatment center is suing the school."

"That's fucked, man, I'm sorry."

"Yeah, whatever. Stupid fucking kids. And yesterday, I had to hear from about five of them that I look like Norman Bates. These morons haven't seen a movie made before 1999, and then spring semester, Richard always shows them *Psycho,* so I have to hear it every year, like they've made some great fucking discovery. Okay, I look like Anthony Perkins, big whoop, blame my fucking dad."

"Sorry, man," said Marc. Ty was always complaining, and it was best to cut to the chase with him or he'd go on forever. "Listen, I have a job for you. I want you to hack into someone's email."

"Oh shit, illegal shit from the big producer. How about giving me a real job, like editing a studio movie?"

"I'm working on it, but do this thing for me, okay?" Marc told him the situation.

"Whoa, The Actor?" Ty said "That fucking guy went through the treatment center over here. Weird dude. Quiet. I'd always see him across the fence, standing alone in the courtyard like he was a junkie Jimmy Dean. I never heard him say anything, but I am almost positive he fucked a couple of the students. It was a pretty big deal when he was there. Everyone tried to keep it quiet, but all the students knew..."

"Okay, okay, what I'm interested in is any emails that are to or from his father, about his father, or the death of his father. Will you find me anything on that?"

The rest of the day passed without Marc hearing anything from Ty. That night, after work finished, Marc went to Cent's trailer where she was changing out of her teenager character clothes into her teenager real clothes. Usually Marc wouldn't be anywhere near her trailer if she were changing, but things were getting desperate. And then, before he could say anything, she told Marc that she was not feeling up to staying at his place again.

"Oh, what the fuck?" he said.

"What? What is your problem, Marc? I'm not your wife! Or your daughter! I just want to stay at home tonight, okay?"

"To what? Cuddle up with those sketches?"

"Are you serious? What is it with you guys? You can't get over the fact that I like The Actor's sketches?"

"They're dangerous, Cent! They're dangerous! You don't know what you're dealing with! And wait, what do you mean, 'you *guys*'? Did you show them to someone else?"

"I showed them to Zack, and he got all weird about them too. He said they were terrible, but it was like he was jealous or something."

"You showed them to Zack? Fucking great!"

"What?"

"Why are you showing that idiot anything? He's an idiot!"

"Oh, God, I don't want to get into another thing about Zack."

"What do you mean, 'another thing about Zack'?"

"Nothing, this is stupid. You just get all uptight when I talk about Zack, just like you're doing with these drawings. I don't know what your problem is. It's like you think I'm cheating on you or something, and I'm not. This is stupid. I'm going home."

"Cent, you don't know what these drawings are."

But Cent was already leaving.

Something came over Marc. He grabbed the sketchbook from her hands and started ripping the pages. She screamed and tried to take it back. The sketches fell on the ground and Marc started stomping on them like they were roaches.

"Stop it! Stop it, Marc!"

Finally, she slapped him. He slapped her back, and the struggled ended. Cent was crying as she picked up the torn sketches and got into her car.

That night Marc called Cent five times, but she didn't answer. He rented one of The Actor's films. It was a weird movie, almost a comedy, about heroin. The Actor wasn't bad, but he wasn't good. Just a handsome sensitive guy without any backbone.

At 1 a.m., Ty sent him an email:

I did it. His password turned out to be "mock-me." I figured he must be really insecure, so... Anyway, there was not much stuff on his father, but the following two letters were written last December. They were the last two in his box. After January it seems like he didn't write anything. I don't know if he's dead or what? Here you go, I hope it helps,

Ty

12/31/xx—11:30 p.m.

Dad,

I am sorry for how my trip ended. I did not enjoy leaving like that, I was angry and I didn't want to say anything that I would later regret.

I am sorry if I embarrassed you at the dinner. Of course it was not my intention to do so. I agree that the dinner was awkward, and I apologize for my contribution to that awkwardness. But I am still unsure about what I did. You said I acted like a dope. I suppose that means that I was not engaging or talkative. If that is so, I agree; I was not talkative, because I was uncomfortable. I did not know those people, and I was immediately introduced to the director and producer of the play (I think they were the director and the producer, I still don't know), which made me think that there had been some planning for the get-together of which I had not been made aware. Because they were show business people, it made me think that I was expected to talk about show business.

I like to go to Palo Alto because I can relax. I did not feel relaxed at that dinner. If you want to spend one of the few nights I have with the family out with your boss, that is fine, but please don't expect me to be the life of the party. I am not that kind of person, and I usually don't like to discuss my work, especially with a whole table of strangers.

And if it has to do with my level of enthusiasm rather than the amount that I spoke, you're right, I was not very enthusiastic. One of the nice things about coming to Palo Alto is that I get to spend time with the family, and I don't feel any pressure to be anything other than a family member. I am happy to spend time with your friends, and maybe it would be a good thing, but I can't help but feel like there was a spotlight on me that night. It was *not* just a friendly dinner; there was pressure to "perform." To tell stories about movies, or, if I was not expected to talk, I was expected to be interested in what the director and the producer had to say. I am interested in what they had to say. I think that the play was very good, and I was not lying when I said it was the best play I had seen in the Bay Area. But, because I felt like there had been planning done without my being made aware, I shut down. I was just uncomfortable. I didn't try to be rude, or show anyone that I was uncomfortable, I just tried to get through the dinner as best as I could. If there had been no expectations of me, I think my conduct would have been fine. The fact that we are talking about this and that I am being singled out shows me that there was some expectation put on me.

I was not excited about this dinner. The first I heard about it was the night before. I wish you had told me that it was an important dinner for you. I am still not sure if it was. At first you said that "you didn't mind playing the fool," but when the person you have to work with every day is there, it is embarrassing. That sounds to me like your business was involved. Of course I don't want to hurt your business, and I would love to help in any way that I can, but I like to be informed when I am doing so. Like with the premiere. Those tickets were very valuable, not only because the movie had a lot of interest, but also because it was a charity. I think the tickets ran from $300 to $1,000. I had many friends that I could not invite. When I saw that you had put your partner and his wife on the list, without even asking me, I questioned it. I was told that it was important for your job that they come, so I allowed it. That is something that I am happy to do, but you didn't even ask me, you just slipped them in. That is how this dinner felt, that something was being set up without asking me.

If I am completely off base, I am sorry. If your only complaints are the two that you mentioned—that I said "bad meat," and that I didn't sign an autograph—then I think this situation has been blown out of proportion. I absolutely meant nothing about her cooking when I said "bad meat." She said that she cooked the apples in honor of *Apple Train*, and then Ryan said, "Do you have any *Coffee*?" So I jumped in and said "bad meat," for no other reason than it was a bad joke on the title of Ryan's movie. I was just being a stupid older brother, I hadn't even tried the meat. Maybe it was ill-timed, but I am sure that we are all guilty of a badly timed joke. And I absolutely meant nothing by it, I don't know how you could think that I did, my manners are not so bad that I would insult anyone's cooking. Or maybe, as you said, she was already feeling insecure, which gave the comment more significance than it should have had. Why she might be feeling insecure at that point, I don't know, unless I was supposed to be behaving in some manner other than I had been. Up to that point I was fairly quiet, but I had not said anything that could even be considered rude. So I am not sure why she was insecure, unless she was expecting more enthusiasm from me for some reason. If the stupid joke, that had absolutely no significance as far as her cooking went (it was *good* meat), was ill-timed or unnecessary, I am sorry for that. But I don't think it was so heinous as to ruin a whole meal, which makes me think that something else had already ruined the meal.

If the complaint against me is that I didn't sign an autograph, then that is another gross misunderstanding. I sign autographs for anyone! I never refuse, unless I am being rushed into a premiere. I would have been happy to have signed *ten* for her. She never asked! She put a card with a bunch of celebrities' signatures in front of me and asked me to identify them! If that was my cue to offer my own signature, then I didn't catch it. Maybe I didn't feel worthy to sign next to

Warren Beatty or Russell Crowe. I never presume that anyone wants my autograph. If that is what she wanted, and you saw that she was too scared to ask, then you could have easily spoken up. For the record, I am always willing to sign autographs for any friends. I think I even signed stuff for charity drives for their theater in the past!

You said that it was my responsibility to talk to you about the dinner if I was feeling uncomfortable about it. I am not sure about that. I think it was your plan, and you were the one that had expectations. I am an adult now; if you want me to behave like an adult at your partner's house, then tell me what the situation is. Don't just drag me along and expect me to behave in a certain way. And frankly, I *hate* dinners. I just don't like having them, especially with strangers. Believe me, I get asked all the time, but I don't like to go, even with people that I *am* interested in. But I would be willing to go for you, if you told me it was important. You said you tried to talk to me in the bookstore, but you didn't ask me about the dinner, you asked me what I was reading lately. Regardless, I will go to you in the future and try to discuss anything that sounds uncomfortable to me.

As far as your work, I am happy to help you in any way that I can. I don't know much about what you are doing, but I am very interested and would love to hear more about it. I am proud of you for winning that award, and the relief work you do sounds amazing. If I can help by being a good guest at your partner's house, then I am happy to do so, but it would make me feel more comfortable to know that there were no expectations of me. I socialize better that way.

Another issue arose before I left. You said that we don't talk. I am sorry for that. I would love to talk to you more. I said that I didn't like to talk to you about books because you never liked the books I was reading back in high school. And now when I do, I still feel like I am a kid talking to an adult. It feels like I'm trying to communicate something that won't be entirely understood, or would be looked down upon, so I don't try. Maybe that is all due to my insecure projections. It probably is. Before we had our heated discussion, when I was driving to the house, I was thinking about how you and I didn't talk enough, and how I would love to spend more time with you. I am willing to get over my childhood insecurities, because I really would like to talk to you more.

As far as you "willing to play the fool," I don't know what that meant. I never want you to feel like a fool. It sounds like you have felt that way in the past. If that has anything to do with how I treat you, or anything to do with my behavior, please tell me and I will amend the situation as best as I can. I never want to embarrass you.

—The Actor

(I think this next one is from his girlfriend. -Ty)

1/1/xx—1:30 a.m.

hi big bear

I don't know if anything i say is helpful, but i just wanted to say a couple things that i'm thinking about all this. i hope i can be helpful. I'm so sorry he said those things to you. i would have stormed out too, those are really hurtful comments he made, and i think very immature. they were inappropriate. he shouldn't be talking to you like you are a little boy.

but i also think that maybe this is a good thing. it seems like maybe this was less about this one event and more about your guys relationship, built up things between you and your dad. i think that you have said a number of times that you don't have a lot of respect for him, and you have good reasons (i'm not criticizing those feelings of yours). i think on some level he probably feels that. so he has probably been harboring hurt feelings toward you. maybe this is what you guys needed to get through some of the stuff between you.

i think you can use this situation to your advantage and be the bigger person. you might in some ways have to be the father figure, you know? show him how you want things to be. the fact is, you did go into the evening angry because you felt (again, with good reason) manipulated and uninformed. he could and should have said to you up front that this was an important dinner for him, and could everyone be on their best behavior. i think there's a lot of miscommunication on both ends. and now is a good opportunity to maybe be more open and honest with him about how this relationship is for you and how you want it to be different.

i think it would be a mistake to ignore this and let it stew. it's so much better to have this on the surface than brewing underneath, even if it doesn't feel that way.

Mark read the emails and read them again. What could he do now? Obviously there was strife between The Actor and his father, but the emails didn't prove that The Actor murdered his father. He was certain that the sketchbook contained answers. He would have a serious talk with Cent in the morning and tell her that she must hand over the sketchbook. He would apologize for being jealous and immature, but there were bigger issues involved now.

At her small apartment in West Hollywood, Cent spent the night transcribing the reversed writing from the sketchbooks. The writing told a frightening, albeit somewhat inscrutable story. It seemed to be a confession of murder, but it was unclear. Cent was aware of the shooting of The Actor's father and The Actor's possible guilt in the affair, and she knew that the *Spider-Man Journals* (as she now called them) could implicate him in the crime.

It was strange, but she felt an affinity with The Actor, even though she had never met him. She was ten years younger than him, and she had grown up watching his movies. The Actor had been her first Hollywood crush. The damaged sensitivity she saw in his movie roles made her ache, because she felt sensitive and damaged too. She also knew from interviews that The Actor painted in his free time. She loved to paint too, not that she thought she was any good.

Although the journals spoke about murder, they also had an endearing sensitivity, and she found herself siding with The Actor against his father. It was all so weird. She knew that she was possibly dealing with the life and death of real people, but it also felt like it was all a movie.

Cent made a decision. She would help The Actor and fuse herself with The Actor at the same time.

She cut out the pictures from the journal and began to make a collage. She loved to make collages. In addition, she painted over much of the reverse writing, to obscure the incriminating sections. In the end she had five large pictures.

At 1 a.m., she called her costar Zack and asked him to come over to look at the pictures. He came, and despite his earlier criticism of the sketches, he admired the new pictures. He thought they were cool.

Cent talked to him about Marc and how she knew she shouldn't be with him, but that she was always looking for a father figure because her own father had abandoned her and her family. She talked about how her brother Butch was suffering from the lack of a father.

Zach seemed to understand. He said nice things, and when he kissed her, it was sweet and romantic, just like he did in their scenes in the movie. Zach wasn't as deep as The Actor, but he looked a little like him.

They made love that night.

On a small piece of paper that she kept under her mattress she had written down what was in the journals, painstakingly reversing The Actor's backward scrawl:

I don't know what I'm writing, or even how to write, but I thought I should put a few things down, just so the record is clear from my side. The death of a father is a significant event in most people's lives, albeit of varying degrees depending on the history between offspring and parent. The murder of a father is an even more poignant event, which can be inflated to exponential degrees, depending on the identity of the executioner. Patricide is the ultimate expression of a son's maturation, whether it is realized physically or not. I recall from my high school English class that Oedipus stabbed himself in the eyes after realizing the identity of his murder victim. Well, that, and the fact that he was screwing his mother. I have not slept with my mother (the closest I got was a proposal of marriage when I was eight) and I have not stabbed out my eyes, and I am still uncertain of my guilt.

A few things are clear: 1) My father is dead. 2) He died on Christmas morning. 3) There is a bullet hole in the front widow of my parents' home.

I am still piecing this story together, so please forgive the mystery; I assure you it is unintentional. And please forgive any sloppiness in the craft of the story itself, I have never written anything like this before. Although I can boast of a lifelong love of literature, an affinity that developed in the midst of a neglected childhood. This neglect is not introduced here to elicit any pity; it is just a fact that my early reading was not encouraged by my father. He was too busy working on a business plans for his big Silicon Valley company to care about my discovery of Dostoevsky's Underground Man, or Raskolnikov, or Hamsun's *Hunger*.

I can recall one conversation when I was twelve:

"What are you reading there?"

"*The Stranger.*"

"That existential shit is crap. You should be worried about science. Those French writers are full of shit. It will get you nowhere but murder."

Maybe so, Dad, maybe so.

To my father, my heroes were all nuts writing meaningless words in a void. So I spent my childhood in books and found new fathers.

When I went to school, I got into acting. As an actor, I got to play many roles. I got to kill fifty fathers. Every thug I killed in every cheap crime drama I acted in was my father. I shot him and I shot him.

If I killed him, then I am a criminal, but only because it took place off screen. If I didn't kill him in life, didn't I kill him anyway? I killed him in my mind and I killed him on screen. He's dead to me. My emotions tell me that I've killed him. But then again, when I "act," I use *real* emotions.

Hard to tell where the acting ends and life begins. They don't always say action or cut.

I can see the Christmas tree flashing its red, blue, green, and yellow in its corner by the window. I just can't decide if it was a Christmas tree from my memories of childhood, or from last weekend. I guess the fact that I saw myself in the window, floating like a phantom over the bent figure of my father, says that I was standing outside.